WRONG TURN

WRONG TURN

A Lucinda Pierce Mystery

Diane Fanning

Severn House Large Print
London & New York

This first large print edition published 2018
in Great Britain and the USA by
SEVERN HOUSE PUBLISHERS LTD of
Eardley House, 4 Uxbridge Street, London W8 7SY.
First world regular print edition published 2012 by
Severn House Publishers Ltd.

British Library Cataloguing in Publication Data
A CIP catalogue record for this title is available from the British Library.

ISBN-13: 9780727893383

Severn House Publishers support the Forest Stewardship Council™
[FSC™], the leading international forest certification organisation. All
our titles that are printed on FSC certified paper carry the FSC logo.

Typeset by Palimpsest Book Production Ltd.,
Falkirk, Stirlingshire, Scotland.
Printed and bound in Great Britain by
T J International, Padstow, Cornwall.

To
Julie Rea

One

Lieutenant Lucinda Pierce had one foot across the threshold of the homicide department when the voice boomed out, 'My office, Pierce!'

She watched the back of Captain Marcus Holland receding down the hall. For the first time, she noticed that the red bristles on his head were speckled with white and a spot on the crown of his head was thinning. She shook her head and sighed. It was no time to think about the ageing of her commanding officer. The order had been given; she'd lost track of the number of times she'd heard those words. They were always the precursor to bad news. She followed him down the hall with apprehension dragging at her heels.

As she entered his office, Holland was scanning through a stack of file folders on his desk. Most of them had worn-out, tattered edges and bent tabs as if they'd been wrapped in rubber bands for quite some time. Without looking up, he said, 'Please have a seat, Pierce.'

Lucinda started. Holland never said 'please'. Must be really bad news, she thought. Still, her instinctive urge to remain standing whenever she was told to sit down kept her on her feet.

Holland looked up at her. 'Please, Pierce,' he said, gesturing to the chair in front of his desk.

Lucinda looked at him. No throbbing in his

1

temples. No redness blotching across his cheek-bones. No evident signs of anger. He looked more defeated and sorrowful than irritated or wrathful. Definitely not his typical demeanor after calling her into his presence, raising Lucinda's level of apprehension but stirring her curiosity, at the same time. She slid into the chair and regarded him with wary fascination, her fight or flight response on high alert.

Holland looked back down at his desk, fiddled with his files and cleared his throat. She'd never known him to be at a loss for words unless he was too enraged to speak. 'Sir?'

He cleared his throat again, raised his head and twisted his neck in the collar of his shirt. 'Do you remember when you joined Homicide, Pierce?'

'Yes,' she said, recalling that dreadful, pivotal moment captured by Court TV cameras. Lieutenant John Boswell had been on the stand all morning, and for most of the afternoon, in the trial of Martha Sherman who'd been charged with first-degree murder in the death of her step-daughter Emily. The judge had decided to dismiss the court for the day and leave Boswell's cross-examination for the morning. Boswell had risen from his chair, then the color had drained from his face and he'd slumped back down. He'd struggled to speak as his face turned gray and he'd keeled forward, his head making a loud thump as it hit the rail of the witness box.

Heart attack. Boswell was dead before he reached the hospital. A thirty-year law enforcement veteran with more than twenty years in

Homicide, he'd brought some of the most dangerous men in their jurisdiction to justice. He'd survived bullet wounds, head trauma and countless tense situations in the field. So many risky situations; so many opportunities to die and yet it was the betrayal by his own body that ended his life. If it weren't for his death, she wouldn't have gotten the job – at least, not at that time, and she had to admit, maybe never.

'Yes, sir. I most certainly do. It was because of Boz. That bothered me a lot at the time; in fact, it still does when I think about it.'

'Do you remember what happened after Boz died?'

'There was a delay in the trial. Then, the funeral. I escorted Mrs Boswell that day. When I finished with my duties, I got the message that I was wanted in your office.'

'Did you know why?'

'No, not really. Frankly, sir, I assumed that as Lieutenant Boswell's next-in-line, you wanted a report on how well his family was holding up; I thought you wanted to know if there was anything you could do. I was more than a little surprised when you offered me a position in Homicide. I really wanted it, but I thought it would be years – even with the vacancy created by Boz's death.'

'Remember I told you that Boz had spoken highly of you and that you were on my shortlist for an opening?'

Lucinda nodded, 'Yes, sir.'

'I didn't tell you the complete story at that time and I never planned on telling you. But now, there have been some developments that make it necessary – regrettable, but necessary.'

Lucinda's brow furrowed. Would he ever get to the point?

'Remember Sergeant Carmody?'

She remembered him only vaguely. 'The one who left about a month after Boz died?'

'Yes. He took a job in Homicide down in Raleigh. He was not pleased that he was passed over in favor of you. We lost a good man when he left; he's done some good work down there.'

'And now he wants to come back? And he wants my job?' The thought flew out of Lucinda's mouth before she even had a chance to absorb it.

'No. No, Pierce. Nothing like that. Please bear with me.' Holland pulled a hand across his face, leaving a weary expression in its wake. 'At the time, Carmody was one of my top two choices. I was also considering hiring from the outside. Getting some fresh blood into the department. And, honestly, you were the third option – but you were a distant third.'

Red tinged Lucinda's cheeks. That bald statement of fact wasn't all that surprising but it certainly was embarrassing and humbling. She had a thousand questions in her head but she sat mutely waiting for Holland to continue.

Holland sighed. 'I'd already decided that I needed a replacement for Boz sooner rather than later. I planned on Carmody taking his place. I was going to tell him after the funeral. But before I left for the service, once the DA walked through my door with the Chief of Police, everything changed.'

4

'Something was wrong with Carmody?'

'No. Absolutely nothing. He had excellent performance reviews. His outside life was squeaky clean. By rights, he was next in line to move up to Homicide. He earned it. But the DA and police chief convinced me that there was something bigger at stake. The judge had ruled on the motion submitted by Martha Sherman's defense team. He'd thrown out the testimony of Detective Boswell since the defendant no longer had the opportunity to cross-examine him. The state had to present that evidence all over again. Of course, that meant you.'

'Yes. I'd been assisting Boz since the first day of the investigation. I was with him all the way. I knew the case inside and out. I was on the witness list from the beginning but the DA had said he wouldn't be calling me because Boz could cover it all. I was ready and willing already. Did he think I needed to be bribed with a promotion to do a good job on the stand?'

'No. He didn't have a doubt that you'd do an excellent job. In fact, he remarked on the eye patch you wore back then as something that would add to your gravitas while simultaneously tugging at the sympathies of the jurors.'

Lucinda rolled her eye. 'Then what are you saying, captain?'

'He insisted that I give the job to you and the chief concurred. They believed it was vital that whoever took the stand to deliver the evidence was a detective – someone who would be addressed that way by the state. And if the defense refused to use that honorific with you, they could appeal to the female majority on the jury by pointing out that lack of respect at every opportunity.'

Lucinda's palms flew to her temples, her fingers sticking through her hair on either side. This was awful. In a quiet voice, she whispered, 'I only got the job so the state could use me as a political tool in the courtroom? I got the job because my gender was right – not because of anything I'd done?'

'Not exactly, Pierce. No matter who assisted Boz on that case, male or female, they would have found a spin for it. The DA was just using what you were to their best advantage. They were determined to get a conviction in that case and they knew you were the only person who could get them there.'

'And you went along with this?'

'You've got to understand, Pierce. Andrew Sherman, the dead girl's father, could apply a lot of pressure. He was powerful, wealthy, and a major political contributor. He wanted his second – and soon to be ex – wife to spend the rest of her life behind bars for killing his daughter. I really had no wiggle room.'

'Really, captain,' she sneered.

'Really, Pierce,' he said giving her a hard stare before continuing. 'They did give me an out, though. They said after the trial was over, I could demote you as fast as I promoted you. And they'd back me up all the way.'

Lucinda exhaled sharply through her nose and pursed her lips. She was well past the embarrassment and humility phase now. She was flat-out pissed. She moved her focus away from the captain and stared at the wall behind him.

'Well, I didn't, Pierce, did I?'

Lucinda turned her head towards him then jerked it back facing the wall. She didn't trust herself to speak. Too often words she'd spoken in the heat of the moment had come back and knocked her off her feet. She was trying to get some control over her temper, but it wasn't easy.

'I didn't because I didn't believe it was fair. You did perform admirably in the courtroom. The state did get a conviction. It only seemed right to give you the opportunity to prove yourself.'

Lucinda jerked back. 'Or fall on my face?'

'Yes, Pierce. Or fall on your face. I gave you control of your own destiny and quite frankly, I think that is significant. And you did prove yourself. Every time. Never once did you give me reason to regret my decision.'

'Oh, stop, captain, you know that isn't true. Stop patronizing me.'

'OK, Pierce, there were times when you made me doubt the wisdom of my decision. You caused me to question it from time to time; but in the end, you always came out on top. Not for one moment did I ever regret offering you the job.'

'OK, I'll take your word on that, sir,' she said, not really certain whether she should believe him or not. 'But why are you telling me all of this now?'

'The body of Emily Sherman has been found.'

'That's wonderful – I thought we'd never find her.'

'Actually, the circumstances surrounding the

7

discovery of the body are a bit problematic for all of us.'

Lucinda tilted her head to the side. Why would he be conflicted by this? Andrew Sherman would finally be able to bury his daughter. Isn't that what we always wanted – to bring a missing victim home? 'I don't understand, sir.'

'Emily Sherman is now part of the Mack Rogers case.'

'What? That is ridiculous. Why would anyone come to that conclusion?'

'Last night, the forensic anthropologist identified one of the skeletonized bodies you found in the basement.'

'No! That can't be true.' Lucinda jumped to her feet and rested her hands on Holland's desk. 'It couldn't be her. It just couldn't.'

'It was, Lucinda. The forensic odontologist suspected it when he compared the dental X-rays, but couldn't be positive about his identification because of the rodent damage to the skull that dislocated some of her teeth. But the DNA results are in now. There's absolutely no doubt that one of the bodies in that basement belonged to Emily Sherman. And very, very little doubt that Martha Sherman was wrongfully convicted.'

Two

The basement. How she hated basements. In fact, if the negative subterranean experiences continued much longer, she feared she'd develop the same phobia of the space that little Charley Spencer had. She had found the body of Charley's mother in a basement; the little boy she accidentally killed had been held in the range of fire, unseen, behind a dirty basement window; the serial killer who sliced her Achilles tendon was in a basement.

And now this basement. She had first arrived at the house on DeWitt Street, filled with the same solemn, optimistic enthusiasm she possessed at the inception of every homicide investigation. Sergeant Robin Coulter, the newest addition to the homicide squad and the only other woman, briefed Lucinda in the front yard. The horror she prepared to face chipped away at her positive attitude. Actually entering the basement destroyed it.

The landlady, whose cleaning of the house for a new occupant prompted the discovery, sat on the front porch of the small white bungalow with dark green trim. A home that looked much like any of the others on the block – nicely painted, unassuming with a freshly mowed front yard. Before the patrol cars swarmed around it, there had been no indication that it bore any difference to its neighbors. The landlady's minister sat on one side of her, the police psychiatrist on the other. She was as close as anyone could get to hysteria without running stark, raving mad into the street.

The pest control company employee, who actually discovered the first body, sat stunned on a bench beside the drive. A patrolman sat beside him trying to get something more than yes or no answers to the questions posed, but requests for elaboration seemed to generate nothing more than a faraway stare.

She walked through the front door choking with dread. She could smell the faint whiff of the basement's contents the second she stepped inside. An officer handed her a jar of mentholated gel to smear in her nostrils before she descended the steps. Usually she didn't bother, but this time was an exception. The smell by the door to the lower floor was so intense, so nausea inducing, she could not resist. It diminished the odor but could not eliminate it.

At the foot of the stairs, the semi-finished section appeared perfectly normal. Along one wall, a washer, a dryer and a large utility sink looked ordinary. The rough concrete floor was typical. The air felt damp and she imagined, without the odor of decomposing bodies overwhelming all else, it would smell a bit musty and dank.

She walked toward the entrance to a peculiar kind of hell. The door was three-quarters of normal height. A broken hasp canted crookedly from the frame. A busted padlock lay on the floor. She bent down and eased her way onto the dirt floor on the other side. She couldn't stand upright and didn't want to brush her head against the dust, cobwebs and grime on the rafters, making her duck lower than necessary. The floor rose gradually in front of her, narrowing the gap down to cat height before reaching the foundation on the other side.

To the left of Lucinda, and about four feet from where she stood, the toes of a pair of shoes broke through the ground. The pest control employee had brushed away the dirt over the legs to make sure that what he thought he saw was really what was there.

Further back in the crawl space, a figure in a Tyvek suit, booties, gloves, head covering and a face mask with a breathing filter, raised a head and shouted out a muffled, 'Lieutenant!'

'Marguerite, is that you?'

'Yes, lieutenant. Let's talk outside.' Forensic specialist Marguerite Spellman duck-walked across the dirt until she reached a spot where she could stand, albeit it in a crouched-over posture. 'I've now found a fourth body. It's nothing more than a skeleton. I think I should get out of there and let a forensic anthropology team take over.'

'You sure we can't manage without calling in the state guys?'

'Hate to say it, lieutenant, but we might need the Feebs – and not just our local buddy Special Agent in Charge Lovett, but the experts on forensic excavation from headquarters in DC.'

Lucinda's face twisted into an expression of extreme distaste. She sighed.

'I'm sorry,' Marguerite said, 'but we really

11

need an anthropologist here. These remains need to be meticulously extracted if we're going to have any hope of preserving evidence in a manner that the defense can't rip to shreds. They already have a little ammunition because the pest control guy touched the first body and some of us have entered the space – that probably was not wise.'

'Let's go topside and get away from this stench for a while and then I'll make the calls. You'll need to be here, though, while they work. You need to observe every little thing they do.'

'I'd planned on that, lieutenant.'

Lucinda nodded, gave her a tight smile and led the way up the stairs. They removed their protective gear and stepped out into the front yard. The first inhalation of fresh, outdoor air was intoxicating. Any of the city pollutants churning through the atmosphere now smelled as clean and pure as snow compared to the cloying, sweet, sickening smell from the crawl space.

Marguerite leaned her head to one side and sniffed the sleeve of her shirt. 'Eeew. I probably will never get the smell out of these clothes. I'll have to toss them out when we're through. Somebody needs to invent a body suit that blocks odors.'

'Why don't you handle that in all your spare time, Spellman?' Lucinda asked with a chuckle.

'Spare time? Could you define that alien phrase for me?' she responded with a grin.

'Tell me about it,' Lucinda said and pulled out her iPhone and called the state lab. They delivered the bad news that Marguerite had warned her they would. A request would have to go to FBI headquarters but they assured her that the agency would scramble to get someone on the ground as quickly as possible.

'I'm sure they will,' Lucinda said. 'They just love this sensational, banner headline producing stuff.'

'Watch the attitude, lieutenant. You're going to have to work with these guys.'

Lucinda disconnected the call without comment. Everyone knew how difficult and vainglorious the federal guys could be, but they all got so sensitive about it when anyone said it out loud.

She decided to tackle what was probably the easier of the two interviews first. With a toss of her head, the officer rose from the side of the pest control man and Lucinda slipped into his place. She put a hand on his lower arm. 'How are you holding up?'

He shrugged but kept his head down, eyes focused on the ground. His shaggy brown hair blocked any view of his features. She noticed his company overalls were embroidered with 'Russ' over a pocket on the upper left side. 'Your name's Russ?'

He shifted his weight to one side and pulled the wallet out of a rear pocket. Without a word, he handed her a business card.

She read, 'Russell Englewood, Pest Control Specialist. We Knock 'Em Dead.' She turned to the man beside her, 'Mr Englewood?'

He nodded and muttered, 'Russ is fine.'

'I really need you to talk to me about what you saw and what you did. Can you do that?'

13

Russ shrugged again.

'I know this is difficult, Russ, but I need your help to catch this guy.'

Russ didn't move or say a word.

Lucinda sighed. 'I know you've had a traumatic experience, Mr Englewood, but I'd going to need you to man up here. After all, you're an exterminator; you need to get a grip.'

For the first time, he lifted his head. A pair of bright blue eyes glared at her.

'You can be angry with me for the rest of your life, Mr Englewood. You can hate my guts for eternity. But you are going to have to give me information – detailed information. I don't want to start looking at you as a suspect but if you don't open up, I won't have any choice.'

'Damn you,' he shouted, rising to his feet. 'Yes, I've seen a lot of dead bodies in my line of work – mice, rats, snakes, possums, cockroaches – but I ain't never seen no dead woman before – no dead person of any sex. This ain't right. It just ain't right.'

Lucinda remained seated, placing a calming hand on his lower arm. 'No. It isn't right, Mr Englewood. Why don't you sit back down and tell me about it.'

He squeezed his eyes shut. 'Russ is fine, ma'am. Please, Russ is fine,' he said, sinking back down on the bench. 'Where you want me to start?'

'How about when you pulled up in the driveway?'

'Miss Plum met me outside here. She pointed to the skiff over yonder,' he said indicating the scarred, blue, tractor/trailer-sized container in the front yard. 'She say, "I done moved all that furniture out thinking it was causing the stink but it just won't go away. I think I gotta dead critter in the wall." And I say that I'll go see what I can find.'

Lucinda was certain that retired English teacher Veronica Plum didn't put it quite that way, but she didn't interrupt.

'So I followed my nose down into that there basement. Sure enough, there was somethin' dead down there. Didn't take me much time to narrow it down to that crawl space. I figured I'd find me a dead possum or coon or maybe even somebody's cat got trapped in there – that happens more times than I like to remember. I hate that. My old lady's got a cat and it's a pretty nice little thing.'

'And then, Russ?'

'Well, I ask Miss Plum for a key to the padlock and she told me she ain't never put a padlock on that door. And if I needed to pry it open to go for it. So, I reckon I did. I used a tire iron from my truck, I started levering it. It didn't wanna budge. So I found a sledgehammer in the corner and beat on the lock till it broke off. But then, I still couldn't pull back that hasp so I went to levering it again. Finally, it popped.'

'What did you see when you opened the door, Russ?'

'Damn, that smell almost blinded me at first. Never smelt nothing like it. I figured I was fixin' to find more than one dead critter down there. I shone my flashlight round the place and spotted somethin' stickin' up through the dirt. I brushed that off and it looked like a shoe. I'm thinking, I'm hoping, that someone just left a pair of old shoes down there. So I kept brushing away dirt until I touched skin. I didn't want to believe it. So I brushed a little more. And I rushed out of there to upchuck in the sink.' Russ gave a big smile.

The smile was more than unsettling. 'You got some pleasure from that discovery, Russ?'

'Pleasure? You crazy? Made me sick. I thought you might be right pleased with me. I watch some of them shows on the tee-vee. I know about contaminatin' a crime scene. In nothing but a split second, I done realized what a dead body meant. I got out of there without puking out my guts all over the evidence.'

Lucinda repressed the bubble of laughter that rose in her throat and forced a serious expression on her face. 'Yes, Russ. That was quick thinking. I am impressed that you reacted the way you did. Not everyone would think twice about contaminating the scene. I appreciate that very much.' As she very well did: vomit near the body would have been another bone of contention in the courtroom – *if* they ever found the perpetrator.

'What happened then, Russ?'

'I got up those steps as quick as I could and called 9-1-1. Miss Plum was circlin' me, askin' one question after another. But I just talked to the dispatcher. When I told that 9-1-1 guy that I found a dead body in the crawl space, Miss Plum started squawkin', throwin' her hands up in the air and pacin' round the room. She must've said, "Dear, sweet Jesus" a hundred time or more 'fore those officers got here.'

'Is there anything else I need to know, Russ?'

'Not from me, ma'am, I don't rightly think. That's 'bout all I know. Didn't know nobody who lived here. Don't know who them bodies belong to. Don't know nobody'd do a thing like that – leastways, I sure hope I don't.'

'Thank you, Russ. You just sit right here. I'll get the officer to come back over and make arrangements for your written statement, OK? You did very well. Thank you very much.' Lucinda patted his forearm, rose, spoke to the officers and headed toward the landlady Veronica Plum on the front porch. Odds were whoever had lived in this house had given her a false name, but hopefully she'd have enough additional information to narrow down the field.

Three

With the support of a spiritual advisor on one side and a mental health professional on the other, Lucinda was pleased to see that Veronica Plum was far more composed than she'd been when the detective arrived on the scene. Nonetheless, Veronica did look a bit worse for wear. Lucinda suspected that the up-do at the back of the woman's head was usually prim and proper with every hair in place. At the moment, strands – even clumps – of brown and gray hair stuck out in every direction as if someone had grabbed her by the bun and spun her around in circles.

'Ms Plum, gentlemen, I'm Lieutenant Lucinda Pierce, and I am the lead investigator in this case. Ms Plum, I know this will be difficult for you, but I need to ask you a few questions about your tenant, your home and your actions that led up to the discovery in your basement.'

The minister raised up his hands palms out. 'Lieutenant, I am sorry but—'

'And you are?' Lucinda interrupted. Coulter had already provided this information but he didn't know that and she sure didn't want the pastor to get on enough of a roll to run her over.

'Excuse me, ma'am,' he said, rising to his feet and stretching out his hand. With his tiny wire-frame glasses, his boyish facial features and his hair slicked from one side to the other, in a futile attempt to conceal his bald spot, he looked more like a teenaged nerd gone to seed than a stalwart defender of the faith. 'I'm the Reverend Paul McManus, leader of the flock at the James River Methodist Church.'

Lucinda was surprised by the warmth and firmness of his handshake. She'd expected something colder, limper – the kind that always made her feel the need to wipe off her hand. 'I'm sure your presence here is a comfort for Ms Plum.'

'Thank you. I must insist that your questioning wait for another time. Miss Veronica is quite distraught.'

'I'm very sorry, Reverend, but it simply cannot wait. And I'd prefer to speak with Ms Plum alone.'

'That is not possible. Not at this time.'

Lucinda glanced over at Steve Carroll, the department shrink. He took her cue instantly, reaching for the minister's elbow. 'Paul, come along with me. The sooner the lieutenant gets started, the sooner the ordeal will be over.'

Reverend McManus began to bluster but Steve spoke to him in soothing tones, firmly guiding him across and off the porch. The minister looked back over his shoulder at Veronica Plum as he walked away. The expression on her face gave the impression she thought he was being marched off to an unwinnable war against the forces of evil.

Veronica turned and looked up at Lucinda, her eyes growing wide. 'That stuff on your face, whatever happened to you?'

Lucinda grimaced. That stuff on her face was the remaining scars of her injury, the ones that Dr Burns had not yet repaired. Sometimes now she almost forgot about it; the appearance of that side of her face had been drastically improved by earlier surgeries. Then, another insensitive clod would point it out to her again. 'We need to talk about what we found in your house today, Ms Plum.'

'I might own this house, but I have not lived in it since I went off to college. It used to be my parents' home before they passed – and that was quite a while ago. I know they didn't do this. I know it.'

'Relax, Ms Plum, we realize that it's been a dozen years since you assumed the title for this home. I imagine that's when you lost your last parent. We are interested in your renters. Who has lived here since you acquired the property?'

'My momma died twelve years ago. She lived only five years after Daddy was gone. And I swear, she cried every single day. But she kept this house immaculate – at all times – she would have never tolerated that smell.'

'Ma'am. Once again. I do not suspect your parents had anything to do with what we found in the house.'

'I should hope not. They were a fine Christian couple. Went to church every Sunday – and any other day the doors were open for Bible study or prayer. They never harmed a soul in their whole lives.'

'Yes, ma'am. I have no doubt about that but I need to know who has lived in the home since

20

they've been gone. Can you please give me that information?'

Veronica gave Lucinda a wary look as if she feared it was all a trap. 'I can't say I remember all the names. I'd have to look in my papers. In the beginning, I had a lot of turnover. Most stayed a year; a couple of them broke their leases, just leaving without letting me know. That is so rude and inconsiderate. I try to be a good landlady. I try not to get into their business. And instead of gratitude, they sneak out in the night without letting me know. I thought about selling this house and getting away from all the aggravation. And now . . . and now . . .' Veronica put her face in her hands and her shoulders heaved as if she were sobbing.

Lucinda wasn't sure how much of Veronica's evasiveness and emotions were real and how much were merely the phoney, helpless, Southern woman façade; but she knew bullying would get her nowhere. She sat down next to Veronica and put an arm around her shoulders.

Veronica shuddered and lifted her head, dabbing at the corner of dry eyes with a tissue. 'Well, I'll tell you what I can. My first tenants – I can't remember their last name or the husband's name and certainly none of the children – there were six of them, or maybe seven. Not one over eight years old. Can you imagine raising that many in this little house?'

Lucinda shook her head and hoped her silence would spur Veronica to continue.

'Well, now I remember her, Betty Ann was her name and she was the most mealy-mouthed woman I ever met. She came to tell me they wouldn't be renewing their lease. Her husband lost his job and they didn't have any money for the next month's rent – last one on the lease. I know it wasn't good business, but I felt sorry for the woman and I told her they could stay until her husband found another job. But she said that he wouldn't accept any charity. They were moving back to Alabama to live with his parents until they got back on their feet. Now, I thought that was charity in a way, too. But I knew she could never stand up to that man so I let it go. She promised me that they would pay that last month's rent as soon as they could. I told her not to worry but she insisted that they would just as soon as they had it. She said her husband didn't want "to be beholden to anyone". And they paid the rent – it was nearly a year later but I got a money order for the full amount. Quite frankly, I wished they'd just kept it and bought some shoes for those kids – they were barefoot half the time. But, you can't force—'

'Ms Plum. Ms Plum,' Lucinda interrupted. 'Who moved in after Betty Ann and her family left?'

'Worthless couple. I almost got in trouble on their account, too. They were cooking methamphetamine in the back tool shed. When the police came to arrest them, they were gone. Two months behind on the rent and gone. The shed's not back there any longer. Too contaminated with the fumes. I had it torn down and hauled away. After that, it was some college boys. They signed a full year's lease late August but just moved out

22

when school was over in May without a word. I don't know what's become of young people these days. You know they were raised right and yet—'

'Who was after that, Ms Plum?'

'That sweet, little Minnie Culver. She was eighty-four years old and still as bright as a cardinal in the tree. I was coming by to get her to sign a new lease for another year and I found her, sleeping in her bed. But she wasn't asleep, she was gone. Broke my heart. I can still see her gray hair spread out on that pillow . . .'

'And then, Ms Plum?'

'Then was my biggest mistake. He seemed like such a nice young man. It was nine months before I realized what was really going on in my house. His room-mate was really his boyfriend. Now, I knew there were laws against kicking them out because of their sexual preferences but I sure wasn't going to renew their lease. I was still teaching then – what would happen if the PTA president found out I was renting to homo-sexuals? I simply shudder to think . . .'

Lucinda sighed. 'Who was your next tenant, ma'am?'

Veronica smiled. 'That's when I got lucky. Brad Loving was the next one to sign the lease. He renewed year after year.' Veronica's face darkened and creases formed around her mouth as she frowned. 'Well, I thought I got lucky until today. He always paid his rent on time – early more often than not. If anything went wrong in the house, he didn't call me, he just fixed it. He'd tell me about it when the work was done.

I told him to deduct the costs of the repairs out of his rent. He'd send me all the receipts and deducted the cost of supplies from his payment, but never once charged for the work itself. I thought he was the perfect tenant and now . . .'

'Brad Loving, you said? Did he give you any references?'

'No,' Veronica said with a sigh. 'I almost didn't rent to him because of that. But when he explained that he'd been living with his mother because she was so sickly and stayed there in her apartment until she died – well, it made sense. And how can you not believe in a young man who nursed his mother so faithfully?' Veronica sighed again. 'I'd like to sell this place now, but who in their right mind would want it?'

'You certainly are not in an enviable position, Ms Plum. I empathize with you. But, back to the matter at hand, could you please describe Mr Loving?'

'Let's see,' she said, tapping an index finger on her chin. 'He wasn't what I'd call a handsome man, but he had a very appealing face with a smile that must have made younger women melt. And his voice, so lovely. I could listen to it all day.'

'His eyes, Ms Plum, what color were his eyes?'

'Brown, deep dark brown – so dark you could hardly distinguish his irises from his pupils. A woman could lose herself in—'

'Yes, Ms Plum. What about his hair color?'

'A golden brown – looked like the sun kissed it every morning as it rose in the sky.'

Oh boy, Lucinda thought, she had a crush on

her tenant. 'And his face – the shape of it, the contour of his nose, any facial hair?'

'Oh, no beard or mustache or any of that. His sideburns were a little bit long but not too long. His face was a perfect oval, his lips were wide with a prominent, almost French-looking lower lip, and his nose was – well, it was just right for his face.'

Lucinda didn't think she could trust her glorified assessment – not one little bit. 'How tall was he? About how much did he weigh?'

'He was something over six foot tall – nice height in a man, don't you think? Oh, well, I suppose maybe not for you. You're that tall yourself, aren't you? You'd need someone with a bit more height, wouldn't you?'

'His weight, Ms Plum?'

'My, I'm no good at that sort of thing. He wasn't thin but then he wasn't fat. He looked fit but not muscle-bound, if you know what I mean?'

'So, you're saying, basically, he was just perfect?'

Veronica smiled. 'Now that you mention it, that's right. He was just perfect.' Veronica scowled. 'I just can't see that he could have had anything to do with . . . with . . . with this . . . this horror.'

'Ms Plum—' Lucinda began.

'No listen. He moved out a month ago – his lease was up, his rent paid in full. Why, he even told me to keep his deposit to care for any cleaning up I might need to do. I'd had a touch of the flu and hadn't been able to get over here and do that till this week. Someone could have come in here and put those bodies in the basement after he left. I bet that's what happened.'

Lucinda sincerely doubted that theory but she wasn't about to argue with a smitten woman. She'd lay odds that Brad Loving moved out when the smell got to him or when he thought he'd put as many bodies in that basement as he possibly could.

'I'll certainly keep that in mind, Ms Plum. Now, you won't be able to get back into this house for a few days at least. Do you need me to get a patrolman to drive you to your home?'

'I don't ever want to go back in that house again, lieutenant. Not ever. Thanks for the offer but the reverend said he'd give me a ride when you all said I could leave.'

'I understand that, Ms Plum. I'll let you know when everything is finished up here and you could decide what you want to do with the property then.'

'Right now, I'd just like to watch it go up in flames.'

'I'm sure you would, ma'am,' she said, waving the minister over to her side.

Lucinda had then watched Veronica slip an arm into the crook of Paul McManus' elbow, get into his car and drive away.

Since that day, a month ago, much had happened. Fingerprints in the home were linked to Mack Rogers, a man with a long criminal record but with very little time spent behind bars. It appeared that since his last release from prison, he'd been living right here in Veronica Plum's house.

At first, Veronica refused to believe that her 'Brad' had anything to do with the carnage in the basement. Then, Lucinda showed her his photograph, and Veronica gasped and crumpled to the floor. She swore she'd never trust another human being as long as she lived. The FBI still had not released the house and Veronica was counting the days until she could send a bulldozer to knock it down.

And Mack Rogers was still on the loose. Every law enforcement agency was on the lookout for him but no one had reported a verifiable lead. He was still out there – free to hunt for new victims. The fact that he hadn't been caught yet disturbed Lucinda's sleep more nights than not.

Now, the identification of Emily Sherman's body. Martha Sherman had spent seven years in prison for a crime she did not commit. And Lucinda had helped put her there. The guilt for that alone nearly overwhelmed her. What made it even worse – what haunted her waking hours and her nightmares – was the other consequence. By putting the wrong person behind bars, she'd allowed a ruthless killer to take more victims. At least four of the bodies found in that basement were young women killed after Emily – women who died because somewhere in the early stages of the investigation, she'd taken a wrong turn.

Four

Special Agent in Charge Jake Lovett rose from his desk and opened the door to his office wondering why someone from the state Attorney General's office would want to meet with him. He stretched out his hand as the man approached. 'Special Agent in Charge Jake Lovett. How can I help you?'

A lanky man who looked more like a college freshman than someone who had actually graduated from law school and passed the bar reached out to return the greeting. 'Will Hunt, sir. I'm here to talk about developments in the Chris Phillips case.'

'Chris Phillips – you mean former United States Representative Chris Phillips?' Jake said, gesturing to a chair in front of his desk.

'One and the same,' Hunt said as he slid into the seat and pulled a file folder out of his briefcase in one smooth move.

'I thought he was in the state prison for life.'

'He was – still is for that matter – but not for long. He got a favorable ruling from the federal appeals court this morning. His release is being arranged as we speak. He'll be let out on bail awaiting a second trial on the charge that he murdered his third wife, Patty.' Hunt used the fingers of his right hand to comb strands of his blond hair away from his forehead. 'Personally,

I think we ought to charge him with the homicide of his first wife Melinda, too, this time around; but that decision will happen somewhere above my pay grade.'

'That's a real shame, but it was a state crime. What does that have to do with me?'

'This morning, Phillips' attorney referred to his client as the rightful, duly elected representative of the citizens of his district to the United States House of Representatives. He vowed to use the courts to regain the seat that was stolen from Phillips after his wrongful conviction.'

'Sounds like typical defense lawyer B.S. to me,' Jake said with a shrug.

'Perhaps,' Hunt acknowledged, 'but since he once was, and is now claiming that he still is, an elected federal office-holder, it seems that the federal government ought to have some oversight in this matter. We'd like you to direct the re-investigation, working with the local lead detective in the case.'

'I can't just push myself into a case like that; I don't see any jurisdictional imperative.'

'The Attorney General has already spoken to your regional director. She has approved of this plan. I wanted to get you on board before I spoke to the trial prosecutor.'

Jake rolled his eyes at the mention of his loathed supervisor. 'You should have started with that fact. Why did the appeals judge throw it back for a new trial?'

'He ruled that the statement of his ex-wife – formerly wife number two – was prejudicial and should not have been admitted at his trial.

The prosecutor should have never put her on the stand. She'd accused Phillips of trying to kill her by pushing her down the stairway but he'd been acquitted of that charge. I suppose the state thought they needed her statement to demonstrate a pattern of behavior in order to get a conviction; but I cannot understand why the trial judge allowed the admission of that testimony.'

'So the appeals court is basically saying that he was railroaded in this first trial?'

'You could put it that way. I assure you that law enforcement and the legal community are united in their belief in Phillips' guilt, not just in the case of his third's wife's death, for which he was convicted; but also in the demise of his first wife Melinda. However, since she was cremated, we can't even exhume to look for more evidence. The autopsy photos and the report itself contain information that indicates that the cause of death was homicide, according to our experts, but the first pathologist labeled it an accidental death.'

'I'm still not sure why you need me involved.'

'This is the Attorney General's call. From his point of view, the local prosecutor and the local judge both made errors of judgment in this case. He felt it was quite likely that, somewhere along the line, the local cops did, too. He wants an independent party with a strong investigative background to look into the conclusions reached, find any bias or tunnel vision, and set a clear path for a conviction in the second trial.'

'Alright, I'll do what I can. But some of the

detectives on a local level are very resistant to what they consider FBI interference.'

'You just let me know if you have any problems. We'll pressure the district attorney and I'm sure he'll send that message downhill fast.'

Jake doubted the wisdom of that maneuver. In fact, he was not very keen on the whole plan. 'Who was the lead on the initial investigation?'

'A woman named Pierce – Lucinda Pierce. She was a sergeant then, but I believe she's a lieutenant now.'

Jake closed his eyes and sucked in a sharp breath. This was all he needed.

Will Hunt rose and dropped a file folder on Jake's desk. 'Here's a summary of the case and the contact information for everyone involved.' He stretched out a hand. 'We'll have her report here to you and you can take it from there.'

Jake popped to his feet. 'No! Don't do that!' he shouted.

Hunt dropped his hand and said, 'Is there a problem?'

'Excuse me, I mean, I've worked with her before on other cases. Don't order her here. I'll go to her and brief her on the situation.'

Hunt cocked his head to one side. 'Really? Making her report to you would set up the lines of command pretty clearly.'

And she'd probably never speak to me again, Jake thought. 'Trust me on this. I believe I know the best way to handle the situation to ensure her willing cooperation.'

'Your call. Play the old gal any way you want.'

Inwardly Jake winced at the lawyer's choice

31

of words; but he clapped the other man on the back and led him to the door. He watched until the other man turned a corner and disappeared from view.

He had immediate regrets. Why did I volunteer to tell her? Maybe I should have let them handle it and then apologized for their boorishness later. Jake kicked his trash can and sent it wobbling across the room. He slammed his foot into it again and realized his mistake in an instant. A not-quite-empty take-out coffee cup slung its contents on the beige carpet. He uprighted the waste receptacle and pulled a used paper towel out of it to dab at the mess on the floor. The stain had already set into the fibers, making him want to kick the can again. Instead, he lifted it and placed it by his desk.

He felt as if nothing was going his way lately. He'd badgered every field office across the country in the hunt for Mack Rogers but there was no sign of the man anywhere. Every time he spoke to Lucinda, she asked for an update on the progress. He'd grown tired of having absolutely nothing to report. Right now, he'd settle for any lead he could pursue even if it ended in a dead end. At least it would be something to do – something to make him feel as if there were hope for resolution and a chance at getting a violent predator off the streets.

Now, this. He knew she would not take it well – not now, with Mack Rogers still on the loose. He'd lost count of the times she'd said that getting the FBI into the case was a big mistake. He'd remind her that she hadn't had any luck finding the suspected serial killer either. She'd snap back that FBI headquarters was not keeping her in the loop and accuse him of holding back information, too. He hadn't, but he did understand her frustration; there were times when he thought the profilers were keeping things from him, too.

During the next hour, he'd called Lucinda's cell at least four times and each call went straight to voicemail. He had to admit he was relieved the first time he failed to reach her, but his anxiety rose with each attempt, in anticipation of the challenging conversation ahead. He knew a lot of his dread was personal. Although he and Lucinda continued to grow closer, she always held a piece of herself back and her reluctance to make even the lightest commitment left him permanently uncertain of where he stood with her.

He left messages of escalating urgency and wondered why she'd had her phone turned off for so long. Was she caught up in vital pursuit of evidence in a new homicide case? Or had she been dragged, kicking and screaming, into another mind-numbing round of departmental politics?

Five

Lucinda left the captain's office and trudged upstairs to meet with the district attorney. His office was three stories up and the elevator would have been quicker but she was in no hurry to get there. The captain told Michael Reed that he'd look in the files and send the lead investigator in the case up to his office. She hadn't been in charge of the case; she wasn't even in Homicide at the time, only temporarily assigned to assist Lieutenant John Boswell in the investigation. She was, though, as close to a lead detective as Reed was going to get since Boswell was dead.

When she walked into Reed's office, he bolted to his feet, put his hands on his hips and asked, 'How did this happen?'

'Martha Sherman, sir?' Lucinda asked.

'What else, Pierce? Did you screw up something else, too? Where did you go wrong in the investigation into Emily Sherman's murder?'

'I do not know, sir. I—' Lucinda began.

'You do not know? You are the lead investigator and you do not know? You arrested and charged a woman with a murder she did not commit and "I don't know" is the best answer you can give?'

'Sir, I wasn't the lead—'

'I don't want your lame excuses, Pierce. I want

34

answers. I want to know what went wrong and how it went wrong. If you can't give me more than "I don't know", what am I supposed to tell reporters? They'd skewer me if I repeated that. I need more. But if you can't give it to me, then I'm going to have to say, "I don't know" and if you force me to do that, I'm going to have to add a "but". I'm going to have to say, "But, I've called for the immediate dismissal of Lieutenant Lucinda Pierce from the police force of this fine community." Is that clear?'

Lucinda spoke through a clenched jaw. 'It certainly is, sir. As I was trying to say, I intend to pull all the files on the case and follow every step of Lieutenant John Boswell's investigation to find out where we went wrong on this case.'

'Don't be blaming someone else. Finger pointing is not an attractive characteristic – not in anyone. Particularly not in someone like you who is always convinced she's right in each and every situation.'

Lucinda's hands clenched up into tight fists by her side. She pressed her teeth together with more force and squeezed her eyelids tight. She simply did not trust herself to respond. His assessment of her was unfair and undeserved. Or was it? Was the Sherman case symptomatic or an anomaly? Did she lock into theories prematurely and ignore evidence that did not fit into her preconceived notions? She never thought that about herself before, but now she wasn't sure.

After an awkward minute of silence, Reed asked, 'Can't think of a snappy comeback, Pierce?'

35

'When will Martha Sherman be released?'

'Changing the subject work better for you? Well, her release is not a foregone conclusion. We have to schedule a court date before that can be considered. I haven't gotten around to that yet.'

'I would think, sir, that that would be a priority.'

'Oh, would you? Well, I suppose you didn't have to listen to the howling claims of injustice pouring out of Andrew Sherman, like I did this morning. He is convinced she should remain behind bars. He is certain that she is involved – that she's either an accomplice of Mack Rogers or she killed Emily all by herself and garnered a favor from Rogers, allowing her to put his daughter's body down in the basement of Rogers' house.'

Lucinda stared at him. What a ridiculous allegation. That woman should be released immediately. 'And you're taking Andrew Sherman's wacky theories seriously?'

'I have to.'

'Oh, that's right. He's a major contributor, isn't he?'

'He's one of the citizens I was elected to serve, Pierce. My oath of office does mean something, you know.'

'Oh, please, Reed. Your political pandering is as transparent as your glossy ambition. You wouldn't adopt this attitude for just any citizen – only one with deep pockets and a willingness to dig into them.'

'You,' Reed shouted, pointing an index finger at her face. 'You better get me some answers and get them quick. I am not going to lay down on the sacrificial altar for you.'

'You've never taken a bullet for anyone, Reed, unless you knew it was in your best interests. You sicken me!' Lucinda spun on her heels, grabbed his door and slammed it as she walked out. As she passed the desk outside of his office, she saw a wide-eyed look of horror on the face of Reed's secretary, Cindy, and hoped he didn't take it all out on her. If he did, she'd have to add Cindy to the long list of people to whom she needed to apologize; a roster of names that seemed to grow every day.

As she waited for the elevator, she turned on her iPhone. Stepping inside, the cell pinged at her several times. Four calls from Jake. *I guess he's heard about the identification*, she thought. She certainly didn't want to talk to him – or anyone – right now; but knew he'd keep calling if she didn't.

She punched in his number as she walked into her office and slumped into the chair at her desk.

'Special Agent in Charge Jake Lovett,' he answered.

'Did you call to gloat, Special Agent?' she snapped back.

'Gloat? Why would I gloat?'

'Don't play dumb with me. You all are in charge of the Mack Rogers case. I know you've heard about the latest body identification.'

'Yeah. What about it?'

'Are you telling me the name meant nothing to you? Do you want me to believe that you don't know how this is impacting my job?'

'Lucinda, I swear to you, all I know right now is that I am very confused.'

'If you didn't know, then why the hell were you calling me this morning?'

'I wasn't calling about the Mack Rogers case at all, I swear.'

'Really? Then, why did you call?'

'It's about another case.'

'Which case?'

'It's complicated. Can we please sort out one case at a time?'

Lucinda sighed as a surge of regret climbed into her throat. 'I'm sorry, Jake. I just had an ugly encounter with the DA over the body identification and I took it out on you. I was out of line.'

'What's the problem?'

Lucinda gave a synopsis of the case that led to Martha Sherman's wrongful conviction. 'And now the DA is stalling about Martha's release from prison when we should be turning everything upside down to get her out of there as quickly as possible.'

'It's political, isn't it?'

'Oh, yeah. Andrew Sherman, Emily's father and Martha's former husband, is a major contributor to Reed's campaign. He's still insisting that Martha was involved in Emily's murder.'

'That sounds like a real stretch to me.'

'Tell me about it,' Lucinda said with a sigh. 'So, what case did prompt your phone calls?'

'Remember US Representative Chris Phillips?'

'I'll never forget that bastard,' Lucinda said. 'Oh, no, Jake, don't tell me that – oh, please, please don't say his appeal was successful.'

Jake didn't respond.

After a moment, Lucinda said, 'Oh Jeez, that's it, isn't it?'

'Yes, Lucinda, I'm sorry. The judge released him on bond to await a new trial.'

'I wonder why Reed didn't beat me over the head about that, too.'

'I don't think he knows yet. Someone from the state AG's office will be informing him at some point today.'

'Wait a minute. How do you know all this?'

'A guy from the AG's office paid me a visit this morning.'

Lucinda's chest tightened. 'And why is that, Jake?'

'Well, it's—'

'Complicated, Mr Special Agent in Charge man? You're taking over this case, too, aren't you?'

'No, Lucinda, I'm not taking it over. They've just given me oversight . . .'

'Yeah, yeah, give me a break. Oversight means you're taking over.'

'No! They want me to work with you because Phillips was a federal employee when he committed the murder of his third wife. That's all there is to it.'

'Right. Got ya. You'll come in and if he's acquitted in the second trial, it's all on me. If he's convicted, the mighty Feebs will soar again.'

'You sure are in a pissy mood this morning.'

'Well, wouldn't you be if you just found out you were involved in two cases where the defendants have had their verdicts overturned?'

'Listen, Lucinda, Sherman's not on you – it's on Boswell. And Phillips isn't your fault either; he's walking because the prosecutor made a bad call at trial. Besides, Phillips' guilt is obvious. His taste of freedom will be short-lived and he'll spend the rest of his life in prison.'

'Maybe he shouldn't.'

'What do you mean? The man attempted to kill three wives and succeeded with two of them.'

'Maybe he's not guilty after all.'

'What? How can you entertain that thought for even a moment?'

'Because, as it has become painfully obvious to me this morning, my judgment is not very reliable. My detecting skills are clearly in question. I was certain Martha Sherman was guilty. I was wrong about Martha Sherman – maybe I was wrong about Phillips, too. Maybe I refused to consider the questions that should have been asked. Maybe I had tunnel vision and just plowed forward with my personal theory on the case and just ignored any information that contradicted that theory.'

'You don't really believe that, do you, Lucinda?'

'I don't know what I believe anymore, Jake.'

Six

Lucinda drove over to the building housing the police department archives. It had all been moved a few years ago from the basement of the old police headquarters into a separate warehouse, with climate controlled sections for fragile evidence. She continued to be amazed that the city had won the federal grant against stiff national competition and was now one of two state-of-the-art facilities of its kind in the country. The real irony, she thought, was that Representative Chris Phillips played a major role in making that possible.

At the front desk, she received codes indicating the location of all the evidence in both the Sherman and Phillips cases. She went first to the refrigerated area where forensic evidence, with the potential to contain DNA, was stored. She didn't intend to pursue any of that in depth at this time but wanted to be aware of what was available.

In the Phillips case, the contents comprised clothing and hair samples, bloodstained pieces of glass, chunks of carpet from the stairs and swabs taken from the crime scene in the death of his third wife. Nothing was available from the stairway where his first wife, Melinda Phillips, died, since it had not been considered a homicide until suspicions were raised years later when his most recent wife passed away under suspicious circumstances. Lucinda would have to check the reports in the paper files for more details on the results.

A few bulkier items were available in the Sherman case including a big chunk of the blood-soaked back seat and a major portion of the headliner from Martha Sherman's car – the pivotal pieces of forensic evidence pointing to the stepmother as the killer of Emily Sherman. From that vehicle, technicians had collected an incredible amount of hair and blood samples.

Neither case had any evidence in the weapons area. Chris Phillips, prosecutors alleged, had placed a sharp-edged, glass-topped table on the landing before shoving his wife down the stairs. They theorized that he additionally used a piece of the shattered glass to deepen the slice in her throat; but not one of the fragments recovered at the scene bore any fingerprints, as if the table had been wiped clean after being placed in the path of the victim's descent, and then anything Phillips touched after the fall was removed before the 9-1-1 call.

In the miscellaneous artifacts section, Lucinda found a bounty of trash and papers from the car connected directly to Emily Sherman or Martha Sherman, as well as two cellphones: one belonging to the stepmother, the other to her stepdaughter. It didn't appear as if anything in the vehicle could be traced back to Andrew Sherman but she made a note to check that out in the paper reports.

In the Phillips case, there was also a cellphone belonging to the victim as well as high-heeled shoes and a clutch bag that had been thrown clear of the stairway before any blood was shed.

Lucinda decided to leave the exploration of the original audio and video tapes of the 9-1-1 calls and interviews recorded after the crime until later in her review. For the moment, she'd peruse the written transcripts and then listen to tapes for any vocal nuances or visual clues to hidden meanings behind the actual words. All of those documents should be on the department's database but she was far more comfortable with the physical than the digital. She always worried she'd overlook something when she viewed reports on the computer screen.

She entered the cavernous document room with its high ceilings, harsh lighting and unending stacks of metal shelves where labeled cardboard file boxes collectively contained enough paper to create a national forest. There, she was assigned a stack steward, a young, physically fit specimen – usually male – who was trained in the operation of the electronic, moving ladders and lift platforms designed to locate and retrieve boxes from the high shelves.

Her steward was built like a pole-vaulter with muscular upper arms bulging against the sleeves of his T-shirt, prominently developed musculature in his thighs and calves, but with a thin, lanky torso whose sole purpose seemed to be to hold the all important limbs in place. Lucinda gave him the numbers relating to the Phillips case; knowing the stacks well, he went straight to the correct level near the top and zoomed down the tracks to the right spot without any hesitation. He loaded the three boxes onto the lift and lowered them to the ground. When he returned to the floor, he placed the lift contents onto a flat dolly and he was off again.

The Sherman files were on a shelf that Lucinda could have easily retrieved on her own without a ladder or any other assistance. She started to reach for them but was stopped when the young man, who never had bothered to introduce himself, slid between her and the stacks.

'Sorry, neither the insurance company nor the city attorney approve of anyone but stack personnel pulling document boxes.'

'But, they're right here,' Lucinda objected.

'Liability issue,' he said as he turned to extract another three boxes and place them with the others on the dolly.

Lucinda rolled her eye. As far as she was concerned, it was nothing more than bureaucratic mumbo-jumbo inspired by politicians' over-arching desire to cover their asses at any expense. She had to admit, though, it was nice having someone load the boxes into the trunk and back seat of her car. She hoped she could find a patrolman to help to take them out of her vehicle and into headquarters when she arrived there.

In fact, thanks to two police officers who pulled into the parking lot of the Justice Center just after she did, Lucinda didn't have to lift a box. They asked her to step aside, obtained a dolly and transported everything up to her office. Now she barely had room to maneuver; stacked two high, the six boxes occupied almost all the available floor space.

She sat down on the one clear spot remaining on the floor and, one at a time, pulled the content inventory sheets and prioritized the material review. She thought for a while about where to start. On the one hand, she felt a desire to get to the body of the Sherman case to make right the travesty that had been committed in the name of justice; on the other, Chris Phillips was out on the street after attempting to kill one wife and succeeding with two others. That offended her sense of justice, too. But what if she was wrong about Phillips – just as she had been about Sherman? What if he, too, should be free?

Finally, she decided to start with interview reports and transcripts from the witnesses in the Sherman case, judging it to be of the greatest urgency. The woman's continued incarceration lay heavy on her conscience. She packed up a tall stack of documents into a smaller box and carried them out to her car just after nine o'clock.

When she arrived home, Chester, her gray tabby, greeted her with a vocal interlude and a series of acrobatic maneuvers in, around and over the furniture. She served him a smelly cod, white-fish and shrimp combo that filled him with rapture. Why was his current greatest love the stinkiest excuse for food she ever found in a can? Her nose wrinkled and lips curled as she covered the portion remaining in the tin and shoved it into the refrigerator as quickly as possible.

She slapped together a butter, pickle, ham and Swiss sandwich, grabbed a glass of Merlot and settled at the dinette table with a pile of transcripts. She pulled out the first one but then remembered that she'd gotten an alert when she was in the warehouse that she had a voicemail message on her cell. She pulled it out to see if there was any reason to return the call that night.

She winced when she saw that she'd missed a call from Charley Spencer. The two had bonded tightly a few years ago after the discovery of Charley's mother's body in the basement of the Spencer home and had stayed in touch ever since. Lucinda hit the message playback button.

'Lucy, I think maybe somebody I know did a bad thing but maybe she didn't. Maybe she was just trying to act tough. Maybe she was trying to scare me. Or maybe it's just one big joke. I don't know what to do. I need your advice. Call me anytime, day or night.'

Lucinda smiled at the last sentence; Charley was definitely a drama queen. She looked at the time on the top of the screen: 9:43 p.m. Way too late to call an eleven-year-old on a school night. She made a mental note to try to catch Charley in the morning before she left for school. Back to the stack of papers. More than two hours of reading refreshed her memories of the investigation but brought her no new insights and not a single new fact to the surface.

She looked up at the clock, yawned, and decided she could get through one more witness interview by midnight and then she'd have to get to bed. She picked up the transcript of the exchange between Lieutenant John Boswell and Sherman neighbor Lisa Pedigo.

Halfway in, she encountered three heavily redacted pages. Her alertness snapped to high.

46

Originals should never be redacted; only the publicly disseminated copies should have blocked-out material. Was this a mistake? Or was this the deliberate obliteration of information? Boz wouldn't do that, would he?

She grabbed one sheet of the adulterated document, pulled the shade off the lamp on an end table, turned it on, and held the paper over the bulb in an attempt to read the words behind the black permanent marker. Impossible. It had to be a mistake. Maybe the original had been accidentally distributed and these redacted pages inadvertently placed in the file. But if that had happened, wouldn't there have been a media outlet taking advantage of the slip?

She went to her computer and logged into the department site where she searched for the Sherman files. She went through the detailed list of transcript documents four times before giving up. Maybe, she thought, it's in the wrong folder. She scanned through the complete list – still no sign of the Pedigo interview.

Could it be mislabeled? She opened each document one at a time, viewing every one of them just long enough to determine that the contents were an accurate reflection of the file name. She reached the end of the list with no sign of the interview transcript. It simply was not there. What did that mean? And what did she need to do next?

The first question troubled her deeply. Boz meant a lot to her and to her career. Not only did she get her job because of his death, but she learned an awful lot from him as she assisted him in the investigation – serving as everything from a backboard on which he could bounce ideas off, to a simple gofer, running hither and yon at his command. Did Boz make a mistake or did he intentionally make a decision that was, in all likelihood, illegal and a violation of his oath of office? No, not Boz. Anyone but Boz.

She dug into her memory but could not even recall ever hearing Lisa Pedigo's name or anything Boz said that could have related to the contents of her interview. Every other transcript she reviewed tinkled little bells of recall, stirring up at least some level of familiarity. But not this one. Not the beginning of the interview. Not the few words that remained intact on the redacted pages. Not anything in the final section. Did she simply forget or did she never know?

Tomorrow, she decided, she'd return to the warehouse, find the audiotape or videotape of the conversation and get her answers. There had to be an explanation – a simple, ethical, legal one – for this situation. She hoped that she would be able to find something that did not smear Lieutenant John Boswell with posthumous shame.

Seven

Jake knew Lucinda was being far too harsh on herself but she was right about Martha Sherman. That woman deserved to be released from prison immediately. The fact that she'd spent seven years behind bars for a crime she did not commit was an outrage. Every day she remained there compounded the injustice of it all. He also knew that governments often tried to find ways to avoid paying damages for wrongful incarceration and vowed to do everything he could to make sure that did not happen to Martha Sherman.

He knew that the best thing he could do to speed up her release was to locate Mack Rogers. He began another round of calls to fifty-four of the fifty-six FBI field offices across the country; for now, he was not being proactive with the locations in Hawaii or Puerto Rico because nothing indicated that Rogers had obtained transportation outside of the continental United States. Wherever he went he had to have travelled by road.

Most of the agents he called had nothing to report. Some did have leads that were followed up and then fizzled out to nothing. Jake struggled to keep the discouragement and weariness out of his voice as one fruitless contact trailed after another. Everything changed when he called the Salt Lake City field office.

'We sure do have a lead, Lovett,' the agent told him. 'We got a call from our satellite office in Pocatello, Idaho. Three different individuals claim to have seen him on the Snake River. We're scrambling now to get adequate personnel in place.'

'In Idaho?'

'Yup.'

'You find it credible?'

'As best I know, he's never been known to be this far west but we've got three people who spotted him in roughly the same location and I understand there is a fishing connection. Is that right?'

'Certainly is,' Jake said. 'One of the bodies found in his basement belonged to sixteen-year-old Lindsey Johns. She disappeared from the Fly Fishing Festival on the South River in Waynesboro, Virginia, less than two years ago.'

'Well, there you go. Listen, I'll update you as soon as I know anything. Right now, I need to get back to it.'

Jake got off the phone pumped up and ready for action. He wanted to hop the first flight headed west. He knew, though, that unless Mack Rogers was actually in custody, his travel request would be denied with the generic 'there are plenty of trained personnel on the scene at this time. Your presence is non-essential'.

Not being there made him a bit crazy. Just sitting here and stewing about it would make him totally bonkers. He had to do something. He picked his phone back up and continued the round of calls. It was after six p.m. in Virginia but offices in the Mountain and Pacific Time zones were still open.

The call to the Denver Special Agent in Charge was less than productive. 'Damn it, Lovett, you are draining our resources. Seems like half the population of Colorado thinks they've seen Mack Rogers. Every single lead turned out to be an obvious case of mistaken identity or seemed to be based on some idiot's dream or a psychic's vision. We need to drop the priority on this one, buddy.'

'Hold on a minute. We're talking about a serial predator of teenage girls here. He's been operating for years. He remains a top priority until he's captured; the lives of young women are on the line,' Jake insisted. 'And besides, if you're following up all that many leads why do I not have the paperwork to back it up?'

'Because we're too damn busy to file the reports. It's not like a single one of them amounted to anything.'

'You still have an obligation to keep me informed.'

'Obligation be damned. I'm lowering the priority on this case in my office. And I imagine you'll hear the same thing elsewhere. We can't handle the work load and do everything else that needs to be done. I can't neglect homeland security issues and survive in this job. You got a problem with that, call DC,' he said and slammed down the receiver.

Jake felt a surge of anger building in intensity and rushing its poison through his bloodstream. He got up and paced the room, resisting the temptation to kick the trash can again. He calmed himself with the knowledge that despite what Denver was saying, no one else was complaining. Everyone accepted the seriousness of this capture. Not one of them cared to have Mack Rogers settle into their jurisdiction and start killing again.

What could he do now? He pulled out the interview files and made a list of the best possibilities for a re-interview. He hoped that at least one of those people could lead him to someone who'd not yet been contacted – someone who knew Mack Rogers and might have an idea of where he was now. He'd start the second round of interviews first thing in the morning.

He had a plan to move forward in the search for Mack Rogers as well as one active hunt going on right at that moment. But what, if anything, could he do for Lucinda? He considered calling her and rejected it as quickly as it crossed his mind. Unlike most of the women he'd known, Lucinda needed solitary time to process the new developments and find her comfort level with them. She would not welcome any intrusion on the subject that was troubling her until she gained some acceptance of it.

She was not a whiner, rarely one to vent. Good qualities on the one hand but on the other, it created distance between them – a barrier that he'd tried to cross many times without any success. He knew that finding Mack Rogers was the best thing he could do for her at this time. He hoped he'd be able to report to her on success in Idaho. Short of that, even a hint of a promising outcome would be a good reason to give her a call. He had to find a reason every single day so she'd never forget that he cared or that he was always there for her. He checked to make sure the volume on his cell was all the way up, walked out of his office and headed home.

Eight

Lucinda got into her work space at six the next morning. At seven, she took a break from her review of Emily Sherman's autopsy report to call Charley. The line barely began to ring when it was answered. 'Did you find her?'

'Dr Spencer?'

'Yes. Who is this? Did you find her?'

'This is Lucinda, Evan. Is Charley or Ruby missing?'

'Yes,' he said. 'Did you find her?'

'Who, Evan? Charley or Ruby?'

Evan grunted with impatience. 'Charley, of course. Is she with you?'

'No, Evan.'

'Are you sure?'

'If she were here with me, I would tell you.'

'Are you at work?'

'Yes.'

'Maybe she's sitting outside of your apartment. You remember – she did that once before.'

'She promised she wouldn't do that again but considering that possibility I'm just sending a text right now from my cell to the building super. He's on his way to check. While we're waiting to hear back from him, fill me in, Evan. When did you last see her? And when did you notice she was missing?'

'I saw her last night about nine. She gave me a

kiss goodnight and then went to her bedroom. On a weekday, I usually get up at six, and brew a pot of coffee. She wakes up a little bit after I do. By the time I've gulped down my first cup, she's gotten Ruby out of bed and come downstairs ready for breakfast. But not this morning. I realized that I hadn't even heard a single sound of movement from the girls' bedrooms and wondered if Charley stayed up late reading and overslept because of it. I went to her room to wake her up but she wasn't there. Her bedroom light was on but she was gone. I looked in Ruby's room – Ruby was still sound asleep. I looked in their bathroom. I called her name. No Charley. I ran down to the lobby and no one there remembered seeing her either.'

'Did she say anything last night that might indicate what she's up to?'

'I don't know, Lucinda.' For a moment he was silent and then he said, 'She seemed distracted last night, but she gets like that a lot when she's up to something. More often than not, it just means her mind is on a science project or on one of her creative flights of fancy. Nothing she said indicated that it was anything more than that. And you haven't heard from her?'

'She left me a message but by the time I got home, it was too late to return her call. Something about someone she knew doing something bad. That could be behind her disappearing act this morning but then again, with Charley, logic isn't always the answer.'

'What do you mean a bad thing?' Evan said, the pitch of his voice raising a notch higher with each word.

Lucinda winced. Too late to take those words back. 'I don't know. That's all she said.'

'Is she mixed up with some bad kids?'

'I don't think—'

'Are there drugs in her school? You'd know that, wouldn't you?'

'I am certain Charley is not involved in drugs.'

'You didn't answer my question. Are there drugs at her school?'

Lucinda sighed. 'I'm sure there are some there, Evan.'

'You're sure!' he shrieked. 'These kids are just children! What about DARE? Don't you still have that program in the schools? Aren't they supposed to keep drugs away from the school children?'

'Yes, they still do, but Charley is in middle school now and—'

'So, you're telling me that your DARE program is a failure. It's just a waste of time and money? An opium for the masses of parents? Pabulum for the taxpayers?'

Lucinda was as frustrated with the ineffectiveness of the so-called war on drugs, leaving her without much of a basis to mount a defense. 'Well, Evan, they do believe those programs keep it under control.'

'Oh, that's a comfort – it's under control. And now my daughter is under the control of one of those druggies and that's just some insignificant anomaly?'

'Evan, stop it! You are jumping to unwarranted conclusions. Did you check with the school to see if she was there?'

'Of course, I did, but I got a recorded message that the regular school office hours are from eight to four thirty. They have the whole damn summer off. Can't they get in a little earlier?'

'I understand your concern and how stressful it is when your child is—'

'You, understand? How do you understand? You've never been a parent. You have no idea how I feel!'

Evan's words left Lucinda reeling with the sting of truth. He's right, she thought. How do I know how he feels? I think my love for Charley is as strong as any mother's for her child. But, I've never been a mother. What do I know? The silence stretched long, as Lucinda struggled to find the right words to say in response.

Finally, Evan broke the awkward hiatus. 'I'm sorry, Lucinda. I know how much you care for Charley. I shouldn't have . . . well, what I said . . . I mean, it was unfair and even a little cruel. I am ashamed that I lashed out at you of all people.'

'No, no it wasn't unfair. You're right. I am not and have never been a parent. I should not make assumptions about your feelings. I'm sorry, Evan. But, really, for Charley's sake, you do need to calm down. You need to think clearly right now.'

'Point taken. I'll do my best. But where is she?'

'I wish I knew. Sit down someplace quiet and run through everything she said last night and see if you can remember anything that might provide a clue to what she's up to this morning.

You know Charley – she's got the spirit of a crusader. If she thinks something needs to be done and she thinks she can do it, she'll go galloping off on her white horse without a thought about the consequences.'

'You got that right. And lately she's been growing more obtuse and secretive.'

'Girls get that way when they're growing up. It's going to get worse as she enters her teens. Wait a minute. I've got a message. She's not at my apartment, Evan. The super checked there and circled around the exterior of the building to make sure she wasn't just arriving. I'll alert the patrol squad to keep an eye out for her.'

'Call me if you hear anything?'

'Certainly, Evan. I'm sure everything will be fine,' she said before disconnecting the call. That last statement was a lie. Lucinda was not anywhere close to sure. She just wanted Evan to think that she was. But in fact, she was very worried. Someone Charley knew had done something bad and now Charley was missing? Lucinda hoped the two facts weren't connected but she strongly suspected – and feared – that they were.

Nine

The previous morning Charley had been in a stall in the girls' restroom, when she heard the door to the hall bang open and a loud voice of a girl entering. 'You really wrote that on the wall?'

'I sure did. In big red letters. I love writing with spray paint,' a second voice said.

'And I made a big daisy in the center of that fancy white carpet in the living room,' a third voice added.

'How did you get in there?'

'One of the guys busted out a bathroom window. We climbed up on one of those big rolling trash cans and hoisted ourselves in.'

'What guys?' the third girl asked.

'High school guys – one of them was your brother.'

'Tyler? Really? Who else?'

'Nick and Matthew.'

'That Nick is cray-cray,' the third girl said.

'You telling me? He had this wild idea to pee in the closets, the kitchen cabinets and the bathroom vanities. And all three of them pulled their things out and let it fly.'

'My brother did that?'

'Oh yeah. He sure did.'

Charley belatedly realized that she should have spoken up, made a noise, or come out of the stall when they first arrived. Now it was too late.

Outside her confined space, the conversation continued. The third girl asked, 'What else did you do?'

'Nick had a knife and we all took turns slicing up all the sofas and chairs.'

'Sofas? Chairs? I thought nobody lived there.'

'Don't. It was a model apartment where they show off the place to people on weekends. Nobody's living in the whole complex yet.'

'And then we left water running in every faucet.'

'And plugged up the bathtub. That should be running all through the place by now.'

'I want to see it. Where is it?'

'You know that construction at Twelfth and Jefferson.'

'Yeah, yeah. Which is the model place?'

'You can't miss it – there's signs pointing to it. But make sure nobody's watching so you don't get caught.'

'Hold on a minute,' the first girl said.

Silence followed her remark. Their sudden quiet unsettled Charley as the ominous possibilities for it tumbled through her mind. She held her breath. She thought about stepping up onto the commode to hide her feet but decided any movement at all would give her away. The sudden erupting cacophony of multiple fists banging hard on the stall door made Charley cry out.

'You better come out of there right now,' the second girl said.

'Or we'll come in and get you,' said the first.

Charley slid back the latch and stepped back. The door slammed open just missing her. A hand reached in, grabbing her shirt and pulling her out to the main space where they circled her. Charley looked at their faces: Madison, Ashley and Jessica, all eighth graders – intimidating eighth graders, the kind with boobs and heavy make-up.

'You spying on us, baby bitch?' Madison asked.

'You gonna go running to your mama and tell on us?' Ashley added.

'You tell on us, you are in big trouble, girl-friend,' the third girl, Jessica, said, backing up her friends.

'You tell anybody what you heard in here and we'll make sure everybody thinks you did it.'

'Yeah, there's three of us and one of you – our word against yours. You think you can beat those odds, asshat?'

Charley held up her hands. 'Hey, I don't know what you're talking about. I heard the sound of your voices talking but I didn't get any of the words.'

Madison gave Charley a one-handed shove to the shoulder, sending the smaller girl staggering back two steps but maintaining her balance. Madison leaned into her face, each word sending spit into Charley's face. 'It better stay that way, munchkin, or you're going to regret it for the rest of your life.'

The three girls turned to walk away from her. Charley almost breathed out a sigh of relief but choked on it when Ashley spun back around to face her. Two of Ashley's hands flashed out, pushing Charley hard. Charley staggered backwards and, failing to regain control of her equilibrium, crashed down hard on her backside. The three girls laughed. 'You should have seen the look on your face when we opened that stall, you stupid little shit,' Ashley said.

'Remember that moment of fear,' Madison added.

The three roared with laughter as they exited the restroom, leaving Charley sitting on the floor. Charley felt her fear morph into anger. She'd tell Lucy about what they did just as soon as she could.

She slipped into her American History class trying to be as quiet and unobtrusive as possible, hoping not to be noticed. She realized she'd failed at that, too, when Ms Gardner stopped talking about Fort Sumter and said, 'Charley Spencer. You are late for class. See me after the bell.'

As the teacher laid out the events in South Carolina that signaled the commencement of the Civil War, Charley let her mind wander back to her own conflict in the restroom. What if Madison and Ashley were just trying to impress Jessica? Did they really do what they said they did? And what would they do to her if she told Lucy? They couldn't do anything, Charley thought, because they'd be arrested and they'd be expelled. At that moment, she was certain about her course of action.

However, she changed her mind throughout the day and she encountered the girls over and over again in the hallways as classes changed. She tried to cling to the walls and become invisible but one of them always spotted her, glaring and pointing fingers in her direction. No doubt about it, she knew she now had three sworn enemies. She hoped they wouldn't be waiting for her after school.

In class after class, she was chastised for not paying attention or belittled for not having an answer to a question. Only one teacher, Mr Spinnato, seemed to care enough to ask her if she was OK. She nodded mutely and hurried out into the hall. She could tell no one in school what she knew because everyone would know about it in an instant. She wanted to get home without being cornered again.

When she left the building at the end of the day, she made sure she flowed outside with a large crowd of students, positioning her body next to the tallest, bulkiest guys she could find. Her breath caught in her throat as she boarded her bus, fearful that one or all three of them would be waiting for her in that confined space. She scanned the seats looking for one of their dreaded faces.

Behind her, someone shouted, 'Hey, move it!'

She hurried down the aisle and slid into the nearest seat as she continued to look at the faces of the other riders. No sign of Madison, Ashley or Jessica. A slight edge of tension eroded away during the ride. It ratcheted up again when the bus reached her stop. What if they're waiting for me here? she wondered.

She went down the steps to the sidewalk. The doors to the condominium building seemed so far away. She wanted to run inside and cower behind the security desk until she was sure no one was following her. Instead, she straightened her spine and took deliberate steps, shuddering with relief when she was inside. She scanned the lobby, waved at the security team behind the desk and pressed the up button for the elevator.

The ascent seemed eternal. The walk from the lift to her door seemed interminable. Finally, she was there. Her hands trembled as she struggled to get the key in the lock, missing every time she turned her gaze up or down the hall to make sure no one was creeping up behind her.

At last, she was inside. She pushed the door tightly closed. And then, she shoved on it once again. She threw the deadbolt and stood stock-still feeling the fear and anxiety drain from her body. Home, she thought. Home safe and sound. A nasty little voice in her head whispered, I bet Mom thought she was safe and sound in her home, too. She pressed her skull between her hands and breathed in deeply through her nose, held it in for a moment, then let it out slowly – just like her therapist taught her. She feared she would be haunted by her mother's brutal death for the rest of her life.

Within two minutes, she felt the calm wash over her. But the day's tension left its scar. She wanted a cup of coffee right now more than anything. She knew her dad had forbidden anything with caffeine after school but today simply had to be an exception. It could be worse, she thought, I could have an urge to hit the liquor cabinet.

She brewed a small pot, fixed a cup and went

out on the balcony to await the arrival of Kara and Ruby. As she sipped, a new course of action percolated through her thoughts. Maybe it would be better if I checked out the model apartment first. Make sure that there was a real reason to raise the alarm. Maybe they knew I was in the stall the whole time and everything they said was one big joke. Maybe they wanted me to report what they claimed to have done but actually hadn't to make me look silly and stupid and have me labeled as a crybaby tattletale. Her thoughts were interrupted by the arrival of her little sister and the sitter.

She listened to Kara scold her about the coffee. Charley insisted she was sorry when she really was simply annoyed. Kara still treated her like a stupid, little child. Ruby's prattling had been annoying her of late but today she welcomed it, willingly giving her hand to her sister and allowing her to drag her away from Kara's lecture.

Ruby was on non-stop chatterbox mode. Charley nodded her head and made non-committal responses as Ruby kept the virtual monologue going. It started to give Charley a headache but it beat listening to Kara's admonishments. She was, she believed, far too old and far too mature to have to answer to any sitter. Ruby was a baby in need of supervision, she thought, but not me.

If I want coffee after school to help me get through my homework and studying, then I should be able to have it, she told herself. A tiny internal voice said, That's not why you had coffee today. She suppressed that bit of truth and grew determined to confront her father about the caffeine restriction. After all, she was in middle school; she was no longer a baby.

Dinner was an unbearable ordeal where her dad kept asking what was on her mind and she kept insisting that nothing was. Finally, he gave up, telling her, 'That's never true, Charley, there's always something on your mind. Just remember, when you're ready to talk about it, I am always here ready to listen.'

She thought about all the times he wasn't there when she needed him and almost snapped out a blistering comment. But knew she was being unfair and said nothing. Once the table was clean and the dirty dishes stacked in the dishwasher, she slipped out on the balcony to call Lucy. She tried her home phone first. When she got voicemail she left her a message: 'Lucy, I think maybe somebody I know did a bad thing but maybe she didn't. Maybe she was just trying to act tough. Maybe she was trying to scare me. Or maybe it's just one big joke. I don't know what to do. I need your advice. Call me anytime, day or night.'

She thought about calling Lucinda's cell but decided if she was still at work, she was busy with something. It's time I stopped running to her like a baby every time I have a problem, Charley thought. It's time I stood up for myself and solved my own problems. She formulated her schedule for the next morning. She'd set her alarm to get up before her dad and slip out of the house before he came downstairs. Then she'd go over to Twelfth and Jefferson and find out if there was any truth to what they said. If they were telling the truth, she could deliver an eyewitness account of what she saw. Or, if it was nothing, she would never speak of it again.

She went online and printed out walking directions from her condo to the apartment complex. Just over a mile and a half, she could walk that in half an hour – no sweat. And she should be able to do that, check out the scene and get to the school before the first bell. She fell asleep with a smile on her face; she had a plan of action and that was always better than sitting still waiting for things to happen.

Ten

The moment Charley's alarm started to ring the next morning at five thirty, she slammed it off and got dressed. She made sure she had some money to stop at Starbucks and snuck out of the house. She avoided the lobby by taking the elevator down to the garage and slipping out through the rear entrance.

When she stepped up to the counter at the coffee shop and ordered a grande latte with an extra shot, the barista gave her a peculiar look. 'You know that's three shots of espresso, don't you?'

'Of course, I do,' Charley said.

'Are you sure you're allowed to have that?'

'I thought the customer was always right,' Charley snapped. 'I have the money,' she said, slapping a ten-dollar bill on the counter. 'I don't think there's a law against serving a minor coffee, is there?'

'OK, OK, just don't come back here whining or send one of your parents in here to yell at me,' the barista said as she took the money and returned her change.

The pick-up counter was above her head, but she reached up and grabbed her drink when it arrived. The guy at that end said, 'Hey, little girl, are you sure that's yours, it's a latte with a triple shot.'

'It's mine,' Charley said through clenched teeth.

'Are you sure you don't you want some hot chocolate or something?'

Charley just turned and walked away. She was so tired of being treated like a child. She stalked out of the store, praying for more height soon. When she arrived at the complex, she spotted the model apartment sign displayed just as prominently as the girls had said it would be. She circled around back and saw the big trash can below a busted window.

She tossed her empty coffee cup inside the receptacle and tried to hoist herself up on top of it, but she was too short to get the needed leverage. Looking over the area around her, she spotted a pile of wooden pallets. She dragged one over next to the can, stood on it and realized she still wasn't high enough.

She grabbed another one and struggled to get it up on top of the first. She shoved on it to make sure it was sturdy and then scrambled up on the trash receptacle. She pushed a few sweaty strands of hair out of her face and reached for the window sill. She nearly cried when her first effort to pull herself up failed. Now she was not only angry about the situation, she was mad at herself for being too small and too weak. She tried again, nearly slipped but, at last, with the help of a foot on the wall, she was able to pull herself up on the ledge and look inside.

Below her, water was running in the bathtub, slopping over the edges and flowing like a little stream out the door. She had no choice. If she wanted to get inside, she had to jump in the tub. Do I really need to? she wondered. The water's running; obviously something they said was true. But that could be a coincidence; maybe someone turned it on to see if it worked and forgot to turn it off. She had to be sure. She clung to the sill, and made the small drop. When she pulled her hand away, she realized she'd been cut on a piece of broken glass.

She swirled her hand in the water, watching a little stream of red eddy into the tub. She used her uncut hand to grab the faucet and turn off the water. She stepped out onto the wet floor, grabbed a towel off the rack and pressed it against the cut. She turned off the sink faucet, too, and opened the medicine cabinet, searching for a bandage, but it was empty. No one lives here, dummy, she admonished herself, why would you even look?

She sniffed the air for the scent of urine but everything just smelled musty and damp. She sloshed out of the bathroom and into a bedroom where the carpet was drenched by the ankle high water. She squished across the sodden flooring to the living room where she saw the red writing on the wall and the red daisy on the carpet. The can of spray paint bobbed in the water. She picked it up and went into the kitchen.

She turned off the water running in the kitchen and opened the cabinet under the sink and sniffed. Ewww – pee. She remembered that smell from the stairway in the downtown parking garage. She was standing beside the dining-room table when the door blasted open and four uniformed officers burst into the room, guns pointed right at her.

'Uh, uh . . .' was the only sound Charley could make come out of her mouth.

'Drop everything in your hands, girlie. Drop it all now,' one of the officers shouted.

Charley looked down at the can and the towel in her hands as if seeing them for the first time. She jerked her hands open as if what she'd been holding had just burned her fingers. The can clattered on the top of the table, then rolled to a stop beside the centerpiece. The towel fell to the floor, laying on the watery surface, absorbing it for a moment, before sinking to the bottom.

'Hands up in the air!'

She shoved them up as high as she could.

'Turn around!'

'But, but . . .' Charley objected.

'Turn around!'

She obeyed the order, her knees shaking, heart pounding. She didn't think they'd shoot her in the back but she'd heard some strange stories on television. Her wrists were grabbed from behind. Her hands secured in a pair of cuffs. A hand pushed on the back of her head. 'This way, girlie,' the officer said, maneuvering her around, leading her out of the apartment and into the back seat of a waiting patrol car.

On the way to the Justice Center, she spit out the names of the kids responsible for the vandalism, admitting she didn't know all of their last names. 'Please don't say anything else,' the officer in the passenger seat said. 'We need to read you your rights but before we do that, we need to have one of your parents present.'

'No,' she insisted. 'I just need Lucy – I mean Lieutenant Lucinda Pierce.'

'You want Pierce?'

'Yes. She's my best friend. Don't call my dad. He worries about me too much.'

'Lieutenant Pierce is your best friend?'

'Yes, sir.'

'Yeah, right,' he said with a chuckle.

'No, really, she is, honest,' Charley pleaded.

'Just shut up, kid, before you get yourself in even more trouble.'

Charley simmered. She'd gotten pretty disgusted with adults over the last twenty-four hours. But these two were the worst. Wouldn't even let her explain anything. She hoped nobody called her dad.

She rode up in the elevator to the fifth floor with an officer by each side. She took turns staring at them but neither one would look her in the eye. They walked down the hall and stopped outside of an office marked 'Sgt. Cafferty.'

One of the officers went into that room, leaving her there with the other one. She followed the conversation inside. 'Got another little criminal on the line, Cafferty. You might have to throw this one back, though; I think she's too small to keep.'

'Deadly kids come in small packages,' she heard the other man, who Charley assumed must be Sergeant Cafferty, respond.

'She claims Lieutenant Pierce is her best friend.'

'Pierce? Oh, give me a break. How old is this kid?'

'Looks about ten.'

Out in the hall, an indignant Charley shouted, 'I'm eleven. I'm in middle school. I'm not a little kid.'

'Zip it, kid,' the officer with her said.

'Whoa, officer, sounds like a hardened criminal to me,' Cafferty joked. 'Empty her pockets and put her in an interrogation room. And if you have cuffs on her, take them off. It really freaks parents out, with the little ones especially.'

'Sergeant Cafferty, sir!' Charley shouted. 'I need to see Lieutenant Lucinda Pierce. Don't call anybody until I talk to her.'

A dark-haired man in a suit came out of the office and looked down at her. He had those spooky blue eyes, the kind that always made her feel like a butterfly pinned to a board. 'You want me to call Pierce?'

'Yes, sir,' she said. Then, quickly added, 'Please, sir.'

'What's your relationship to Pierce?'

'She's my friend.'

'Really, what did she bust you for?'

'She didn't bust me, she's my friend.'

'Right. What's your home phone number?'

Charley pursed her lips tight.

Cafferty crouched down on his haunches. 'C'mon, what's the number?'

Charley shook her head. 'I'm not telling you anything until you let me speak to Lieutenant Lucinda Pierce.'

Cafferty rose back to his full height, a look of disgust on his face. 'Take her away.'

The two officers hustled her down to an interrogation room. Once inside, they removed the handcuffs. 'Now, everything out of your pockets. Everything.'

Charley pulled out her cellphone, a pen and the change from the ten she spent at the coffee shop, laying it on the table. As an officer started to scoop it all into the palm of his hand, she said, 'Wait! That's my stuff. You can't just take it.'

'You're under arrest, kid; we can take anything you've got.'

'Can you leave my cellphone here?'

The two officers burst out laughing and one of them said, 'No way.'

'I promise I won't make any phone calls without permission. I just want to play a game while I wait for the sergeant guy to come back.'

'Kid, we don't want you entertained in here; we want you bored. Now sit down and shut up or we'll cuff you to the table.'

Meekly, Charley took a seat and stared down at the surface of the table. She wanted them to think she felt defeated. She could think better if they got out of the room and left her alone.

When they were gone, she raised her head and saw her reflection in the glass across the room. She knew that it wasn't a mirror. Lucy had told her about the two-way glass. They'll be watching me, she thought. I can't forget that. She swore that when she was grown up, she'd treat everyone with respect no matter how old they were or how tall they were and she wouldn't let anybody laugh in anyone's face in her presence – no matter what they did or said.

Eleven

Jake had a fitful night wondering what was going on out in Idaho. He woke up every two hours; reaching for his cell to check if he'd missed an incoming call. At seven thirty that morning, he decided he'd waited long enough. He picked up his phone and called the cell of the Special Agent in Charge at the Salt Lake City office.

'Do you know what time it is, Lovett?'

'Seven thirty or so,' Jake answered, puzzling over the question as he spoke.

'That's on the east coast, Lovett. Out here, we have what we call Mountain Time and it's just five thirty – the sun hasn't even come up yet.'

'I'm sorry. I wasn't thinking about the time difference. Did I wake you?'

'No, Lovett. I've been awake all night, sitting in the ranger station overlooking the campsite where we've narrowed down the location of Rogers.'

'Why don't you go in and get him?' Jake asked.

'Listen, Lovett, I don't know how you handle things out east but out here in God's country, we place a value on women and children and kind of think we ought to protect them.'

'What's that got to do with anything?'

'At the campsite, there's a woman and two small children. We were hoping to avoid turning all three of them into hostages. So we're waiting for him to come out of the tent for a morning whiz or a bit of early fishing. You got a problem with that?'

'No, of course not. Sorry to have bothered you. You will keep me posted on any developments?'

'Don't call me. I'll call you.'

Jake hung up, disgusted with his western colleague. He had to keep busy. He got dressed and drove to his office. On route, he called Lucinda and updated her on the latest in the hunt for Rogers. 'You sound distracted, Lucinda.'

'I am, Jake. I've got two things bothering me. One is an anomaly I found in the Sherman case files last night but I can hardly think about that now because of the other thing – Charley is missing.'

'Anything I can do? Do you think she's been abducted?'

'Honestly, Jake, I think she's up to something and we are going to find her safe and sound before we know it. But, in the meantime, no matter how unlikely, I can't help but worry that something else is behind her disappearance, or that whatever she's gotten into this time, she's not going to come out of it unscathed.'

'Let me know if you need my help at any point. I'm following the developments out in Idaho but aside from that I'm at loose ends – nothing that can't be dropped to help you and Charley.'

'Thanks, Jake. Let me know when Rogers is in custody.'

Arriving in his office, he asked one of the agents to keep an eye out for any mishaps involving a young girl that might possibly be Charley. 'It's not official. We're not involved in the case but if we can find out anything to help them locate the girl, I don't think anybody will mind where the information comes from.'

At his desk, Jake pulled out Rogers' file and once again went through it looking for any small item he could have overlooked that could point the search for the fugitive in the right direction. Finally, at nine his cellphone rang. It was an agent in the Pocatello satellite office. 'Sir, I've been asked to give you a call and let you know we picked up Rogers. He's being transported in as we speak. You will receive an update after the completion of his interrogation.'

'The woman and the kids – are they OK?'

'They were still in the tent asleep when we left. They don't even know we were there.'

'What about Rogers?'

'Scraped up a bit when he tried to resist – but nothing all that serious. He keeps insisting he is not Mack Rogers but he sure looks just like him. As soon as he gets into the station, we'll get his fingerprints for confirmation.'

'Can you let me know as soon as that's happened?'

'I don't know. I was told we'd call you after the interrogation.'

'Ah, c'mon . . .' Jake pleaded.

'OK. OK. I'll call once the prints are checked. But keep it to yourself, all right?'

'You got it,' Jake said. He was pumped. He wanted to be there – and maybe he'd get to go once Rogers' identity was beyond question. He hated sitting here so far away with nothing to do but wait. He was thrilled that it was all about to be over but the pent-up energy was making him crazy. He had to get out and get moving. He left the office and walked the four blocks to his favorite diner – eggs, bacon and a stack of silver dollar pancakes sounded like just the thing to calm his jangled nerves. By the time he finished eating, he should have an answer – and maybe a plane ticket to Pocatello.

Twelve

Lucinda was on her way out of her office when the phone on her desk rang. Normally, she would have just kept going but now, with Charley missing, she couldn't ignore the call. 'Pierce,' she said into the receiver.

'Hey, lieutenant, this is Brubaker. That little girl you were worried about this morning, someone matching her description came in here in cuffs.'

'In cuffs? I don't think it could be her.'

'Lieutenant, it looked a lot like that photo you emailed down here. You'd better check it out.'

'Where is the kid?'

'Property crimes, second floor.'

'Thanks,' she said, and went down the stairs to the floor below hers and asked the first officer she saw.

'You just bring a little girl in here?'

'Yeah. Sure did.'

'Is her name Charley Spencer?'

'Don't know, lieutenant. But she's in Interrogation Room B; you can go check her out.'

Lucinda went down the hall to the room in question, stretched out her arm to push on the door. 'Hold on a minute, Lieutenant Pierce.'

Lucinda turned around and spotted the sergeant walking her way. 'What's up, Cafferty?'

'The little punk's been asking for you.'

'What little punk?' Lucinda asked, hoping it wasn't Charley.

'Her name is Charley Spencer – leastways that's what she told us before she got stubborn and refused to talk to us until she talked to you.'

Lucinda's hands planted on her hips. 'So why didn't you call me, Cafferty?'

'She didn't kill anybody, lieutenant. It wasn't a case for Homicide. And since I knew she was lying when she said that you were her friend, I didn't want to bother you.'

'You idiot. She wasn't lying. You didn't call me because you didn't want me around to keep an eye on you. I've heard of your division's reputation with minors. Twist their minds up until they confess and then the hell with the truth. I'm going in to talk to her.'

Cafferty glowered at Lucinda as he slid between her and the door. 'I can't let you do that, lieutenant.'

He was two inches shorter than Lucinda and of average height and build. In her heels, she could look down on the top of his head at the brown hair slicked back from his forehead. She lowered her stare to his artificial contact lens blue eyes. 'Out of my way, Cafferty.'

'Sorry, lieutenant, conflict of interest. I am following procedure when I refuse you access to the subject,' he said with a smirk. 'Can't have you interfering with an investigation, now can we?'

Lucinda had a strong urge to punch him in the face but held it back. 'Why did you arrest that child in the first place?'

Cafferty leaned back against the door and folded his arms across his chest. 'It's solid, lieutenant,' he said with a smile. '9-1-1 got in a call saying that there was an act of vandalism in progress.'

'Who made the call?'

Cafferty shrugged. 'Don't know. No identification on the incoming call and the number tracked back to a disposable phone.'

'Oh, that sounds real credible.'

'It panned out, lieutenant. We sent out two squad cars. When the four officers got there, she was inside the apartment. She was caught with a can of red spray paint in her hand – kind of like catching literally red-handed,' he said with a chuckle. 'She also had a cut on one of her hands that she admitted was from the broken window and she was standing with her feet ankle deep in water. They figured she had to have been there all night to flood the place. They're trying to estimate the damages right now – only a broad estimate of twenty to sixty thousand at the moment, they're working on narrowing that down. No doubt, though, it's a major crime. Your little friend is in a shitload of trouble.'

'You've got the wrong kid. She was not out all night. She was home in bed.'

'You know that for a fact, lieutenant? Were you there, too?'

'No,' she sighed, regretfully accepting the fact that he was completely within his rights as lead investigator to block her from having any contact with Charley; in a similar situation, she would do the same. She was determined, though, to get other concessions. 'Can I just see her through the glass?'

Cafferty eyed her suspiciously as if he thought it was a trick. 'OK. Come on into the observation room.' After stepping inside, Cafferty warned her, 'Stay clear of the control panel. I don't want you getting a wild hair and pressing the intercom button to deliver a message to that kid.'

Lucinda suppressed the urge to lash back at him and turned her focus to the little girl on the other side of the glass. It was Charley all right. But Lucinda could not believe that Charley was responsible for destroying that apartment. There had to be another reason for her presence at the scene.

She studied Charley's posture. Her shoulders were slumped, her head bowed and her hands folded neatly on the table in front of her. It broke her heart when she realized Charley's little legs were too short to reach the floor. They just dangled from the seat, dripping water from her shoes and the cuffs of her pants. Anger rushed in to replace her sorrow. The least they could have done was get the child – any child – out of wet clothes.

At that moment, as if Charley sensed Lucinda's eye upon her, the girl raised her head and stared straight at the glass. Everything about her demeanor said she was docile, cowed, ready to cooperate – perhaps on the verge of making a confession – except for one thing: Charley's eyes flashed bright. Lucinda knew that look. Charley was thinking and planning, and biding her time. The expression on her face indicated her determination to find a solution and her commitment to never, ever giving up. A smile crossed Lucinda's face.

She spoke to Cafferty without turning to face him. She forced herself to restrain her involuntary smile. 'OK, Cafferty, would you at least let me be the one to inform her father?'

Cafferty paused for a moment and then said, 'All right. But make sure he understands he needs to get down here so we can question his daughter.'

When Lucinda reached the stairwell, she called Evan on her cell.

'Lucinda?' he answered.

'Yes, Evan. I found Charley.'

'Oh, thank God! Is she OK?'

'She's unhurt, Evan.'

'Where is she?'

'She's here at the Justice Center.'

'I'll get there as quick as I can.'

'No, Evan, wait.'

'What do you mean "wait"?'

'She was arrested on a serious charge – felony vandalism.'

'What?'

'I don't think she did it, Evan, but she's in one heck of a mess.'

'Well, get her out of it, Lucinda.'

'I can't. They will not let me talk to her. I got to see her through the glass and she's doing fine – I can tell because the fire is still in her eyes.'

'Isn't there something you can do to get her out of there?'

'No, Evan. They know of our personal relationship and because of that, my opinion is irrelevant; it's the way it should be, but it certainly has me frustrated.'

'OK. Fine. I'll take care of it. I'm on my way.'

'No, Evan. There are two things you need to do first.'

'You're trying my patience, Lucinda.'

Lucinda wanted to say something sarcastic about that but knew it wasn't the right moment. 'You need to do two things before you drive over.'

Evan's exasperation was apparent in the quality of his sigh. 'What?'

'Charley needs a change of clothing, including shoes.'

'Shoes? Good grief, what happened to her?'

'She walked through some water, Evan, that's all. She's not hurt but still I think she needs to get out of her wet things.'

'Oh, I see they're taking care of her really well—'

'Evan, don't worry about that now. Just get the damn clothes.'

'What's the other thing?'

'She needs a criminal attorney – a good one. She's up against a division that has a long history of success in obtaining confessions from minors and doesn't seem overly bothered if the kid's story matches the facts at the scene. She needs the protection of a skilled attorney.'

'I didn't pick a winner for myself, when I was in trouble. I really don't trust my judgment here, Lucinda. Who would you call?'

'Bill Waller. I don't know if you can get him. He's really picky about the cases he takes on.

But if you tell him that a Detective Cafferty in the property crimes division is pushing your daughter, I imagine, if he's available this morning, he'll at least get you through this initial phase.'

'What's the name of his firm?'

'Waller, Clutter and Rea. And if Waller is not available, try for one of the other partners. They're all good but Waller has the most experience with the tactics that division has used with minors in the past. He'll know what he's up against and won't need to waste time assessing the situation.'

'OK. OK. I'm on it. You sure Charley's going to be OK until I get there?'

'I'll make sure Officer Brubaker keeps an eye on her. He's a good guy. If anything looks questionable, he'll let me know right away. I've got to run out to the warehouse but I'll have my cell on and will not turn it off. Call me if you have any problems.'

The call ended and now Lucinda felt helpless. She'd done what she could do to protect Charley but it didn't feel like enough. And what if her instincts were wrong? What if Charley was somehow involved? How could she help her then?

Thirteen

At the warehouse, Lucinda went straight to the audio/video-tape storage area. She pulled the box for the Sherman case and rummaged through until she found a set of three tapes labeled 'Lisa Pedigo'. She signed them out and went back to her office, double-checking her cellphone along the way to make sure she hadn't missed a call.

She stopped at Brubaker's desk before going up to her office. 'Hi, officer, have you been able to check up on Charley Spencer lately?'

'Better than that, lieutenant, I have a buddy up there keeping a close eye on her. But the big news is that her father got here just a couple of minutes ago and he came with an attorney.'

'Did you recognize the lawyer?'

'Oh yeah, couldn't miss him – it was Bill Waller.'

What a relief, Lucinda thought. 'Are they questioning her now?'

'Not yet. A policewoman took her down to the restroom to change into the dry clothes her father brought in for her,' Brubaker said and then grinned. 'I hear that the officer gave Cafferty a piece of her mind for letting that child sit in that room so long in wet clothes.'

'I bet that didn't go over well.'

'Sure didn't. Cafferty got up in her face and threatened to write her up for insubordination.'

'Oh, dear,' Lucinda said.

'Not to worry. Apparently Lieutenant Overby overheard the conversation, stepped in, and told Cafferty to shut his pie hole and get back to work.'

Lucinda applauded with delight.

Brubaker grinned. 'Another good day for the good guys, lieutenant. You want me to call when Cafferty starts questioning her?'

'Just let me know when they finish up. Thanks again,' Lucinda said, and ascended the two flights of stairs to her office.

At her desk, Lucinda slipped the first of the tapes into a cassette player. All she heard was hiss. She waited. It would start soon. Two minutes later, the sound hadn't changed. She fast-forwarded, stopped and listened again. Still nothing but tape noise. She repeated the process several times until she reached the end. She flipped it over, concerned but convinced that it was only one-sided and she'd put it in the wrong way. But she got a repeat of the first side.

Something was wrong. She put the second tape in the machine. Again, she ran through one side and then the other. Nothing but hiss. She slammed the third cassette into the slot, hoping her suspicions weren't true. Another blank tape.

By the time she was finished, her heart was pounding. Had the recorder malfunctioned and the interview never captured? Couldn't be. The transcript was here. Someone had to listen to the tape to do that. Maybe that person accidentally destroyed the tape.

Right, and coincidences happen all the time.

But erased tapes and a redacted original transcript in the same case? Not hardly. She pulled out the witness lists from the trial. Lisa Pedigo was not called by the state or the defense. Was there a problem with the witness? Or a problem with the investigation and prosecution?

Lucinda thought back to her initial involvement in the Emily Sherman murder investigation. The homicide division had looked a lot different in the old building – one large room with lots of desks, little room to negotiate the space and absolutely no privacy. She had been talking to a detective about the unproductive door-to-door canvass in the vicinity of a fatal shooting of a young man suspected of drug trafficking.

She paid little attention to Lieutenant John Boswell who answered an incoming call, until he shouted, 'Sergeant Pierce!'

'Yes, sir.'

'Somebody spotted a car abandoned behind Merchants and Farmers Shoe Factory building on Bridge Street. Blood's all over the interior. Wanna come with me to check it out?'

Lucinda had dreamed of joining the homicide squad since before her graduation from the police academy. For now, going on a call with the legendary Detective Boswell was as close as she was likely to get. She agreed without a moment's hesitation.

As they left, the other detective quipped, 'Watch out, Boz, she'll be gunning for your job in no time.'

Lucinda's pride absorbed the sting of Boz's laughter at the remark. The homicide division was an all boys' club and she imagined they all suspected – and hoped – it would stay that way.

Bridge Road was a narrow, twisting street that zigged and zagged for no apparent reason. It was littered with bridges over small creeks that that led directly or indirectly to the James River. Boz drove down it at a speed that she thought was unreasonable, causing him to brake sharply at every curve and causing the car to bounce over each water crossing. She hung on to the strap as if she feared she'd be thrown from the vehicle at any moment.

Gravel flew in the air, pinging on the metal, when he turned into the neglected drive to the old factory. The car jerked and lurched through the smaller potholes and swerved to avoid the mammoth ones. The multi-storey brick building loomed like a blind monster over the weed-filled, pocked landscape surrounding it. The windows on the bottom two floors were covered in plywood; those on the top had been shattered from thrown rocks, birdshot, or whatever projectile trespassers could find to break the glass.

Behind the derelict structure, a patrol car was parked next to a Cadillac of recent vintage. An officer emerged from his vehicle and said, 'The Caddy is registered to Martha Sherman. She reported it stolen six days ago.'

'Andrew Sherman's wife?' Boz asked.

'Think so,' the man in uniform responded.

'Isn't that the guy whose daughter is missing?' Lucinda asked.

'The wealthy guy whose daughter is missing, yeah,' Boz said.

Boz and Lucinda walked over to Martha's car, peering in the windows. Dark, blackened stains covered most of the back seat. Blood spatter splashed across the interior of the windows, all over the headliner and the upholstery on the doors and on the back of the front seats.

'Holy shit,' Boz said. 'If that's the girl's blood in the car, everybody from the mayor and police chief, all the way down the chain of command, are going be coming down on me to get this case closed.'

Lucinda didn't hear from Boz for a couple a days. He called her again to tell her that the tests confirmed that the blood did belong to fifteen-year-old Emily Sherman. 'My captain cleared it with your patrol supervisor. You're assigned to me for the duration of the investigation.'

'Really?' Lucinda said, incredulous at the turn of events.

'Yeah, kid, you wanna be a homicide cop, it's time you learned the ropes.'

Lucinda couldn't think of anyone she'd rather have as her teacher than Boz. He had the highest closure rate of anyone on the force in any division.

Together, they interviewed Martha Sherman on several occasions. They both had difficulty believing that the woman was capable of committing a crime with that much brutality, violence and bloodshed. But Andrew Sherman had the district attorney's ear and he was screaming long and hard for the arrest of his wife, Emily's step-mother, Martha Sherman. The pressure from above was relentless.

One afternoon, Lucinda was drafting a section of the investigative report when she got a call from Boz. 'Hey, Pierce, we were right. Martha didn't do it. I've got the proof that she couldn't have done it – it was impossible. I'm on my way back to the Justice Center. As soon as I speak to the DA, I'll come tell you all about it.'

Hours passed before Boz finally returned to the homicide division. He looked tired, defeated and depressed; strain seemed to drag his whole face downward. 'Are you OK, sir?'

'Yeah, yeah, I'm fine. Just a long day, that's all.'

'So what did you find out? What kind of evidence did you get?'

'False alarm, kid. Nothing but a false alarm. I'm calling it a day. You might as well go home, too.'

She should have pressed him for more details. She shouldn't have accepted his assessment at face value. She should have protested. But she didn't. Instead, the next morning, she accompanied Boz and two patrol officers to assist in the arrest of Martha Sherman.

For days, she was bothered by lots of questions. The seemingly tailored anecdotes from Andrew Sherman about Martha's horrible mistreatment of Emily – tales that no one else could confirm until some of Andrew's friends and employees started popping up at the station to back up his story. She took many of their statements and each one sounded hollow and no matter how much she pressed, every one of them was vague about details.

Whenever she meekly pointed out some of her

concerns to Boz, his dismissive responses caused her to back down right away. She should have questioned Boz's attitude. She should have challenged his judgment. But Boz was the experienced detective and she was just there to observe, learn and assist Boz in any way that he asked. She believed Boz always did the right thing. And that was the attitude that sent her careening around the bend, down a very wrong road.

Now, back in the present, she went to her computer and got an address for Lisa Pedigo. At the time of Emily's murder, Lisa had lived in a house across the street from the Sherman residence and two houses closer to the intersection leading out of the cul de sac. She now lived in Mechanicsville. Did she tell Boz something about the Sherman family that no one above Boz wanted to hear? Did Lisa see something in the neighborhood that didn't fit the official theory? And was Boz complicit in an effort to conceal evidence from the defense? She did not want to believe that about Boz. The only person who could answer her questions was Lisa Pedigo. She had to talk to this woman as soon as possible.

She went downstairs to check with Brubaker for the latest on Charley's situation. 'Lieutenant, I hear that the attorney won't let that little girl answer a single question. The lawyer and the dad have stepped outside several times to talk on the sidewalk and then come back inside.'

'And left her alone with Cafferty?' Lucinda asked.

'No. Every time they left, Waller left specific

instructions that no one could ask her a question in his absence and told the detective to stay outside of the room until he returned. Cafferty's about to have a cow; he knows that Waller and his division have a long history. There's been a lot of shouting going on. I'd say the lawyer's taking real good care of her.'

'Good. Call my cell if you learn anything else. I've got to run up to Mechanicsville. I'll be back as soon as I can.'

A half hour later, Lucinda's cell rang. 'Hey, Brubaker, did Cafferty tire of playing with Waller?'

'No. They're still going at it. Same ol'. Same ol'. I was calling about something else.'

'What's up?'

'You remember Gloria Phillips?'

'The congressman's second wife – the one that survived?'

'That's the one. She asked for you and when I told her you were out of town, she got hysterical.'

'Really, I'm surprised she remembered me – she dealt more with the DA's office than with me.'

'Well, it was you she wanted. She'd just heard about the congressman's release from jail and was certain he was coming to kill her, too. Said she'd gotten four hang-up calls in the last forty-five minutes. During the last one, the person on the other end whispered her name and then said, "My little habanero".'

'What?'

'She said that the only person who ever called

94

her that was Phillips and she insisted it was a veiled threat. She's sure he's going to try to kill her again and this time he'll make sure he doesn't fail.'

'I don't think he's stupid enough to go after her physically so soon after his release – but then, again, he is a politician, so who knows? Tell her to pack an overnight bag and send a patrolman to pick her up and bring her into the Justice Center. Tell her I'll talk to her as soon as I get back, and get her to some place safe for the night. If she gets hungry before I return, send someone out to get her lunch – don't let her go out on her own.'

Charley, Gloria, Lisa, Martha – it was all piling up too fast. And what about Jake? Why hasn't he called? Have they still not taken Rogers into custody?

Fourteen

Lucinda pulled into the driveway of a large two-storey traditional home with a broad front porch flanked by two massive pillars. The grass was a blanket of brilliant green and smelled as if it had just been mowed that morning. She rang the doorbell and heard approaching footsteps.

The door opened halfway and a diminutive woman with envy-inducing skin, smooth, clear and in a light shade of *café au lait*, asked, 'May I help you?'

'Are you Lisa Pedigo?' Lucinda asked.

The woman's brow furrowed as her deep brown eyes looked over the detective. 'Who are you?'

Lucinda pulled out her badge. 'Lieutenant Lucinda Pierce, ma'am. I'm outside of my jurisdiction so you have no obligation to speak to me, but if you would, I'd like to ask you a few questions about an old case.'

The woman nodded, 'Yes, I'm Lisa Pedigo. Please come in.'

Lisa led her to a formal sitting area with soft white carpet, white sofas, red chairs and black lacquered tables. Lucinda wasn't sure how anyone could ever feel comfortable in the room – or how it would be possible to keep that carpet clean and unstained – but Lisa appeared to be in her element and very proud of her home.

'Ms Pedigo, do you remember the Emily Sherman murder?'

'I certainly do. I kept waiting for that Lieutenant . . . uh, I forget his name . . .'

'Boswell?' Lucinda suggested.

'Could be. But anyway. I kept waiting for him to contact me again. He was so excited when he left here. He said that I was a huge help to the investigation and that what I knew would make sure that justice and right won out over power and influence. I asked him for his opinion about the murder; he said he couldn't talk about that just yet.

'When I didn't hear back from him, I called and left messages but he never returned my calls. I even called the district attorney but he never telephoned me either. I thought it was odd that they never wanted my testimony at trial.'

'Did you have any suspicions about that? Did it worry you?'

'It certainly did. In the end, I suspected they didn't want me in the courtroom because they knew I would help the defense raise reasonable doubt about Martha's guilt.'

Lucinda's heart pounded. 'You thought she was innocent?'

'It seemed quite possible. How could Martha have gone anywhere to harm Emily? She didn't have a car. Martha was stuck at the house.'

'OK. How did you know Emily had taken the car?'

'I saw her run out of the house, jump inside of Martha's car and back out of the driveway before peeling off down the road at far too fast a speed. I remember thinking that she was too young for her driver's license but then other people's children do seem to grow up every time you turn your head.'

'You told the detective about what you saw?'

'I certainly did. I also told them that less than a minute later, Martha ran out of the house, looked up the street and then slumped onto the garden bench and sobbed.'

'Did you ever see the car return home?'

'No, never. It was never in that driveway again.'

'Could it have been parked in their garage?'

Lisa chuckled. 'You obviously never saw the inside of the Sherman's garage. Packed floor to ceiling with boxes and stuff. You couldn't have found space to park a skateboard in there.'

The memory of the scene at the Sherman home came rushing back to Lucinda. She recalled the methodical dismantling of the garage and the fear that the teenager's body might be found in the midst of all the clutter. She thought it was odd that Boz entertained that theory, because there was no odor of decomposition present. Now she wondered again: why did they do that? 'What kind of person was Martha Sherman?'

'She seemed very nice. But my children were rather small at the time, and you tend to spend more time with women who have children in the same age range as yours. But I do remember that she always seemed to have a smile on her face. Well, not always. It was often missing when Emily was around.'

'Did she mistreat Emily?' Lucinda asked.

'Oh no. I never saw any sign of that. I'd say the opposite was true: Emily was mean to Martha.'

'Really?'

'Yes, very. Like one time, on a scorching hot afternoon, I was weeding a garden bed when Martha pulled into the driveway. She walked up to the front door carrying two large paper grocery sacks – one in each arm. Emily came running around the side of the house and right up to the porch.

'Martha smiled at her. I imagine she thought the girl was coming to open the door for her. But instead, Emily shoved Martha, knocked her sprawling into a rose bush, sending groceries flying in every direction. Then, that girl hopped on her bicycle and pedaled down the street. When she passed by me, I realized she was laughing.

'I ran across the street to help Martha. I pulled her to her feet. The two of us gathered her purchases up from the lawn and the flower bed. Martha kept saying she was OK but I insisted on going inside and putting something on the cuts she got from the thorns. But Martha only shrugged when I asked her about Emily; she wouldn't say a bad thing about that girl, though, heaven knows, she had plenty of reasons to do so that afternoon.'

'When did that happen?'

'Oh, nine months or so before Emily died.'

'Did you mention that in your interview?'

'I certainly did.'

'What else did you tell the detective?'

'I thought you kept records of those interviews.' Lisa said.

'Yes, ma'am, but, we have a little problem with the transcript document. Apparently, someone filed away a redacted media copy instead of the original.'

'Redacted?' Lisa asked.

'That just means that when a document is made public, someone goes through it and, using a permanent marker, blacks out some of the information not appropriate for release. Most often they obscure people's birth dates, phone numbers, social security numbers – private information. And occasionally, a judge will deem some of the material too inflammatory or prejudicial for public release.'

'Well, don't you keep the tapes of those interviews? I know he recorded it.'

'The tapes were damaged, ma'am.'

'Ah, well, I suppose with the conviction you no longer thought you had any need of that and someone got careless.'

Lucinda didn't correct her on that point; she just waited for her to continue.

'Let's see,' Lisa said. 'It's been quite a few years, lieutenant. I'm not sure I can completely recall.'

'If I showed you a transcript of your interview, would that help you remember?'

'It might.'

Lucinda handed her the thick document and said, 'What I'd like to know Ms Pedigo, is what you said in the places where the words are blacked out, if you can recall.'

'It will probably help if I read the whole thing from the beginning.'

'Take all the time you need,' Lucinda said.

Lucinda leaned back in the sofa watching the woman as her eyes went down a page, flipped it and started at the top of another. At this moment, she knew it did not look good. If Boz listened to what Lisa said, why didn't he raise an objection before or during the trial? If he hadn't been involved in the concealment of Lisa's statement, why did he allow the omission to stand? She had to find out if the defense had even been aware that Lisa had made a statement to police.

Lisa rose out of the chair and sat next to Lucinda on the sofa. She pointed to the largest section of blackout and said, 'This is where I told him about Emily driving off in the car that afternoon before she died.' She flipped a couple of pages. 'Here is where I told him about the time Emily pushed Martha over – like I was telling you. And right here, is something I'd forgotten.'

'What was that, Ms Pedigo?'

'It had slipped my mind but I knew Andrew was having an affair.'

No wonder he placed the blame on Martha; he wanted her out of the way. 'With whom?' Lucinda asked.

'I didn't know at the time,' Lisa said, 'so I didn't tell the detective back then but I found out her name later when I saw the wedding announcement in the newspaper – she is the current Mrs Sherman. She was Dora Canterbury, the heiress to the Canterbury real estate empire – word is her father is rich enough to buy and sell Donald Trump several times over – and she is an only child.'

Lucinda felt her stomach churn. The obvious injustice and the nefarious motives behind the framing of Martha Sherman would be recognizable to a kindergarten student. And Boz was mixed up in all of this? And he never said a single word about it to her? And she'd never questioned a single thing he'd been doing, throughout the whole investigation. How could she have been so naïve?

Fifteen

Now that lunchtime had come and gone, Jake wondered why he hadn't heard back from Idaho. How could a simple fingerprint check take so long? It would be understandable if they were doing a blind database search looking for a match, but this was ridiculous. They probably just couldn't be bothered to communicate, he thought.

The agent out west had specifically told him not to call but his silence had gone on for far too long, making Jake feel as if his patience had been shredded at high speed in a food processor. He picked up the receiver and called to find out what was up.

'I told you I'd call you, Lovett.'

'I'm not a patient man.'

'Well, it's a massive SNAFU and I've been busy trying to calm down the guy that we falsely arrested. In fact, I just dropped him off at his campsite where his wife lit into him for disappearing but when he pointed at me and said, "He arrested me at gun point when I went to take a leak," she jumped on me and let loose the wrath of God. The woman had more obscenity laden ways to tell me I was an irresponsible moron than I heard from anyone since my first wife.'

'Back up,' Jake said. 'What's this about a false arrest?'

'When he told us he wasn't Mack Rogers, he was telling the truth. When he gave us his identification, I told him we'd charge him with identity theft. Turned out the fingerprints didn't match Rogers but did match the ones on file when he was in the Marines.'

'You're kidding. How could you make a mistake like that?'

'I swear, Lovett, you don't need to get on my case, too.'

'Sorry,' Jake mumbled. 'But what went wrong?'

'I'll send you this guy's booking picture. I promise you, you won't be able to tell the difference between him and Rogers either.'

'That close, hunh? Did you check to see if he was related to Rogers?'

'He said he never heard of him and we couldn't find a connection anywhere.'

'What about the possibility that he's an accomplice of Rogers?'

'Before we got word on the fingerprints, we were checking on his whereabouts when those girls disappeared. He was posted out of the country when all but the most recent ones had gone missing. In that time frame, he said he was living in Idaho and hadn't travelled out of state. We couldn't find anything to contradict his statement – no plane, bus or train tickets back east. And looking at his work records, the only periods of time when he had enough days off to drive to Virginia and back did not coincide with any of the deaths.'

Jake sighed. Another dead end. 'Thanks for your efforts. Let me know if anything else turns up.'

'Next time, I'm not going to let anybody know anything until I'm damn sure, Lovett – I don't relish another round of public humiliation, thank you very much.'

Jake almost objected to the agent's attitude but quickly realized that he'd feel the same way and he couldn't blame the man a bit. 'Sorry it all turned out like this. I know you're as disappointed with this outcome as I am.'

'Just find that bastard, Lovett. And nail his hide to the wall.'

Jake had nothing to do but start another round of calls. He heard about a transvestite who was harassed in Alabama. The poor trannie's birth name was Mackenzie Rogers but any similarity to the fugitive ended there. The deputies refused to call her Marie but bullied and insulted her for eleven hours before allowing her to return home. Predictably, they did not offer her a ride back in a squad car. When she hitched and accepted a ride from the wrong person, she was beaten and dumped on the side of the road.

Dozens of ex-wives pointed an accusatory finger at their former husbands – most of whom had never been in the state of Virginia, let alone anywhere near the house on DeWitt Street. They were questioned and released, their days ruined and, in some cases, their jobs imperiled. Many who were acquainted with those temporarily accused would never look at them the same again. Once those kinds of suspicions are expressed, you can't completely take them back; the stain corrupts for a lifetime.

Jake wished that local law enforcement would

be more circumspect in handling potential suspects; but was grateful that the description of Rogers made it clear that he was not Black or Hispanic. The harassment potential if the case involved a person of color would have spread like a virulent infection throughout the South and beyond. Still, despite the description, an officer in Detroit brought in a homeless black man. Fortunately, the patrolman was laughed out of the station house and the poor man was given a hot meal before being returned to his makeshift home under a bridge.

Everyone wanted to be the hero who nabbed Mack Rogers but too many went about the search with reckless, desperate abandon. Jake could only hope that Lucinda was having a more fruitful day.

Sixteen

Back at the Justice Center, Lucinda went straight to the room where Gloria waited for her return. The restless, pacing woman reminded the detective of corralled wild mustangs, high-stepping from one end of the fence to the other, anxious to break loose and head for the hills.

Gloria's mass of wavy, dark auburn hair hung down below her shoulder blades. She tossed it about like a distressed mare as she bounced around the room. Lucinda realized that her first challenge would be getting the woman to calm down enough to sit still and have a cohesive conversation.

Lucinda opened her mouth, ready to issue a bland greeting to Gloria; but before she could utter a word, the woman lit into her. 'How could you do this to me? Is my life that insignificant? I helped you put him into jail and now my life is on the line. When he finds me, I'll just be collateral damage, nothing more!'

'Ms Phillips, please, please sit down and let's talk about what we need to do to keep you safe.'

'Phillips,' she spat. 'Do not ever address me by that name again. I should have done this long ago but I'm doing it now. I called my attorney. I am legally reverting to my maiden name: Martinez, Gloria Martinez. I want that on my tombstone. Do not dare make me bear his name on my grave for all eternity. When he kills me, make sure that does not happen or I will never leave you in peace.'

'Ms Martinez, please, we can't talk while you're ricocheting around the room like this. Please, have a seat,' Lucinda pleaded as she slid into a chair. She patted the table at the space across from her. 'Please, sit here.'

Gloria stopped at the spot and slapped both of her hands down on the surface. 'You promised me!'

'I promised you? I promised you what, Ms Martinez?'

'You promised me that bastard would spend the rest of his life in prison. You promised me that I wouldn't have to worry about him.'

'Ms Martinez, I promised you we would arrest him and we did. I never pretended that I knew what the outcome would be at his trial or that he would never have any success on appeal. I can't predict the courts and I have never pretended that I could.'

Gloria reared back and placed her hands on her hips. 'Well, I didn't mean you personally. I meant the lot of you,' she said waving one hand around in a big circle.

'I do not know what you're talking about. No one in my presence ever made a promise that he would go to prison and stay there.'

'OK, it wasn't you. It was the prosecutor. He promised me. He swore if I testified I'd be safe because that damned congressman I called husband would never leave the prison alive.'

'He shouldn't have said that,' Lucinda admitted.

'And I was a fool to believe him. I should have known I couldn't trust the district attorney when Chris walked free after trying to take my life. But no, like an idiot, I took him at his word. But he only said that, he only made that promise, because he knew I wouldn't have testified if he hadn't. I wouldn't have taken that risk otherwise. And now, what am I supposed to do? Chris tried to kill me once over nothing but my life insurance. Now, the stakes are bigger. He will not allow me to live.'

'Ms Martinez, the appellate court ruled that you should not have testified. Phillips has no reason to believe you would be called to the witness stand again. So you are not a threat to him now.'

'Oh, you think so?' Gloria said shaking her head. 'He is a very intelligent man. He is a very ruthless man. He always sought revenge against his enemies. He would kill me just for spite.'

'We are taking you into protective custody. We will not allow him to get near you.'

'But he still has very powerful friends, wealthy friends. Look at what his buddy Karl Porter did, hiring that zoologist and filing an appeal claiming that it was a bat in the house that frightened Patty and made her fall. He claimed that he found traces of guano in the stairwell. I thought Karl was going to get Chris out of jail then. I breathed a sigh of relief when he was laughed out of the courtroom. But Karl hasn't given up. He's still looking for anything else he can find to get Chris off the hook. And now he is and he will have his revenge. With people like Karl to help him, he will find a way to eliminate me, no matter what you do.'

'We are working with the FBI on this case now. Between us, you will have the best security possible. But the most important thing, at this point in time, is that we make you permanently safe. We need to strengthen the evidence surrounding Patty's murder and we need to find something or someone to confirm your story.'

'Why? So you can put me on the stand again? Right, like I'm still going to be alive when he comes into the courtroom again. He was hardly out of the prison before he was calling me. I've moved. Changed my phone number – it's unlisted! And still within minutes, he found me. If you can't protect me from that, how can you protect me from anything?'

'I know you are afraid, Ms Martinez. I know you can't trust any of us. But please, set aside your fear, set aside your misgivings and focus on helping us get Chris Phillips back behind bars where he belongs. You are the only survivor. His other two wives are counting on you.'

Anger flared Gloria's nostrils and furrowed her brow. 'You think I don't care about Melinda and Patty? You think I don't want justice for their deaths? You think I went up on to that witness stand for myself?'

'No, I don't. I know you were thinking of them and wanted to hold their killer responsible. We talked about that once, remember?'

'You're damned right. I did it for Melinda. I did it for Patty. I did it for . . .' Gloria slapped her hand over her mouth. Her eyes darted from one side to another and then she hung her head.

'Who else, Gloria?' Lucinda asked. She suspected she already knew the answer – the unnamed victim in Patty's trial – young Trevor Phillips, Melinda's son.

Gloria shook her head hard, hair flying in every direction, then slumped into the chair looking defeated.

'Are you thinking of Trevor?'

'I will not talk about him,' she said with another shake of her head. She kept her face turned away from Lucinda.

'Ms Martinez . . .'

'No!' she said, turning towards her long enough for her eyes to catch Lucinda's and then darting away at the first visual contact.

'What are you hiding?' Lucinda pushed. 'What do you know about Trevor that you are not telling me?'

'I will not cause that boy any more pain.' Tears glistened on her eyelashes and travelled down one cheek.

'What do you mean? What could you possibly do to him?'

'I've already done enough. I thought we were close. But when he learned that I had his father arrested after he tried to end my life just as he ended Melinda's, Trevor told me he hated me.'

'I'm so sorry,' Lucinda commiserated.

'I understand. He hurt so badly and he was so young. To believe his father pushed me meant he would have to suspect that his father had killed his mother, too. He couldn't do it. Chris

111

Phillips was the only parent he had left – he had to believe in his innocence.'

'How old was Trevor at the time Phillips attempted to take your life?'

'Six. He was only six years old. And such a sensitive child.'

'That would mean he is now fifteen, right? Do you really think it is a good idea for him to spend the rest of his teens being raised by Chris Phillips?'

'That won't happen. Melinda's parents have custody of Trevor.'

'Phillips' attorney filed this morning to have that ruling revoked. He will persist and, in all likelihood, succeed. He is, after all, the boy's biological father.'

'He can't! Trevor's doing so much better now. I don't bother him but his grandparents keep me informed. The last two years have been good for him. That can't be disrupted. And Chris knows . . . he knows what Trevor saw. He will destroy that boy.'

'What does Trevor know, Gloria?'

'Ohmigod,' she sobbed. 'I shouldn't have said that. Omigod!'

'Ms Martinez, I cannot protect Trevor unless you tell me why he needs protecting. Help me. Help me, help Trevor. What does Trevor know?'

Gloria choked on a sob and raised her tear-stained face to Lucinda's. 'He saw it. He saw his father push me. He saw the concrete blocks his father put on the landing. He was right there when I twisted my body toward the banister, hoping I could get far enough to the side to miss

112

hitting the blocks. And when I thrust myself a bit too hard, he saw my body slam into the spindles and break them before crashing to the floor below just two steps above the landing. He saw it all.'

Lucinda was stunned. There had been an eyewitness. 'You didn't tell anyone about that?'

Gloria shook her head. 'After I recovered from surgery, I asked if they spoke to him. They told me they did but that Trevor said he had been asleep and didn't wake up until he heard the sirens from the ambulance.'

'And that wasn't true?'

'No. No.'

'How can you be so sure he saw his father push you?'

'As I started to tumble, the last thing I saw was Trevor's little face. His eyes wide. His mouth opened in a scream. I can never wipe that image from my mind.'

'Why didn't you tell the investigators or the prosecutor?'

'He was such a little boy – such a sweet, little boy. He had to deny it to himself to survive. He couldn't help it. I would not betray him – I didn't think I needed to. When Chris was acquitted, I had my regrets but I knew no matter what I said then, Chris could not be tried again. I almost spoke up when Patty died.'

'But you didn't?'

'He was only ten then, how could I?'

'I'm going to have to speak to Trevor.'

'No. You can't. It will destroy him.'

'If Trevor was there when his father pushed

113

you down the stairs, he may well have repressed the memory of seeing Chris do the same thing to his own mother – or to Patty. He could be carrying around a festering burden of unacknowledged guilt for his silence. If he never confronts the truth, he will never conquer the burden he carries for what he knows.'

'Ohmigod!'

'I promise you, Ms Martinez, I will make sure Trevor gets professional help to cope with the situation. Melinda's parents will be very supportive of him. They are good people, smart people – you know that. They will help us all help Trevor recover and build his life anew.'

'You need to let him know I don't blame him. I don't hold him responsible in any way. I understand.'

'I will. I promise. And, maybe, if Trevor is willing, we can bring the two of you back together again.'

At that, Gloria broke down completely, dropping her head to the table and cradling it in her folded arms as she cried out her anguish. She stretched out one arm and fumbled for Lucinda's hand. When she found it, she squeezed it hard. Lucinda returned the gesture and left the room to make arrangements for Gloria's care.

Seventeen

Lucinda made a beeline for Captain Holland's office. She needed his help and guidance with the placement of Gloria Martinez, the interview of Trevor Phillips, and the inappropriate documentation in the Sherman case. When she said his name, Holland raised his head and narrowed his eyes.

'Did you find what you needed to get the DA to take steps to have Martha Sherman released from prison?'

'Not exactly, sir. But, right now, I need to talk to you about a couple of other matters that I think can be wrapped up more easily – then I'll get to Sherman, if that's OK.'

'Sit down, Pierce. I should have known you'd have more than one problem to complicate my day.'

'First of all, sir, I have Gloria Martinez, Chris Phillips' second wife, in an interrogation room. She is afraid that Phillips will come after her now that he's been released from prison.'

'Do you think she has grounds for her fear?'

'I think her reaction is a bit extreme, but it's not groundless. She's received hang-up calls and at the end of one of them, the caller used a diminutive that only Phillips ever called her.'

'Is it possibly a friend of the congressman who knew about it?'

'Possibly,' Lucinda conceded with a nod. 'But

I still believe there are strong grounds for taking her into protective custody.'

'I don't know, Pierce. Doesn't seem as if the state would make the same mistake by calling her to the stand in the second trial.'

'That could change, captain, now that there is a witness to the attempted murder.'

'A witness? Now? And you find that credible?'

'That brings me to my second problem, sir,' she said and explained about Trevor's presence at the crime scene. 'We need to talk to him.'

'He's still a minor, Pierce.'

'Right now, the parents of his deceased mother are his legal guardians but we have to act fast. Phillips has filed to regain his parental rights and custody of his son. And I am not betting that the courts will protect Trevor from his biological father.'

'Go see the grandparents. Find out if they'll cooperate – without any coercion, Pierce. Play good cop for a change.'

Lucinda exhaled with enough force to make her lips buzz. 'Captain!'

'OK, OK, I know you can do that but sometimes you get too jacked up when you have a goal in your gun sights.'

'I think I ought to take a child psychologist with me, too. Getting the truth from him is going to be a traumatic experience. I want someone there to help him afterwards.'

'The in-house shrink won't do?'

'I think we need someone who specializes in children, sir. I realize that this is an added expense, but . . .'

116

'Just do it, Pierce. But don't hire someone right away. Make sure you have the go-ahead from the grandparents first. It would be a total waste to take someone out there only to be turned away at the gate.'

'Yes, sir. I'll make the first visit during school hours so that Trevor won't be present.'

'Good thinking. Now. You said there was a third thing – something to do with the Sherman case?'

Lucinda wiped both hands across her face. 'There appears to be deliberate tampering and cover-up of evidence. I would have to speak to Martha Sherman or her trial attorney to be certain.'

Holland stared at her, his left eye twitching, color rising in his neck.

After a few moments, Lucinda said, 'Sir?'

'Have you lost your mind?'

'Sir?'

'Do you have any idea of how the DA would react if you contacted those whom he considers his enemy?'

'But, sir . . .'

'It is one thing to review our records, our investigation. It is quite another to approach the other side.'

Lucinda lurched to her feet. 'You said that woman was, in all likelihood, wrongfully convicted.'

'Yes, I did. Sit back down.'

Lucinda remained standing. 'You said she should be released immediately.'

'Yes, I did, but attacking the DA's office is not the way to go about resolving this issue.'

'It is not this DA.'

'But it is his office and his predecessor was his mentor.'

'Yes he was. But Boz was mine. And now, I look at the evidence: erased interview tapes, redacted statements, and the information from Lisa Pedigo that was contained in the missing or altered files, and where else do I go.'

'You will destroy Boz's reputation.'

'Maybe that's what should happen. It makes me hurt,' Lucinda said, pounding her chest with her fist. 'It makes me want to cry, but it also makes me feel stupid and outraged. But this cannot stand, captain. It cannot stand.'

'Martha Sherman will be released eventually, Pierce. Just have patience. The courts will release her in due time.'

'You expect me to put faith in the courts? You expect me to be patient? That woman should have never been put in prison. And she should not remain there one minute longer,' she said, bashing her fist against the surface of his desk.

'Back off, Pierce. Sit down. Now. That's an order.'

Lucinda glowered at him as she slowly sank down on the edge of her chair.

'You cannot expose one of our own.'

'Oh, really?' Lucinda said. 'No matter what?'

'I wouldn't say that, Pierce. Short of a crime involving physical harm to another human being – yes, anything but that.'

'And you don't think Martha Sherman has been physically harmed?'

'Emotionally maybe, but not physically. She can be compensated for her loss of freedom.'

Lucinda popped back up to her feet. 'That's lame, captain. How long has it been since you've been to a prison? They are brutal, violent places. Even women's prison. There are nasty individuals – lifetime criminals – locked up with her. Women with a history of drug use, assaults and murders.

'And there Martha was, a sheltered woman raised in a normal, middle-class home, married to a wealthier man. How much exposure do you think she had to the raw side of life? How well do you think she was equipped to deal with profes-sional manipulators and cons – women who'd kill their own grandmothers for pocket change?

'We have no idea of the physical torment she has suffered. Even if she wasn't beaten or assaulted, there's still damage. Only time will tell how much the stress of that environment will impact her health, shorten her life. But without a doubt, there is physical damage, captain. You can't deny it.'

'But I can tell you this, Pierce: you cannot attack an honorable, deceased officer and destroy his family's memories when his only crime was following orders.'

'I can't?' she said, turning from him and walking to the door. In the threshold, she stopped and spun back to face him. 'Just watch me, captain,' she said and fast-walked out of his office and out of the building. She heard him shouting, 'Pierce! Pierce! Get back here this minute! Pierce!' But she did not break her stride.

In her car, she sped out of the parking lot and headed down the street. A mile away she pulled into a parking space behind a dumpster at the public library. Her temper had flared hot and uncontrollable. But now, her sanity reasserted itself. She needed time to think – and time to cry.

Eighteen

Once Lucinda felt her self-control and composure had reached a point of equilibrium, she pulled out of the lot and drove to the Spencer condominium to check on the situation with Charley. She was greeted warmly by Charley's father Evan.

'I am so glad to see you. This has been a nightmare.'

'Charley's home, right?' Lucinda asked.

'Yes, she's in her room. She won't talk to me.'

'Really? What happened?'

'I told her no matter what she did I would always love her and then asked her about her involvement in the vandalism.'

'Oh, no.'

'Yeah, well, sensitivity has not always been my strong point.'

'That's not what I hear from your patients, Evan.'

'Somehow it's different – I'm different – when it's so close to home. I saw the anger flash through her eyes. The moment she turned from me, I apologized. I tried to take back my words but she would not stick around to listen.'

'Let me go talk to her,' Lucinda offered.

'I don't know. Her lawyer told me not to let her talk to anyone connected to the prosecutor or to law enforcement.'

Lucinda stared at him. 'I can't believe you're saying this to me, Dr Spencer.'

'Oh Jeez, there I go again.'

'Don't play pathetic with me, Dr Spencer.'

Evan slumped against the nearest wall. 'Oh, c'mon, can we go back to Evan?'

'I doubt it. Can I talk to Ruby? Or is that forbidden, too?'

'Of course, you can. She's in the family room watching *Kung Fu Panda* for the millionth time.'

Lucinda walked into the room and spotted six-year-old Ruby's eyes riveted to the screen, her mouth hanging open, her little fingers mindlessly fidgeting. 'Hey, Ruby,' she said. 'Could we pause the movie and visit for a bit?'

Ruby did not respond, not even flicking her eyes from the animation before her eyes.

Lucinda lowered herself to the floor next to the little girl.

Ruby jerked her head, saw Lucinda, turned back to the screen and then back to her visitor. 'Lucy,' she squealed, throwing her arms around the detective's neck.

Lucinda wrapped one arm around her and grabbed the remote with the other hand, pressing the pause button. 'I'd say you're glad to see me,' she said with a laugh.

'Lucy, nobody talks to me. Charley won't let me in her room. Daddy just sits still and tries to be nice but he doesn't do real smiles. I ask him questions and he just pats me on the head and says, "I love you, Ruby". I don't understand and nobody will explain nothing.'

'Well, Ruby, Charley's gotten into a little

trouble and she's very upset about it and so, your daddy is upset, too.'

'Charley? In trouble?' she said, her eyes wide and filled with disbelief.

'I do not think that Charley did anything bad but some people think she did.'

'Bad people?'

'No. Some policemen think she did a bad thing because the bad people said she did.'

'Why do they listen to bad people? Why would they be mean to Charley? Charley is good.'

'Yes, she is, Ruby. But the bad people don't want anyone to know that.'

'Will you tell them?'

'Yes, I will Ruby.'

'Will you put the bad people in jail?'

'I'll make sure everyone knows that they are responsible for the bad things, OK.'

'Put them in jail, Lucy.'

'They're little kids, too, Ruby. Jail's probably not the best place for them.'

'I don't care. They're mean to Charley. I want them in jail.'

'Ruby, I promise you, I will do the right thing. For now that will have to be enough, OK?'

Ruby's eyes scanned Lucinda's face. She blinked several times and then said, 'OK,' and turned back to the screen. Grabbing the remote, she pressed the play button.

Lucinda rose from the floor and walked back to the front of the home. She planned to leave without saying goodbye to Evan but he intercepted her. 'I called Charley's lawyer—'

'The attorney I recommended?'

Evan winced. 'Yes, I called Bill Waller. He said you were the exception. You can speak with Charley – if she'll talk to you.'

'Nice, Dr Spencer. As well as you know me, you did not trust me to put Charley's best interests first.'

'Lucinda, it's not—'

'Oh, yes, it is, Dr Spencer. That's exactly what it is about. Now, if you'll excuse me, I'll go talk to Charley.'

'If she talks to you, I'd like to know what she says – and so would Waller.'

'If she talks to me, Dr Spencer, I will decide exactly what is in Charley's best interests and then take the appropriate action.'

'But—'

'Just go see to your own business, Dr Spencer. Don't worry about me. I can let myself out.'

In the hall outside of Charley's room, Lucinda took a couple of deep breaths to clear any signs of anger or irritation out of her voice and off of her features. She knocked gently on the young girl's door.

'Go away!' she shouted from inside the room.

'Charley, it's Lucy,' Lucinda said and waited. Two full minutes passed before the door creaked open.

'What do you want?' Charley asked.

'I just want to come in, sit down and talk to you a bit, Charley.'

'Have you been sent to interrogate me?'

'No, Charley.'

'Did the police think you could get a confession from me?'

'No one in the police department knows I'm here.'

'Oh, Daddy sent you up here to find out how much damage I did to that place. He probably just wants to get an estimate so he can write a check and make it all go away.'

'Oh, Charley please let me help you.' A single tear rolled down from Lucinda's eye.

Charley's lower lip trembled. Her face crumpled up and sobs followed. She threw her arms around Lucinda's waist and wailed. Lucinda led the girl over to the small love seat and sat down with her, stroking her head as she sobbed out the accumulated stress of the last couple of days.

Her emotions exhausted, Charley pulled back and sighed. Her eyes were red, her cheeks blotchy and her nose running.

Lucinda pulled a tissue out of a nearby box and handed it to her. 'Could I go to the kitchen and get you a glass of water?'

A weak smile crossed Charley's face. 'Daddy put a little 'frigerator in here,' she said, pointing to the appliance on the floor beside her desk. 'I'm not allowed to keep soda in it but it's got lots of water and juices. Could you get me a Fusion?'

'Sure can,' Lucinda said, crossing the room.

'And get something for you, too. Anything you want.'

'Thank you, Charley,' she said, grabbing a bottle of water along with Charley's drink.

Charley took a long swallow, smacked her lips and said, 'OK, fire away.'

'Fire away?'

'Ask me any questions you want?'

'Charley, I was just kind of hoping, you'd tell me what happened? I mean, I'll ask questions if I'm not clear about what you're saying but really, I just want to know what happened.'

'And you'll believe me?'

'Of course, Charley. You've never lied to me before. And I have no reason to believe you'll start now.'

'You mean that?'

'Yes, Charley, I do.'

Charley smiled and told Lucinda the whole story from the moment she heard the conversation in the restroom to the minute the cops walked in on her in the apartment. 'And that's how I got myself in this big mess,' she concluded with a sigh.

'Oh, Good grief, Charley. I hope you've learned a lesson.'

'Yes, when you hear someone coming, run – even if it is the cops.'

'Charley!' Lucinda admonished.

Charley burst into a giggling fit. 'Just kidding, Lucy.'

'Seriously now. What did you learn?'

'That you and Daddy and probably everyone else would be a whole lot happier if I told an adult what I thought was happening instead of investigating it myself.'

'But do you get it? Do you see how it's better that way?'

Charley hung her head and twisted her neck to look at Lucinda. 'I can't lie to you, can I?'

'I sure wish you wouldn't.'

'No,' she said. 'I don't realize that because it's not true. I know it went bad this time but most times I do OK. And besides, I didn't know if they did anything wrong or not. If I start telling every time I think I know about something without knowing for sure, it'd be like that boy – you know the one who cried wolf. And then everything would be an even bigger mess.'

'Oh, Charley,' Lucinda said putting an arm around her shoulder. 'I know you mean well but you sure scare me to death sometimes. Promise me one thing?'

'What?'

'Don't do any investigation of anything until we get this disaster cleared up first. OK?'

'OK. I think that's a promise I can keep.'

'You better, girlfriend.'

'I will,' she said and laughed out loud. 'But don't tell Daddy.'

'About what happened? Why not?'

'Because he thought I did that vandalism thing.'

'Charley, I just think he needed to know for sure. He needed you to tell him that you didn't.'

'I don't care. He needs to suffer a little longer.'

'Charley . . .'

'OK. I'll talk to him at breakfast. But not tonight. I'm still mad at him.'

Nineteen

Back at her apartment, Lucinda flipped on the eleven o'clock news. The teaser at the opening of the show mentioned both the Sherman and the Phillips cases. She sat on the edge of the recliner through too many commercials to wait for the story.

The announcer began. 'Although there is no connection between the murder of teenager Emily Sherman and the death of Patty Phillips, the two cases do have something in common. The same member of law enforcement was involved in the investigations of two people who may have been wrongfully convicted by the state of Virginia. We have an exclusive interview with the sister of Detective Lucinda Pierce.'

The color drained from Lucinda's face. Not again, she thought. What did I do to deserve this?

Lucinda's younger sister Maggie faced the camera and said, 'That detective is dangerous. I know her really well – she's my sister. She's killed people – even kids. She'll do anything to get what she wants. She wanted Martha Sherman and Congressman Phillips in jail and she didn't care what she did to put them there. She didn't care whether they were innocent, she just locked them up and threw away the key. Something needs to be done to stop her. If she is not fired, it only proves that the whole police department is corrupt.'

'There you have it,' the interviewer said, 'an unvarnished look at a member of law enforcement from the person who knows her best. This is Shawna Scott reporting from Albemarle County.'

Lucinda hit the off button on the remote. She felt nauseous and her head was pounding. Quickly, her rage built in intensity. She wanted to call Maggie and shriek at her but knew she would not give her sister the satisfaction of knowing she even saw the story. Instead she called Jake, struggling to put a measure of nonchalance into her voice.

'Hey, Jake! How was your day?'

'A whole lot of running hard and standing in the same place,' Jake groused. 'I'm sorry about what just happened.'

'Oh, you saw the news. I imagine a lot of others did, too. Damn that woman and damn that reporter. Why can't they just leave me alone?'

'She just wants what you have.'

'Oh right. She has a husband, kids, a lovely farm and the respect of her community. I'm sure she'd like to come home to a cat, an empty bed and constant vilification in the press.'

'She is envious that you got away. She is dissatisfied and feels trapped. She thinks the only way she can be noticed is when she attacks you.'

'No, Jake, it's much simpler than that. She hates my guts. She wishes I were dead and if she can't have that she's settled for making me miserable.'

'That's not what's driving her, Lucinda.'

'And you know all about it in your sibling-free universe.'

'Being the only child is not all it's cracked up to be,' Jake objected.

'I'd love to walk in your shoes.'

'You'd give up your brother to get rid of Maggie?'

'That's not fair, Jake.'

'Yes, it is. Would you give up Rick?'

'Noooo,' she admitted, dragging out the syllable as long as she could.

'All righty then. How about we move on to other things? What else is going on with you today?'

'Are you copping out?'

'Yeah, humor me, OK?'

Lucinda sighed, finally accepting that Jake was only trying to help her get past the pain and anger of her sister's repeated betrayals. 'I'm bouncing from one case to another at such a rapid pace, I can't hardly keep them all straight – from Sherman to Phillips to Charley and back again, although not in any particular order.'

'How's Charley? Is she in serious trouble?'

'Pretty much but I don't think she did anything wrong except try to act like a hotshot investigator.'

'Just following in your footsteps,' Jake said with a chuckle.

'Don't remind me. I try to set a good example for her but she always makes the assumption that she's good enough and smart enough to take on any challenge – in a way, she is. But this time she got in over her head. I wonder why the police showed up so soon after she arrived. I suspect one of the girls responsible for the vandalism made that call. Makes me wonder if one of them was watching her or if one of them showed up to retrieve evidence and just happened upon Charley in the apartment. Anyway, tomorrow afternoon, I'm going to have to catch up with the investigators in her case and see if I can do any damage control. I imagine they have her fingerprints on the can of spray paint and that doesn't look good.'

'She picked it up at the scene?'

'Yeah. Collecting evidence, she said. But, at least she realized her mistake in retrospect. A lot of good that does her now.'

'Something's up with the Phillips case?' Jake asked.

'Yes,' she said and gave him a rundown of her interview with Gloria Martinez. 'Anyway, about midday, while Trevor's still at school, I plan on visiting Melinda Phillips' parents and trying to convince them to allow me to interview their grandson about Gloria's so-called accident and then move on to the death of his mother and his stepmother Patty. I thought you might want to go along.'

'Why don't you wait until Trevor's home from school? If he's there when you ask, it would probably be more difficult for them to say no,' Jake said.

'I'm under orders to talk to them first.'

'Ha, Lucinda! Since when have orders interfered with your better judgment?'

'Sometimes you have to choose your battles, Jake. First thing in the morning, I'm going to Fluvanna Correctional Center to talk to Martha Sherman in violation of a direct order. I do try not to do that more than once a day.'

'Just don't become all bureaucratic on me,' he teased.

'Oh, you're a fine one to talk, Mr Special Agent in Charge.'

'OK, I give. But what's up with Martha Sherman? Isn't she getting released soon?'

'Don't know, Jake. The DA is trying to delay that and the only reason that makes any sense to me is that he is responding to pressure from Andrew Sherman, the dead girl's dad and Martha's ex-husband.'

'What's the DA throwing out there? The possibility that Martha was Rogers' accomplice?'

'Yeah, that and maybe they were buddies and Rogers let her stow a body in his little storage facility.'

'That's absurd.'

'Tell me about it. But what makes it all even worse is the strong possibility of prosecutorial misconduct at the trial – erased audiotapes and a redacted transcript where the original should be. I can't ignore that even though Captain Holland is insisting that I do.'

'What do you expect to get from Martha?'

'I need to know if she and her attorney were aware of the contents of the interview in question. If they did have knowledge of it, then all we have is someone's careless screwup. On the other hand, if the state concealed that exculpatory evidence from the defense, we have a serious legal problem.'

'Are you sure you want to take the risk of exposing that misconduct? There's a long and colorful history of shooting the messenger.'

'I have to take this risk, Jake. I need to do everything I can to make this right. I hope you'd feel the same way if you were in this situation.'

'I won't argue with you on that point, Lucinda. I'd probably do everything I could, too. But that doesn't mean it would be the wisest decision. Think about it for a minute. It's one thing to violate an order and achieve your goal. It's quite another to do so and get nothing.

'What if she refuses to see you? She'll certainly tell her attorney that you attempted to visit her and you know that will get back to your captain. You'll face the consequences of your actions and still not get anything you want – maybe even make the situation worse.'

'I know this could go all wrong. I know I could damage my career – maybe even destroy it. And I realize that if I screw this up, it'll probably make Reed dig in his heels and try to delay Martha's release even longer. But I could not live with myself if I didn't try. I was part of the problem. I need to be part of the solution.'

'OK,' Jake said, 'Just so you know what you're up against here. Listen, I'm at a standstill in the search for Mack Rogers. So, while you're out at the prison stirring up trouble, is there anything I can do help you out with Charley's case?'

'How good are you at digging up dirt on middle school girls?'

Jake laughed. 'Can't say I've ever tried that, but I'm willing to give it a shot.'

'Great,' Lucinda said and rattled off the names of the girls involved in the vandalism. 'The principal's name is Camilla Stovall. Charley's a good student, so I'm sure she'll want to do anything she can to help – particularly if you ply her with a bit of your natural and irresistible charm.'

'You find me irresistible, Lucy?'

'You know I do, Jake – even against my better judgment.'

'Are you ever going to learn I'm not a threat to you – I'm not your ex-husband? I know I'm an FBI agent just like he was. I know I am now working in the same office he was when you were married. But, really, we are very different people – ask anybody here.'

'You've been talking about me and my ex with your staff?' Lucinda said, feeling the bright flare of anger spark in her chest.

'Not in that context. I never mentioned that you were married to him.'

'And you think they're not bright enough to make the connection?'

'No, Lucinda. But, really, c'mon, quit changing the subject. Back to my original questions: will you ever—'

Lucinda sighed. Why couldn't he be satisfied with the way things were? Why did he have to keep pushing? 'Jake, not now . . .'

'OK, babe. I'll wait for your call after your

visit to Fluvanna. Just don't forget I love you, Lucy,' he said and hung up immediately, before Lucinda could utter the protest that formed automatically on her lips.

Twenty

As Martha Sherman entered the interview room and waited for her handcuffs to be unfastened from behind her back, and instead have one wrist connected to the U-bolt on the table, Lucinda thought back to the Martha Sherman she'd met during the investigation into Emily's death all those years ago. She recalled a soft face, easy smile and tender eyes of a woman who appeared to be filled with kindness, compassion and understanding. At the time, Lucinda had great difficulty reconciling that exterior image to the act of murder that everyone seemed to believe she'd committed. Lucinda had accepted that reality, albeit with reluctance, because she believed everything Boz told her.

Now, only the shadow of that woman remained. Martha sat across from her with wary, hard eyes, deep furrows in her brow and around her mouth and a sneer where there once was a sweet smile. Lucinda wondered if any little bit of the old Martha would ever resurface once she had been freed.

'You got rid of your patch,' Martha said. 'That's a prosthetic eye, right?'

'Yes, it is, but—'

'Your face looks a lot better, too. As I recall your lips were pretty messed up and now they look almost normal and your skin's a bit smoother.'

Lucinda nodded. 'Yes, I've had some surgery.'

'I liked you better the way you were. It was more honest. Your scars revealed the ugliness of your character. The patch hiding the mutilation of your eye seemed to symbolize your unethical willingness to participate in covering up evidence. It was more you, really it was,' Martha said, curling her lips into an expression of disgust.

Lucinda knew she deserved some measure of abuse for the role she'd played in the injustice perpetrated on this woman. She felt she had no reason to defend herself or anything she had done.

'So, you here to gloat because I'm still locked up?' Martha asked.

'No, not at all, Ms Sherman,' Lucinda said with a shake of her head. 'I want to help you get out of here as quickly as possible.'

'Oh yeah, right. What's the catch? What are you after?'

'Justice, Ms Sherman. You didn't get it. Emily didn't get it. I want to do what I can to set things right but, first of all, I want to apologize—'

'Oh, please, shut the hell up. Who cares how sorry you are? You're only sorry that you were proved wrong. You were nothing but the lap dog of that damned detective. He spoke, you sat up and begged. He called all the shots. Why the hell isn't he in here apologizing?'

Was the ordeal so traumatic that she'd forgotten the most dramatic moment of the trial, Lucinda wondered. 'Surely you remember that he died during your trial.'

'Yeah, yeah, right. Sorry, can't say I care. From

where I was sitting, he deserved it and, besides, I've been a bit too preoccupied with my own situation. It's not exactly a picnic having your freedom stolen from you, your character maligned and your life destroyed for a crime you didn't commit. I'm surprised you bastards didn't cover up the identity of the body when you found Emily in that basement.'

'No matter what you think of me, Ms Sherman, I take absolutely no pleasure in seeing you still in prison. I am appalled by what happened to you and my role in it.'

Leaning forward to put her face as close to Lucinda's as she could, Martha said, 'So it's all about you, then?' She glared at the detective for a moment, then she leaned back in her chair.

'I won't lie to you, Ms Sherman. I admit that I am feeling a bit sorry for myself and ashamed that I was not more discerning and didn't ask more questions. Sure, I wish I hadn't been involved in this travesty of justice. But I am not here because I am feeling sorry for myself.'

'You know, I thought I cared why you were here. That's why I agreed to talk to you – curiosity about the reason for your visit. But you know what? I just realized I don't give a flip what's on your mind. You are letting me sit in here and rot when you know damned well I'm innocent. So why should I give a damn about you at all?'

Lucinda realized this sparring was going nowhere. It was time to cut to the purpose of the visit and jettison everything else. 'Do you remember Lisa Pedigo?'

'Are you not listening? I am not here to answer

138

your damned questions. I came out of curiosity and now that's all shriveled up – gone! Poof! Into thin air. I'm ready to go back to my cell.'

'No, please. Please. Help me, help you.'

'Why? So you can sleep better at night?'

'No. So that you can get the hell out of here,' Lucinda said through clenched teeth.

'As if you care.'

'I know you can't trust me. I know you have no faith in the system. And I don't expect you to suddenly embrace us all. I'm just asking you to give me a chance to help you. What do you have to lose?'

She sat silent for a moment, studying Lucinda's face. 'OK. I'll buy that. I don't have a thing to lose other than these luxurious surroundings,' she said, her free arm waving around the room at the cold, gray walls that enclosed them. 'Lisa Pedigo. Yeah. I remember the name. Lived in my neighborhood. Didn't know her much better than to say hello when I saw her on the street. What about her?'

'Did you know she gave a statement to the police?'

'No, but what does it matter?'

'If you didn't know and your attorney didn't know, that means the prosecutor withheld that information from you.' For the first time, Lucinda saw a spark of life in Martha's eyes.

'Exculpatory information?'

'Yes, Ms Sherman. She corroborated your story that Emily stole your car that morning. She witnessed Emily's treatment of you. And she knew of Andrew Sherman's affair.'

Martha absorbed that information, looking as if she didn't understand its significance. Then her whole face brightened. 'So Andrew, the righteous, was having an affair?'

'Yes, he was.'

'With that vapid secretary of his?'

'I don't know if he had an affair with her or not,' Lucinda said. 'I have been told, though, that he had one with Dora Canterbury.'

'The new Mrs Sherman? Son of a bitch. I didn't know he'd met her before my arrest. Hard to believe that Miss Hoity Toity Money Bags had an extramarital affair with that weasel. But then again, he took me in, too. But she acts like she's everyone's superior, as if she is not subject to the foibles of human nature like us lowly creatures, as if she never has the need to perform normal bodily functions like the rest of us. Does my lawyer know about all of this?'

'I doubt it. I think he would have told you if he had.'

'Are you going to tell him?'

'I was hoping you would,' Lucinda admitted.

'But, I have no proof. What good would that do?'

'Tell him to come to my office. Tell him to confront me in the reception area. It would be best if he approached me when there were witnesses to that encounter.'

Martha narrowed her eyes. 'I can't help but think this is a trick, detective. But at this moment, I am inclined to believe you are going out on a limb for me. It sounds as if no one wanted you to give me this information.'

She leaned back, her eyes looking as if her thoughts were far, far away. She sat upright and said, 'Unless my lawyer tells me otherwise, I will do what I can to protect your confidence. If you are taking a professional risk for me, I really do appreciate it. But, honestly, if my lawyer tells me you're full of shit, I will trust him more than I could ever trust you.'

'I'd feel the same way, Ms Sherman, if I were in your position. Do whatever you need to do. You owe me nothing.'

'Maybe not yet,' Martha said.

Twenty-One

The moment Jake opened the door to the crowded hallways of Jefferson Middle School, he regretted his offer to help Lucinda. Half the milling kids were trying to look like tough characters and the other half looked frightened of their shadows. A swirl of unpleasant experiences during his middle school years ricocheted through his thoughts, filling him with a desire to cut and run. But he'd volunteered. He couldn't back out now.

He went straight to the school office, flashed his badge and asked for Camilla Stovall. The receptionist's eyes grew big at the sight of his shield and she scurried down the hall behind the counter.

A middle-aged woman, with no-nonsense, short red hair and blunt green eyes, wearing sensible black pumps and a gray suit with a huge ring of keys jingling at the waist, bustled out to greet him. Stretching out her hand, she said, 'Camilla Stovall. What can I do for you, sir?'

He took her hand and held it as he looked around at staff members behind the counter and students in front of it. 'Well,' he said, with a shrug.

'Oh, of course. Come on back to my office.'

Sitting in front of her desk, Jake said, 'I want to talk to you about Charley Spencer and the charges of vandalism that have been filed against her.'

'The FBI is involved in that?'

'No. Not at all. I am simply assisting a colleague at the police department who has a bit too much to handle right now.'

'From watching television, I didn't think you federal guys and the local cops ever cooperated with each other.'

'Some TV dramas exaggerate the conflict a bit. There are problems, but we can all rise above our jurisdictional squabbles more often than not in my experience,' Jake said, while hearing Lucinda's voice in his head contradicting him and saying he wouldn't know because somehow he'd missed the indoctrination course on how to be an obstinate, glory-seeking ass like most Feebs. 'So, tell me, what are your thoughts about Charley?'

'It's ridiculous. I cannot believe Charley Spencer would do anything like that. To be honest, if it had happened right after her mother died, I wouldn't have been surprised. Kids act out like crazy in the face of a sudden, horrific loss like that. Even good kids like Charley. But now? I thought she was doing very well. I'm baffled, Agent Lovett.'

'What do you know about Madison Sinclair, Ashley Dodson and Jessica Pruitt?'

'Troublemakers. Pure and simple. Well, at least Madison and Ashley are. Jessica is more of a follower and she is so easily led. Sometimes I think the other two spend half their class time in the office making my life and the life of their counselors miserable. Heaven knows what havoc they cause at home.'

'Would it surprise you to know that they have been accused of being responsible for the act of vandalism that Charley was accused of?'

'Not at all. To be honest, I will be amazed if all three manage to graduate from high school without at least one of them being busted for one crime or another. But I can't imagine Charley getting mixed up with those girls. For that matter, I can't imagine them having a thing to do with her. They have nothing but disdain for well-behaved, high-achieving students like Charley.'

'I agree, Ms Stovall. I don't believe Charley was involved with the vandalism at the apartment complex. I think Madison and Ashley were, with the help of some high school boys. I think they're pinning the blame on Charley and, right now, the investigators seem to have fallen for their scam.'

'Oh, dear, what can I do to help?'

'I'd like to speak with one of the girls – the one that you think would be most likely to succumb to the pressure to talk.'

'Oh my, I couldn't allow you to do that without a parent's permission. It most definitely would be Jessica; as I said, she is easily manipulated. But I just can't.'

'How about if you talked to her? If I just sat in the corner and kept my mouth shut?'

'That still makes me a bit uncomfortable . . .'

'Listen. Just ask her about Charley's arrest. Ask her about Charley only. She may say something that I can use or that would confirm Charley's story. Could you do that?'

Camilla Stovall's brow furrowed. She folded

her hands on the desk in front of her and sat quietly for a moment. 'You don't think that Jessica was involved in the vandalism.'

'No. I don't think she even knew about it until after the fact.'

The principal exhaled. 'OK. But because you are not accusing Jessica of anything. And because I do not want to see Charley with a record she doesn't deserve, based on those girls' lies. I can't believe she was involved, but if I was wrong . . .'

'This is not official, Ms Stovall. I will make that clear every step of the way and I will do everything I can to back you up.'

'OK. I'll send someone down to get Jessica from class.'

While Jake waited, he slipped over to the chair in a corner next to an end table. He turned off the lamp there, hoping to be as inconspicuous as possible. The principal returned and sat behind her desk. 'She should be here any moment,' she said.

Jessica slouched into the room with a defiant look in her eye. She glanced at the man in the corner but then dismissed him, to Jake's great relief. 'What now, Missus Stovall? I didn't do nothing. I swear.'

'Have a seat, Jessica.'

The girl slumped in the chair, bent her head, sending her long, blonde hair cascading around her face. She stared at the floor.

'Thank you, Jessica, for coming so promptly. I didn't ask you to visit with me because I think you did something wrong. I asked you into my office to get your opinion on something that's bothering me.'

Jessica raised her head and cocked it with a quizzical expression on her face. 'Yeah? Really?'

'Really. Do you know Charley Spencer?'

'I don't hang out with sixth graders.'

'But you do know her, don't you?'

'I know who she is.'

'Did you hear about her arrest?'

'Yeah. Everybody has. Nobody can believe that little nerd actually did something wrong.'

'Why do you think she would do that?'

Jessica shrugged. 'For kicks, I don't know. Who knows what those geeky little twerps think?'

'You weren't there with her?'

Jessica exploded from the chair. 'Who told you that? That is a lie. I wasn't there when they did that.'

'Please be seated, Jessica,' the principal said, folding her hands on her desk and waiting for the girl to comply.

Jessica sank back down, shaking her head. 'This isn't right, Missus Stovall. I wasn't there. I swear.'

'Who was, Jessica?'

'Well, I guess it was Charley. The police arrested her, right? They caught her in the act.'

'Jessica, a moment ago, you said "when they did that". Who was there besides Charley?'

'I did? Well, I didn't mean it. Not they – Charley Spencer.'

'Jessica, if you are not telling me the truth, this is not a little white lie. You could be arrested.'

146

Jessica spun around and stared straight at Jake. 'Is he a cop? Is he here to arrest me?'

'Jessica! Turn back to me,' Stovall ordered. 'Ignore him. He is not the investigator in the vandalism case.'

Slowly, Jessica turned back to face the principal. 'Honest?'

'Yes, Jessica. But that does not change the fact that if you lie about what happened, you can be charged with obstruction of justice. That is very serious.'

'But I wasn't there. I didn't see anything,' Jessica protested.

'But you know something, don't you, Jessica?'

Jessica dropped her head and shook it back and forth.

'Look at me, Jessica. Tell me to my face that you know nothing.'

Jessica raised her head. Her lips trembled. 'I can't tell, Ms Stovall. If I do I'll have to drop out of school. You don't want me to do that, do you?'

'No, Jessica. Just answer one question.'

'Oh, please, Missus Stovall, I can't be a rat.'

'I'm not asking you to do that. I am not asking you to turn on anyone. I just want to know one thing. Do you know whether or not Charley Spencer was involved?'

Jessica squirmed in her chair, looking at the floor, the wall, out the window – anywhere but at the principal's face.

'Jessica, if Charley Spencer did not do what the police said she did, you have to tell me. It's not right to punish her for what someone else did. How would you feel if you were blamed for something you didn't do?'

'Man, Missus Stovall,' Jessica whined. 'OK. I know who did it. It wasn't Charley Spencer, but please don't make me tell you who it was.'

'I won't ask you that, Jessica. You can go back to class now. Get a hall pass at the front counter before you leave.'

'Yes, Missus Stovall. Thank you.'

When she'd gone, the principal said, 'She's tight with Madison and Ashley right now. She has to be covering up for them. She follows them around, begging for crumbs.'

'I suspect she's also covering up for her brother, too.'

'Really? We never had any problems with him when he was at this school. That is surprising.'

'Well, maybe he's just a follower, like his sister.' Jake rose to his feet and shook the principal's hand. 'Thank you. That bit of information will give the investigators sufficient reason to bring all three girls in for questioning.'

'Do me a favor, Agent Lovett. Try to get what you need from Madison and Ashley before you drag Jessica into the situation any further.'

'I'll do what I can, Ms Stovall, but it probably won't be my decision to make.'

Twenty-Two

'Jake, are you finished at the middle school?' Lucinda spoke into her cellphone as she drove down the highway.

'Sure am. And it looks good for Charley. You done at the prison?'

'Yes, although my ego's a little battered from the experience. Where do you want to meet up?'

'I'm at my office. You want to swing by here?'

'OK. But meet me in the parking lot. I don't want to go inside.'

'Afraid you'll catch some Feeb cooties?'

'I believe that I am the one who invited you to tag along.'

'Yes, ma'am. I'll meet you out front. Do you want me to drive?'

'Once again, Jake, who invited whom?'

'All right. You're driving. Don't know why I bothered to ask.'

'Do you want me to tell you – again – why I'm driving?'

'Nope. Got that one down pat. I'm a man. My driving sucks. But really, I do have a cooler car.'

'Remind me of that when I am suicidal and want you to drive me into a concrete wall. See you in twenty,' Lucinda said, disconnecting the call. A smile stole across her face. She really loved working with him. Loved talking with him. Loved doing nothing with him. Loved – whoa, she told herself, uncomfortable with the trajectory of her thoughts.

When Lucinda pulled into the lot, Jake was waiting with his thumb stuck out in the air. She rolled down the passenger window and shouted, 'Hey, buddy, want a lift?'

Jake climbed into the car and she added, 'Didn't your mama tell you not to take rides from strangers?'

'I don't think my mother would find you all that strange, Lucinda. In fact, I'm pretty sure she'd like you a lot.'

'I doubt that,' Lucinda said. 'OK, fill me in on your middle school visit.'

Jake detailed his meeting with the principal and his conversation with Jessica. 'I'd say that is sufficient grounds to pick up all three of the girls.'

'Hopefully, one of them will confess.'

'Jessica's close to it but I don't think she was there so we really do need one of the other two to take responsibility. Or maybe one of the high school boys involved. Do you know who they are?'

'I know one of them is Jessica's brother but Charley only knew the others by their first names.'

'Well, maybe one of the girls will give them up. So what happened at the prison?'

Lucinda ran through the conversation with Martha Sherman and laid out her plan to move everything forward.

'You're staging a confrontation with Martha's attorney in your office? Are you nuts?'

'I probably am nuts but it was the best thing that came to my mind.'

'You're playing with fire, Lucinda.'

'If no one ever played with fire, we'd all still be gnawing raw, bloody meat off of bones.'

'I don't know. It seems awfully risky.'

'I know that, Jake. But I am willing to pay any price, even the loss of my job, to make sure justice is done for Martha Sherman. Ah, here's the street.'

'The names? What are the names of Trevor Phillips' grandparents?'

'Henry and Marilyn Makowski.'

Lucinda pulled up the driveway of a long, white brick ranch house set up on a hill. The large oaks and maples in the yard testified to the home's vintage.

'Looks like sixties construction,' Jake said.

'Yes, I believe the Makowski's built this home early in the decade and have lived here ever since. They're both retired. She used to do local television and radio shows and he worked as an engineer at Standard Electric.'

'You've done your homework.'

'Actually, I didn't do any of the work. Lara Quivey in the research department dug up the information and prepared a background report. I just read what she wrote.'

On the porch, Lucinda rang the doorbell and was greeted by Marilyn Makowski. A soft blonde shade covered up her gray with only a small indication of roots at the base of the scalp. Her make-up was subtle but obvious, particularly in the wrinkles around her mouth and eyes and the

151

blush on her cheekbones. It was all accented by a deep rose lipstick. Lucinda estimated her height at five foot eight or maybe nine inches – tall for a woman, but definitely short next to Lucinda. 'May I help you?' Marilyn asked.

'Yes, ma'am,' Lucinda said, holding up her badge. 'I'm Lieutenant Pierce with the homicide division of the police department. And this is Agent Lovett with the FBI. We would like to talk to you and your husband about your grandson.'

'I think I know you, lieutenant. Did we meet at Chris Phillips' trial?'

'Yes, ma'am, I believe we did. I am surprised you remember.'

'There's something different about you, though.'

'The passage of time changes us all, ma'am,' Lucinda said, hoping to deflect the conversation away from another rehash of her eye patch and scars.

Marilyn narrowed her eyes, looking closely at Lucinda's face. 'I think it's more than that, but, well, please come in.' She opened the door wide, gesturing her welcome with a swing of her arm. She led them into the living room. 'Please make yourselves comfortable. I'll go get Henry – he's tinkering in his shop. And I'll grab the coffee pot.'

'Don't go to any trouble for us, ma'am,' Jake said, as he and Lucinda sat down on a brocaded teal sofa.

Marilyn smiled at him, 'Oh no trouble, agent, actually it's more for me than you to be honest.

I just made a fresh pot and I'm dying for a cup. It's been a rough morning.' Without an explanation of the meaning of her last remark, she glided out of the room and out of sight.

'So far, so good,' Jake said.

'Yeah, but Henry is a lot tougher than she is. We'll see.'

'I'll follow your lead.'

A tall bear of a man lumbered into the living room, wiping his hands on the legs of his pants. Jake and Lucinda stood and both shook his hand. 'Please, please, make yourself at home. Marilyn will be back with the coffee in a moment.' He sat down in a chair kitty-corner to the sofa.

As if on cue, Marilyn walked into the room carrying a tray. Henry jumped back to his feet. 'Here, Mother, let me get that.' He took the burden from her hands and set it down on the coffee table. Marilyn filled cups, offering sugar and cream, and within two minutes they were all settled with a mug of coffee in their hands.

'OK, detectives,' Henry said. 'I'm sure you did not come out here for coffee and idle conversation. What's on your minds?'

'Chris Phillips,' Lucinda said.

'Oh, dear,' Marilyn choked and appeared as if she might cry.

'Calm down, dear,' Henry said. 'It's all going to work out.' Turning to Lucinda and Jake, he said, 'Marilyn's a bit emotional right now. We just visited with our attorney about the child custody case that man filed. So, we know all about that – and so does our grandson.'

'How's Trevor taking the news, sir?'

153

'Not too well, I'm afraid. He's scared. He promised us he'd not stick around if the court ordered that he return to his father. He is certain that his dad will kill him next.'

Marilyn sighed, 'I told him that they would not give his dad custody while his criminal case was still pending. I didn't tell him about the possibility that the prosecution might not take it to a second trial and it could all be resolved very quickly – he was upset enough as it was.'

'Phillips filed an emergency motion for visitation,' Henry added. 'You'd think he actually cared about the boy the way it was worded: "deprived of the affection of" and "denied the comfort of the presence of his son" for all these years. What a pile of horse pucky! A hearing is scheduled for tomorrow so we got an appointment for Trevor to see his psychologist today after school.'

'He was doing so well,' Marilyn said. 'He only had to visit her twice last year – more like a mental check-up than anything else. But she is so kind. She worked him into her schedule very quickly. She's concerned his father's release from prison is going to shatter his stability.'

'Is there anything else you need from us?' Henry asked.

'Actually, sir, we haven't touched on why we are here. We are hoping to interview Trevor.'

'What?' Henry said and exchanged a worried look with his wife. 'Whatever for?'

'Like you, Mr Makowski, I want the district attorney to pursue a second trial of Chris Phillips.

I want his case to be as solid as possible. I want Phillips back in prison as much as you do.'

'What does Trevor have to do with that?'

'We have reason to believe that he saw his father push his second wife down the stairs. We want to know about that and if he saw anything suspicious when Phillips' third wife died.'

'Trevor has never said anything about seeing anything,' Marilyn objected. 'You'll traumatize him again, and for nothing.'

'Ms Makowski, I would have a CASA volunteer at the interview as well as the department psychiatrist. We will be very gentle with him. If he's kept something bottled up all these years, it could help him to get it all out.'

'I don't know. I just don't know,' Marilyn said. 'It could open old wounds. I couldn't bear for him to be hurt again.'

'I really hate to say this, ma'am. But being returned to his father could cause even more pain,' Lucinda said.

Marilyn gasped. 'I know. I know. I just want what's best for Trevor. This is a nightmare.'

Henry rose and walked to Marilyn's chair and wrapped an arm around her shoulders. 'If you two will excuse us for a moment,' he said. Leaning down to his wife, he added, 'C'mon, Mother. Let's go and talk this over.' Henry kept his arm in place as he led her out of the room.

'Oh, Jeez, this is as bad as waiting while the jury is out,' Lucinda said.

'What do you think the verdict will be?' Jake asked.

'I don't know. I don't think it looks good. I

155

don't want to force the issue and I don't know if I'd be successful with a judge if I did.'

They both sighed and sat quietly lost in the turmoil of their thoughts. The wait felt interminable but it was only five minutes before Henry returned.

'Marilyn is making a phone call. We'll continue this conversation when she returns.'

The three sat in uncomfortable silence until Jake spoke. 'You said Trevor is doing well. How are his grades in school?'

A smile crossed Henry's face. 'He's . . .' Henry began. 'No. No. I'm not going to discuss my grandson until Marilyn finishes her phone call.'

'Is she talking to your lawyer?' Jake asked.

'Right now, that's none of your business, young man,' Henry snapped.

Again, an awkward quiet descended, broken, this time, by Lucinda. 'You have a lovely home, Mr Makowski.'

Henry smiled again. 'That's all on Mother – uh, Marilyn. She has such a great eye for color. When she wanted to buy that sofa, I told her it's just too loud. But look at it. It brightens the room just like she said it would. She pulled it all together so well. She even had my mother's old rocker reupholstered to coordinate with the rest of the furniture. She's some woman.'

'Yes, she certainly did a lovely job,' Lucinda said.

After a pause, she elbowed Jake.

'Oh, yes,' he said, 'just lovely. I wish I had a room like this.'

Lucinda rolled her eye. Yeah, right, as if he'd

ever tolerate a room in his home with ruffled curtains and embroidered, fringed throw pillows. 'How long have you two been married?'

'It will be fifty years in December,' he said and cocked his head toward the hallway. 'She's still on the phone. Good. Listen, don't tell her but I've arranged a surprise cruise to celebrate our anniversary.'

'When will you let her know?' Lucinda asked.

'Well, I wanted it to be a surprise until we arrived at the dock to set sail. But then I realized that would mean I would have to pack for her and I knew I couldn't handle that without forgetting something important. So here's my plan,' he said, leaning forward with his elbows resting on his knees. 'Two days before we depart, I'm going to go down on one knee and ask her to marry me all over again – I bought her a new wedding band, one with three diamonds on it, to replace the plain one that she's just about wore clear down to nothing. Then, I'll tell her the honeymoon has all been arranged – she just needs to pack for fun in the sun.'

'What if she says no to the proposal or the trip?' Jake asked.

Lucinda jabbed an elbow into Jake's side again.

Henry laughed. 'I know my Marilyn, there's no chance—'

'Sssh!' Lucinda said. 'I think I heard her hang up.'

Marilyn walked back into the room, holding a pad of paper. She looked suspiciously at Henry whose face had turned a startling shade of red.

157

She paused as if she was about to ask him what was going on; then shook her head. 'I just got off the telephone with Dr Craig. She said she would approve of the interview if you will agree to her conditions.'

'What are they, ma'am?' Lucinda asked.

'She said that Henry and I would be witnesses to your agreement and if you go back on your word, legal action will be taken immediately.'

'We understand, don't we, Jake?' Lucinda said.

Jake nodded. 'Yes, ma'am.'

'I wrote them all down,' Marilyn said. 'First of all, she must be free to talk to Trevor this afternoon about the possible interview and you must not try to talk to him before then.'

'OK,' Lucinda said.

'She will not advocate for this interview, she will merely go over the pros and cons with Trevor and allow him to make his own decision. If he decides not to go through with it or if she decides it would not be in his best interests, you will drop the matter entirely and not attempt to maneuver around that decision in any manner.'

Lucinda winced. She did not want to slam the door shut but saw no other choice. 'OK.'

'Tomorrow, after school, she will escort Trevor to the Justice Center, where you will arrange the interview to take place in a comfortable room with windows, not in some shabby, airless cubicle.'

'I'm not sure I can comply with that.'

'Well, then . . .' Marilyn began.

'And why not?' Henry asked.

'I don't think we have a room that would fit

that description. We're kind of bare bones and utilitarian.'

'Mother, why can't she meet with Trevor in Dr Craig's office? Wouldn't that be better anyway?'

'I can ask Dr Craig about that,' Marilyn said. 'Would you be willing to go to Dr Craig's office, lieutenant, if she agrees?'

'I certainly would,' Lucinda said with a nod.

Marilyn looked back down at her list of conditions. 'OK. Where were we? Ah, yes. You may make an audio recording of the conversation but no video.'

'That's fine.'

'If at the end of the interview, Dr Craig decides it is not in Trevor's best interest for you to have that tape, you will turn it over to her without question.'

Lucinda swallowed hard; another difficult concession. 'No appeal on her decision?'

Marilyn's soft eyes turned steely. 'No, lieutenant. In this family, we are not overly fond of appeals.'

Lucinda ducked her head. 'Yes, ma'am. I agree to turn over the tape if Dr Craig requests it.'

Marilyn continued. 'If at any point, Dr Craig chooses to terminate the interview, you will comply without objection.'

Lucinda looked away, shook her head and then turned back to face Marilyn. 'Yes, ma'am, will do.'

'Finally, only one member of law enforcement can be present for the interview.'

'OK. No problem.'

'If you agreed to that, she told me to tell you that it would be best if it was a woman; Trevor does have issues with men in positions of authority.'

Lucinda glanced at Jake; he shrugged. 'I'll handle the interview myself, Mrs Makowski.'

'Fine, lieutenant, I'll check with the doctor on the change of location and if it's OK with her, I'll confirm the appointment for tomorrow afternoon.'

'Thank you,' Lucinda said.

'But I want to warn you, lieutenant: I don't care if this all turns out for the best in the long run if Trevor is damaged in the process. If that happens, I will hold you personally responsible.'

'Yes, ma'am, I have no problem with that,' Lucinda said, rising to her feet.

'Good,' Marilyn said with a big smile, as she shifted back into good hostess mode. 'Would you like another cup of coffee?'

Twenty-Three

Lucinda and Jake drove back to the Justice Center to talk to the lead investigator in Charley's vandalism case. Lucinda didn't know Sergeant Cafferty well but hoped for the best.

Cafferty had made detective a short two months ago in the property crimes division. More experienced investigators got the big splashy cases involving huge sums of money. He was stuck with those that were deemed secondary as he paid his dues.

Folding his arms across his chest and planting his feet, Cafferty said, 'Ah, Jeez, lieutenant, did you come in here to laugh at me or bust my balls?'

'Why would I do that, sergeant?'

'Ah, c'mon, lieutenant. I know you had something to do with Bill Waller's involvement in this mess. What's the deal? The kid's not charged with murder. It's a simple, straightforward investigation of an act of vandalism involving a minor and you sic the big guns on me.'

'Her father could afford it, why not?'

'Because this is nothing. She's never been in trouble before. The worst she'll get is a fine and payment of damages. She'll never get a day in juvie hall.'

'She didn't do it, sergeant.'

'We caught her red-handed.'

'No. You caught her with a can of red spray paint in her hand. Not the same thing as catching her in the act.'

'Aw, c'mon, lieutenant.'

'Look, sergeant, start thinking about the amount of damage done to that place. Do you really think one little girl could do all that? And what about the areas where the techs found urination? On closet walls? You think a girl could do that?'

'There's nothing to indicate that happened at the same time,' Cafferty said, pulling his arms even more tightly across his chest.

'Hey, sergeant, I'm not here to give you a hard time. I brought my friend in to talk to you. He has some information that I am sure you will find very useful.'

Jake stepped forward and stuck out his hand. 'Jake Lovett.'

Cafferty hesitated then brought his hand out to meet Jake's. A quizzical look crossed the sergeant's face. 'You the guy in charge of the local FBI office?'

'Yeah,' Jake said.

Cafferty turned back to Lucinda. 'You brought in the Feebs?' he whined.

'Sergeant,' Jake interjected. 'I'm not officially on this case and the FBI is not involved. I'm just trying to help out.'

'Mmm hmm,' Cafferty said looking him over. He shifted his eyes back to Lucinda. 'Really, lieutenant, the Feebs? The first time I'm ever in charge of an investigation and you do this?'

'I'm here to help, sergeant. Why don't you

162

listen to what he has to say before you get on my case?'

Cafferty sighed and blew out a hard breath. 'OK. Let me have it.'

Jake ran down his conversation with Jessica.

'OK. But it is a bit vague. What am I supposed to do with that?'

'I'll give you a statement, not an official report – a statement as a private citizen. You can get one from the principal, too. That gives you enough to bring in the three girls and Jessica's brother,' Jake said.

'Sure makes everything complicated.'

'I know, sergeant,' Lucinda said. 'But you surely don't want a wrongful conviction on your conscience.'

'You should know about that, lieutenant,' Cafferty said. Once the words were out of his mouth, he winced. 'Sorry, lieutenant. That was out of line.'

Lucinda clenched her teeth, holding back a nasty retort, as the color rose in her cheeks. She reminded herself that she needed to help Charley and she couldn't do that if she became defensive. 'It's accurate, Cafferty. Just make sure you do the right thing here.' She spun on her heels, leaving Jake with the sergeant and heading up to her office before she lost her temper, yet again.

Lucinda sat down and reviewed the Sherman files in preparation for the next day's interview with Trevor Phillips. She wrote down the questions, painfully aware of the need for subtlety and gentle maneuvering. The last thing she wanted to do was to freak out the kid or alienate the psychologist.

Forty-five minutes later, Jake joined her. 'I gave him my statement. He said he was going to talk to the principal and bring in the kids with their parents. He was still whining about you when I left.'

'Of course he was.'

'You intimidate him, Lucinda.'

'Me. How the heck does he think he can interview a real hardass perp if I scare him?'

'Got me,' Jake said and laughed. 'What now?'

'Would you look over the Sherman files and give me suggestions on how to handle the interview with Trevor?'

'Hey, you're more experienced at that than I am,' Jake objected.

'Another viewpoint would be helpful, Jake. I don't want to blow this and besides you were once a fifteen-year-old boy. I wasn't. Your perspective could be very useful.'

'Yeah, sure. Hand me some folders. You know what might be the best help for you?'

'What's that?'

'Think about what happened to you with your parents.'

'Don't want to go there, Jake.'

'But you need to go there. Consider how you would have reacted if your father shot your mother but didn't commit suicide afterwards. Would you have accused him? Or would you have remained silent, going along with whatever story he presented by default?'

'I don't think I would have let him get away with it, Jake – he killed my mother.'

'OK, but take it one step further. Pretend you're Trevor. Pretend you are not a girl whose identity is wrapped up in her mother's, but a boy who identifies with his father. You think about that and it will guide you. And let him know you've been there, too. It will help you understand him and help him relate to you.'

'I think I already knew that, Jake. I was just resisting it. It's hard.'

'I know,' he acknowledged. 'Let's dig in and see what else we can find.'

They lost track of time as they buried themselves in the pile of paper, growing oblivious to anything or anyone outside of their circle of two. They both started when Captain Holland shouted through the doorway, 'My office, Pierce. Now.'

Lucinda winced. As she left her office, Jake whispered, 'Good luck.'

The captain was already back behind his desk, his attention absorbed by the papers he signed and initialed as Lucinda waited for him to turn his focus onto her. When he did, she wished he hadn't.

He looked up from his work and stared up at her as if surprised she was there. 'What's wrong with you, Pierce?'

'Sir?'

'I just got a call from the captain down in property crimes. He chewed out my tail because you're bullying one of his detectives. And to make it worse, it's over a case that's none of your business and in which you have a clear conflict of interest. I ask again, Pierce, what the hell is wrong with you?'

'Sir, I—'

'I don't want to hear it, Pierce.' He pointed his finger at her, jabbing with every word. 'You stay clear of this case, clear of Sergeant Cafferty and clear of the Spencer family. Until this is over, you are not to see, talk to or otherwise communicate with any member of that family. Is that clear?'

'Yes, sir.'

'Get out of my office.'

'Yes, sir.'

'And stop causing problems for me,' he shouted. Then he muttered as she left, 'All over a vandalism case – a stupid vandalism case. Why can't I have one peaceful day?'

As Lucinda made a beeline back to her office, the captain's voice faded away. She walked into her space, shut the door behind her and leaned her head back against it. 'Whew!'

'Well, that was short,' Jake said.

'But definitely not sweet,' she added.

'While you were gone, Dr Spencer called.'

'I can't talk to him.'

'Why can't you talk to him?'

'Direct orders – I can't talk to anyone in the family.'

'Seriously?'

'Yes. And he really means it. He didn't even give me a second to explain myself.'

'Doesn't he understand you have a personal relationship there?'

'Oh, yeah, he understands. That's the problem.

But wait . . .' Lucinda said, a smile slowly building on her face.

'What are you thinking?'

'He never said a word about Bill Waller. He never said I couldn't talk to Charley's lawyer.'

'You're asking for trouble, Lucy.'

She snorted. 'What's new?'

Lucinda waited until that evening to contact Bill Waller. She used the phone in her apartment and called him at his home. His wife answered.

'Bill Waller, please,' Lucinda said.

'May I tell him who is calling?'

'Just tell him I have important information about one of his cases.'

'Why don't you just call him at the office in the morning? He's usually in by eight. Do you have that number?'

'Ma'am, I cannot call him at his office.'

'Why not?'

'Ma'am, this really can't wait.' Only silence. After a moment, Lucinda said, 'Ma'am?'

'Very well. I'll go see if he can take a call right now.'

Nearly a full minute had passed before she heard the phone pick up and Waller said, 'Who is this?'

'Lieutenant Lucinda Pierce.'

'Well, why didn't you say so, lieutenant? I suppose you're calling about Charley. That little girl thinks the world of you.'

Lucinda smiled. 'Glad to hear it. Yes, sir. I wanted to let you know what I learned today.'

'Oh, I can see why you don't want anyone

to know you called. Don't worry, I won't give you up.'

'Thank you, sir,' she said and related the day's events to the attorney.

'Do you think that detective will follow up on the information you provided?'

'Don't know. I think he will. I think he has to do it to some extent. He did take Agent Lovett's statement.'

'True. And if he hides that bit of evidence, I'll be able to specify it. But he's pretty new on the job. Would he think he could get away with that? Would he go along if his supervisor or the state told him to bury it?'

'I don't think so, sir. Sergeant Cafferty might be inexperienced but he has never done anything to make me doubt his ethical standards.'

'OK, that's good enough for me for now, lieutenant. Anything else?'

'I'd like to ask you to do me a favor.'

'And what might that be?'

'Could you let Charley and Evan know that I've been forbidden to talk to them? And tell them how sorry I am? And that I'll be back in touch as soon as I can?'

'Be glad to do it, lieutenant.'

'And tell Charley I love her.'

'I think she knows that.'

'Please. Tell her anyway.'

'Will do, lieutenant. And if you need to call me again, here or at work, just say you're from the bar association. They're lobbying me to get on the board right now. You'll have no problem getting put through.'

As soon as Lucinda disconnected the call, she felt pangs of regret. She would do anything for Charley, but she'd just put her trust – and her fate – in the hands of a defense attorney. If he ever thought it was in Charley's best interests, he'd turn on me in a heartbeat, she thought. If word got to the department, she might not lose her job but she'd be painted as a traitor – a betrayer of fellow officers – a Benedict Arnold or worse.

She sighed and scooped up her gray tabby, Chester, and let the softness of his coat, the vibrations in his chest and the sweet sound of his purr comfort her as she walked down the hall to her bed.

Twenty-Four

The next morning, as Lucinda stepped into the homicide division and passed the desk of Kristen, the division receptionist, the young woman smiled at her and said, 'Captain Holland would like to see you right away, lieutenant.'

Lucinda rolled her eye and trudged down the hall.

'Lieutenant, did you hear me?' Kristen asked.

Without looking back, Lucinda lifted a hand in the air and waved an acknowledgement. She slipped into the captain's office expecting the worst.

'Please, Pierce, take that lamb-going-to-slaughter look off your face. I just wanted an update on your progress with the Phillips case. The DA is ragging on me about it.'

Pierce related the conversation with Trevor Phillips' grandparents, the demands of his psychologist and the upcoming interview with Trevor that afternoon. 'And that's where we stand right now, sir.'

'Good,' he said as he nodded. 'You actually followed my orders. This could be a first.'

'Not fair, sir.'

'Aw, Pierce, you don't really want me to start listing all the orders you've violated. If I do that I might convince myself that you need to be terminated for gross insubordination.'

Before she could answer, Kristen's voice came over the speaker in the phone on the captain's desk. 'Sir, there is an attorney downstairs . . .'

'I'm sure there are a lot of them down there, Kristen, but don't worry, they usually won't bite. It'll have to wait. I'm in conference with one of my detectives right now.'

'But sir, he said if he doesn't see Lieutenant Pierce in the next ten minutes, he's contacting the police chief and if he can't get through there, either, he's calling the mayor – and he said that his wife and the mayor's wife are good friends so he knows that the mayor will take his call.'

Holland shook his head. 'Tell them to send him up and escort him into my office when he gets here.' Holland glared at Lucinda. 'What's this all about?'

Lucinda suspected it was Martha Sherman's attorney but she wasn't certain and would not say if she was. 'What was his name?'

'She didn't say, Pierce. What case is this about?'

'Without the lawyer's name, sir, I don't know how I'd know.'

'I heard you were somehow involved in getting Bill Waller to defend your little friend. I hope that's not who's on his way up here.'

Lucinda hoped so, too. If Bill Waller was about to sell her out already, last night's call was a major blunder. To her great relief, Kristen appeared in the doorway with a scrawny little man with a sharp nose, beady eyes and thin lips. She wondered if he always looked like he was ready to throw a punch.

'Mr Nelson Culver, sir,' Kristen said and backed away.

'Come in, sir, and have a seat,' the captain said.

He zeroed in on Lucinda. 'The fact that you are not willing to face me one-on-one, lieutenant, tells me a lot – confirms many of my suspicions.'

'It was my decision, Mr Culver. Not the lieutenant's.'

'I suppose that's a marginal improvement. Very well. I am here on behalf of my client, Martha Sherman.'

'Perhaps it would be more useful for you to speak to the district attorney, Mr Culver. He's the only one that can authorize your client's release.'

'I just have a few questions of the lieutenant, captain. If you'll just give me a moment.'

'I may not allow her to answer all your questions.'

Culver nodded. 'Understood.' Then he turned to Lucinda, who was marveling at his acting abilities. 'Am I correct that the lead detective in the investigation of my client is deceased?'

'Yes, sir, Lieutenant Boswell had a fatal heart attack on the witness stand at your client's trial.'

'Just for clarity, I was not her trial attorney. She became my client during the appeals process. Now. Lieutenant. You took Lieutenant Boswell's place on the witness stand, correct?'

'Yes, sir, I did.'

'And you were involved with the investigation from the beginning, correct?'

'Yes, sir, I responded with Lieutenant Boswell on the first call and assisted him thereafter.'

'Fine. Now tell me about the interview with Lisa Pedigo.'

The captain jerked to his feet. 'This is a conversation you need to be having with the district attorney.'

Lucinda had prepared for that question and wanted to answer it but if she did now, she'd give herself away.

Culver ignored Holland and blurted out another question: 'Why did you withhold that interview from the prosecution?'

'Don't answer that, Pierce.'

Nothing was going as planned, Lucinda thought. This was really a dumb idea. She prayed that Culver would not blow his cool and blow her cover.

'Fine, captain. But there's one more thing—'

'There's no more thing. I am calling the district attorney and arranging for you to continue this conversation with him.' He picked up his phone and asked for Michael Reed.

'I do have one more thing,' he said, pulling a folded document with a blue cover out of his suit pocket. 'A subpoena for the lieutenant to appear about this matter for a hearing before the trial judge's bench on Monday afternoon.'

Holland spoke into the phone. 'Martha Sherman's attorney is down here and he's asking questions that I don't think Lieutenant Pierce should answer,' the captain said, then paused to listen. 'No, sir, she didn't answer any inappropriate questions.' He ran a beefy hand through the gray and red bristles on the top of his head. 'He has served her with a subpoena for a hearing on Monday afternoon.' The captain winced and held the phone away from his ear.

Lucinda heard the anger in Reed's voice but could not distinguish his words.

The captain pulled the receiver back to his ear. 'Do you think that's wise, Reed?' The captain winced again. 'I'll do it. No problem.'

Holland hung up, rose from his seat and gestured Lucinda out into the hall. 'Just give us a moment, Mr Culver, if you please?'

They walked away from the office far enough not to be overheard. 'Reed wants you to escort Culver upstairs. I think that's pretty stupid. It gives Culver time to confront you alone in the elevator. But Reed insisted.'

'I can handle myself, captain.'

'I know. I just wanted to make you aware.'

'Thank you, captain,' she said and walked back to his office. 'Mr Culver, would you please come with me?'

She didn't say another word. Culver kept his mouth shut, too. In the elevator, they both stared straight ahead in silence as if afraid to look each other in the eye.

She led the lawyer to the doorway of Michael Reed's office and said, 'Sir, Mr Culver is here to see you.'

Reed smiled. 'Why, thank you, lieutenant. Would you mind waiting here for just a minute? I'll get Mr Culver settled in the conference room and have someone bring him a cup of coffee and then I'll be back for a quick word. OK?'

Lucinda listened to Reed's jovial banter as he led Culver down the hall. When he returned, the smile was gone. He slammed his office door behind him as he entered.

'I am fed up with you, Pierce. I cannot understand why you are still employed by the department.'

'Excuse me, sir. I brought him up here as you asked and I didn't say a word to him on the way.'

'Oh, you think you're so clever, don't you? Well, while I was waiting for you and your buddy the lawyer, I followed up on a sudden hunch. And what did I learn? C'mon. What do you think?'

'Don't know, sir.'

'I found out you visited Martha Sherman at the jail. Don't deny it.'

'I won't, sir. I am involved in the current investigation in this case and felt an interview with her might be useful.'

'You ought to go into politics, Pierce. You can spin it like the best of them. But you don't fool me. I know that lawyer is here today because you leaked information to Martha yesterday. But I'll tell you one thing, Pierce. If that son of a bitch mentions that Andrew Sherman was a donor to my re-election campaign, your ass is mine.'

'Sir, that's public information.'

'I don't care. You got that. I don't care where he got that information. If he brings it up, I'm hanging it on you. And another thing. You will not show up for that hearing on Monday.'

'I've been subpoenaed, Mr Reed.'

'I don't care. You will not be there.'

'If I'm not there, the judge will find me in contempt.'

'I don't care. You would deserve it.'

'He could put me in jail.'

'It won't kill you. You can spend your time thinking about why you betrayed us all.'

'I have done nothing wrong. I have pursued the path of truth and justice – nothing more, nothing less.'

'Bullshit! You're probably working for that damned ass who's running against me in my re-election campaign. How much did he pay you? What did he promise you? An investigator's job in this office after he's elected?'

'I hope Culver does figure out the contributions Sherman made to your campaign. And I hope he gets it smeared all over the damned front page.' She jerked open the door, slammed it behind her and headed downstairs.

Twenty-Five

Lucinda went straight to her office and sat down, breathing in and out, slowly and deliberately, focusing on nothing but the flow of air, until she felt she was calm enough to speak. She then went back up the hall and knocked on the captain's open door.

He looked up. 'How did it go?'

'Not well, sir. He ordered me to not show for the hearing.'

'Did you remind him you'd been served?'

'Yes, sir. He seemed to think a citation of contempt of court would look good on my resume and a jail sentence would be good for my character development.'

'Listen, Pierce, no one under my command is going to refuse to respond to a subpoena, so you can put that thought out of your head right now.'

'I have every intention of showing up, sir.'

'And don't even think of claiming the fifth,' he said.

Lucinda smiled. Oh what a relief, she thought. 'Of course not, sir.'

'You don't have grounds.'

'No sir.'

'Unless you were involved – unless there is something you are not telling me.'

'No, sir. I knew nothing about Lisa Pedigo

177

until the last couple of days. I had no awareness at the time of the trial.'

'Good. But listen, Pierce. If you ever get pressured to do anything by the prosecutors that you don't think is right, come to me. I won't guarantee I'll stand with you every time. I'll only do that if I agree with your assessment. If I don't I'll tell you – and explain why. Is that clear?'

'Yes, sir. And thank you.'

'Now, get out of here before I think of some reason to yell at you.'

Lucinda grinned all the way back to her office. Holland might give her crap day and night but underneath that he was a decent, honest man and a righteous cop. She knew his moral compass was steady and dependable. She was lucky to serve under him. Now, if she could only get what she needed from Trevor doing it his way.

She was getting ready to leave for the psychologist's office when her phone rang. 'Pierce, Homicide,' she answered.

'Barbara Craig. Dr Barbara Craig.'

In that moment, Lucinda was certain the interview was off but she steeled her voice and said in as upbeat a tone as she could muster, 'Yes, ma'am, what can I do for you?'

'I've been having second thoughts ever since this morning's custody hearing.'

Lucinda felt something inside of her coil up tight ready to strike. She breathed deeply and waited for the doctor to continue.

'I testified that Trevor was emotionally fragile and afraid of his father. I told them that contact with him at this time could destroy all the

178

progress he'd made in the last couple of years. Chris Phillips' attorney tried to get me to admit that he could be more traumatized by the separation from his father and that a reunification with him would heal Trevor's wounds. The judge nodded as if he agreed.'

'You're kidding me.'

'I wish I were, lieutenant. Some of these family court judges can't see beyond the biological connections as if the answer to everything were bringing the family back together no matter how poisonous that environment might be. Trevor's legal team objected to the judge overruling the best judgment of the professional who had been treating Trevor. The judge scowled and ordered an interview with a social worker from CPS to give an independent analysis of Trevor's state of mind. Then, he turned to Chris Phillips and said, "I'm sure we can get resolution here soon, Congressman".'

'When's the interview?'

'A time was not set then and I don't think CPS will be able to set a time this late on a Friday. But I would expect considering the judge's urgent regard of the matter that they will take care of setting the appointment on Monday and, in all likelihood, it will be scheduled for Tuesday. You need to get Phillips locked up again before then.'

'I doubt if I can make that happen – the decision is in the district attorney's hands.'

'I know you have influence there. I need your commitment to apply pressure to make it happen, lieutenant, or I can't agree to this afternoon's meeting.'

'You've got it, doctor,' Lucinda said while thinking that the only influence she had there now would be to push the DA in the opposite direction from what she suggested.

'I also was calling to make sure that you do not arrive here early. Trevor is coming in to talk to me at quarter till and I don't want him to run into you in the waiting room. I want to speak to him before your first encounter.'

'No problem, ma'am.'

'Thank you. I'll see you at four sharp then.'

Lucinda left the office right after the call. She couldn't bear to be stuck inside her small space just sitting around waiting. She decided to stop at a coffee shop and get fortified with a latte before showing up at Craig's office.

She arrived in the waiting room ten minutes before the hour, a time she was fairly certain that Trevor would have already gone into the inner sanctum. The minutes seemed to refuse to move forward, but, finally, at precisely four o'clock, the door opened and Dr Craig invited her inside.

The psychologist was an attractive brunette in her late thirties or early forties. A simple, no-fuss haircut downplayed the striking beauty of her face, giving her a very accessible look. She wore a shirt dress covered with blue tulips and wind-mills, a pale yellow scarf around her neck and a mile of bracelets running up her right arm. And she was a tiny woman, definitely less than five feet tall with an equally petite bone structure. She made Lucinda feel like a marauding giant.

Trevor slouched in a chair beside her desk, his

legs stretching out long in front of him. An arti-
ficially manufactured wear pattern ran down the
front of his jeans; the kind of holes that don't
come cheap. His shaggy hair looked like it
needed a cut but Lucinda thought he probably
liked it that way. His lower lip stuck out as if
in contemplation or a pout and his eyes followed
Lucinda's every move. He held an open, folded-
over, spiral notebook in his hands.

'Trevor, this is Lieutenant Lucinda Pierce, the
detective we discussed. I want you to remember
if, at any time, you grow uncomfortable or wish
to terminate the interview, you let me know and
it's over. No one will harass you for that. Will
they, lieutenant?'

Lucinda swallowed hard. 'Of course not,
doctor.'

'Now, lieutenant, I have told Trevor that he
could ask you some questions and you would
answer them before proceeding with your questions. I trust you will be willing to accommodate
him.'

Lucinda didn't like it but she had little choice in
the matter. 'I'd be glad to answer his questions.'

'You can start your questions, Trevor,' the
doctor said.

Looking down at his notebook, he said, 'Do
you think my dad is guilty of the murder of Patty
Phillips?'

'Yes, I do.'

'Do you think I saw something when my stepmother Patty died?'

'I don't know, Trevor. Did you?'

'No questions yet, lieutenant,' Dr Craig

snapped. She softened her voice when she said, 'Continue with your questions, Trevor.'

Trevor looked down at the page again. 'Do you think I saw something when my mother died?' His lower lip quivered.

'I don't know, Trevor,' Lucinda said, imagining his pain, aligning it with her own.

'Do you think I saw something when my step-mother Gloria went down the stairs and got injured?'

'Yes, Trevor, I do.'

'Did Gloria tell you that?'

'Yes, Trevor, she did.'

'Why do you care if my dad goes back to prison or not?'

'Because, Trevor, I think anyone who takes another person's life should take responsibility and accept the punishment for the crime they committed.'

'If I decide not to testify, will you tell him what I tell you?'

'No, Trevor. I will not. I promise you that I will never tell him.'

Trevor turned to Dr Craig, nodded his head and said, 'OK.'

'You may ask questions now, lieutenant.'

'Trevor, did you see anything when Patty died?'

Trevor squeezed his eyes shut and squeezed his lips together sideways with one hand. 'I can't. I can't. I want to but I can't. They'll all hate me.'

'Who do you think will hate you, Trevor?' Lucinda asked.

'My grandparents mostly. If I tell you what I know, they're going to think I saw what happened to my mother and they'll hate me. But I didn't – I didn't see him do anything to my mother.'

Lucinda wondered if that was true or if the memory was so deeply repressed that he might never resurrect it. If he did see something, she hoped he would never remember. She knew how painful that could be.

'They won't hate you, Trevor,' Lucinda said. 'They know how young you were when your mother died. They know that even if you were there, you couldn't possibly remember anything.' Out of the corner of her eye, Lucinda saw Dr Craig nod in what seemed to be approval of her responses.

'But Patty's parents will. And Gloria will.'

'No, Trevor, they won't. They will understand that you couldn't say anything no matter what you saw. They will realize the quandary you were in.'

'What does quandary mean?'

'A no-win situation – a place where no matter what you did, it would feel wrong. It would damage you whether you spoke up or not.'

'But if I saw something and I didn't say anything doesn't that make me responsible? If I saw what happened to Gloria and didn't tell anyone, doesn't that mean it's my fault that Patty is dead?'

'No, Trevor. It's not your fault. I can understand why you would feel guilty about it. But I know: it is absolutely not your fault.'

'You weren't there. How could you know?

How could you have any idea of what I'm thinking?'

'Because, I've been there, Trevor.'

'What do you mean?'

'I saw my father shoot my mother. I saw her die right in front of my eyes.'

'Did you tell the police what happened?'

'I gave a statement, Trevor, yes.'

'You told them what you saw?'

'Yes, Trevor, but—'

'See you did the right thing. You must really think I'm a pile of crap.'

'No, Trevor, because I don't know what I would have done in your case. You see, after shooting my mom, my dad shot himself. They both died that day. Unlike you, I had nothing to lose.'

Trevor stared down at his shoes. A minute passed. And then two.

'Trevor,' Dr Craig said. 'Do you want me to send the detective away?'

Trevor raised his head and looked straight at Lucinda. 'No, Dr Craig. I want to tell her what happened.'

Both women sat quietly waiting for him to begin. Lucinda doubted the wisdom of remaining silent, but felt unsure. Should she ask a question or just wait on him?

Finally, he broke the silence. 'Like I said, I don't remember anything about my mom dying. I don't remember much about her at all,' he said while tears puddled in his eyes.

'But I do remember Gloria. Dad was putting concrete blocks into the stairwell landing just

184

before he turned and went out into the living room. I asked him why he was doing that. He said, "Insurance, son, insurance". I asked him what he meant and he said, "Someday when you have to deal with women, you'll understand". I asked him what that meant and he shushed me.

'He went upstairs and I followed after him. He went into his bedroom and shut the door and I heard him start yelling at Gloria. I went into my room but left the door open. Then the yelling got louder when Gloria came out of the room. She saw me standing in the doorway and said she was sorry.

'Dad came out and he was still yelling. Gloria said, "Not in front of the boy, Chris". And my dad said, "How else is he supposed to learn what women are like". She said, "Stop it, Chris", and went toward the stairs. He went after her, spun her around so her back was to the stairs and pushed her.

'I ran to the top of the stairs and saw her tumbling. I don't know how she did it but somehow she crashed into the banister and fell through to the floor below instead of hitting the blocks.

'My dad ran down the stairs after her and I followed him. He stood over her with his hands on his hips and started cussing. Gloria lay on the floor moaning. I kneeled down next to her and Dad shoved me and told me to leave her alone. I ran out of the house and went to the neighbors. I told them to get an ambulance 'cause Gloria had fallen down the stairs. But I knew she didn't fall – she was pushed but I didn't tell anyone that.'

Tears ran down Trevor's face. Lucinda wanted to rush to him and wrap her arms around him but she sensed he'd resent it if she did anything to acknowledge that she'd even seen his tears. 'Did the same thing happen to Patty?'

'He didn't put the blocks down there that time. He put a glass top table on the landing. And he didn't push her. He hit her over the back of her head with my baseball bat and she fell. He wiped off the bat with an old T-shirt and handed the bat to me and told me to go down to the river and throw it in the middle. I just stood there.

'He went down the stairs to Patty. She'd hit the table, there was broken glass and blood all over the landing. He dipped that T-shirt in the pool of blood around her head and smeared it on the banister and the post. Then, she groaned. He said the F word and wrapped his T-shirt around a broken piece of glass. I looked away then. I didn't want to see what he was going to do. When I turned back, blood was shooting up in the air like a fountain. And then it stopped, like someone turned it off.

'Then he said, "Get going" and I told him it was dark outside. And he said, "Listen, little scared-of-the-dark baby, I need you to get rid of that and get back here – I'm not going to call 9-1-1 until you do".

'All I could think about was Gloria. And how calling 9-1-1 saved her life and I didn't think anyone could do anything for Patty but maybe I was wrong. So I ran as fast as I could, threw the bat as hard as I could and raced back home. All my dad said was "about time you got back".'

Trevor doubled over, his arms wrapped around his stomach.

'Very good, Trevor. I'm proud of you. You needed to get that poison out,' Dr Craig said.

'He said we're going to take a nice, long vacation on a sunny beach in the Caribbean after he has custody. Don't let him take me. Please. I think he wants to get rid of me.' Trevor cradled himself and rocked back and forth on the chair as he pleaded with Lucinda.

Dr Craig and Lucinda both said, 'What?' Then Lucinda asked, 'When did you talk to him, Trevor?'

'He sent me a text message at school.'

Dr Craig turned to Lucinda. 'Please leave your tape recorder on my desk and wait outside the room while I talk to Trevor.'

Lucinda rose and crossed the room, wondering why she hadn't brought two devices and kept one hidden. She placed the recorder on Craig's desk, her fingers not wanting to release it. She looked up at the doctor.

'We had an agreement, lieutenant.'

Lucinda nodded and walked out of the room. She couldn't sit down. She paced the room, one side to the other lengthwise, then shifted to walking the width of the room.

When the door opened, Lucinda's mouth dehydrated in a flash. She held her breath. Dr Craig handed her the recorder and said, 'Thank you for using restraint. You didn't act like a cop and that's what he needed. I think it went rather well. Well, I need to get back to him but he's ready to testify. I think he needs to do it to resolve his

187

feelings of guilt. And you need to make sure he survives to do that.'

'Thank you, doctor. I will do everything in my power to protect Trevor and with the information on this tape, I am certain I will have the full support of the district attorney. Phillips' message to Trevor has made him a flight risk – that should be sufficient to revoke his bail. Please tell Trevor not to delete that text.'

Dr Craig nodded, turned, went back in the room and closed the door.

Lucinda was buzzing. She got out of the building and pressed the play button. She had to make sure the recording really was still there. She heard Trevor's voice and wanted to shout – she settled for one, slightly subdued, fist pump in the air and a quiet, 'Yeah, me!'

Climbing into her car, she called Jake. 'I've got it, Jake, I've got it.'

'Trevor?'

'Yes. He has a vivid memory of Gloria's accident and Patty's death and he wants to testify. His shrink even said it would be good for him.'

'And good for you, too. This is going to please the DA. You'll be his new best friend.'

'I doubt that, Jake, I haven't told you about this morning yet – I'll catch you later for that. But at least now, I don't have to worry about the DA running me over in the parking lot after work.'

Twenty-Six

Jake sat at his desk getting more frustrated by the moment. His review of the reports on the search for Mack Rogers didn't generate a single idea of where he should look, what he should do next. His phone gave an in-house call buzz and he picked up the receiver. 'Tell me you've got some good news.'

'Look sharp, agent. The press is on line two for you.'

'I don't want to talk to a reporter right now.'

'You rate higher than that, sir, it's a producer calling.'

'Thanks. But no thanks.'

'She says she can help you find Mack Rogers.'

'Yeah and I'll help her find Elvis.'

'Sir, you don't want her telling everyone that she tried to assist the FBI but they wouldn't even talk to her.'

'Crap. OK. I'll take the call.' He disconnected the in-house line, cleared his throat and punched the button two to reach the outside call. 'Special Agent Lovett.'

'Hello, sir. This is Jeanne Jacobs, producer of *Virginia's Most Wanted* for *Eyewitness News*.'

'I was told you believe you can help me with the search for Mack Rogers.'

'Yes, indeed, sir. We'll allow you to come live on our program this evening and make a personal appeal for tips. We'll have a hotline up and running and you can help man the phones.'

'No offense, Ms Jacobs, but Rogers could be anywhere in the country by now. Your show is local – what good will that do?'

'Sir, one of our other guests on the show is a criminal justice professor from Radford University. He makes a very compelling argument that Rogers would still be here in the state. In fact, he believes he would be within our viewing area so that he can keep track of the excavation at his former home.'

'Good for him.'

'Oh, sir, please don't be negative about this. You are vital to the show tonight. We have found in the five years we've been on the air with this program that the response from the public has been far more vigorous when we have had an investigator or sheriff here on the set to talk about his efforts to find a dangerous criminal.'

It was tempting but Jake knew that his supervisor was always looking for an excuse to give him grief. And he knew she'd never approve it if he made a request. 'I'll have to run this by my regional director,' he said.

'Sir, you and I both know what the FBI bureaucracy is like. If they cooperate at all, they'll send a spokesperson. That is just not as effective as someone really involved in the case. People with information are far more likely to call the hotline if the guy in actual pursuit of the criminal is waiting to take their calls. And if he's watching, it would seem a lot more serious if an FBI agent is talking about him instead of one of our announcers. It might push him to do something . . .'

'Like kill another woman? Is that what you want?'

'Oh my heavens, sir. Not at all. But he might feel the heat. It might make him move from wherever he's hiding out, worried that you're getting too close. And I've always been told that it's easier to find a fugitive when he's on the move. And sir, if you're hesitating because you are not familiar with our work, I can give you the name of a few sheriffs who have had very positive results from appearing on our show.'

Jake had no leads to follow. He needed something. Sure, Director Goodman would be pissed but he could grovel for the wicked witch's forgiveness later. If he did get results, she could do nothing but chew on his butt for a while – what's new? 'OK. What would you want me to do if I agreed?'

'We've already written script for you.'

'You want me to read a script? I don't think so.'

'Oh no, sir. It's just a guideline to help you follow the show's point of view.'

'I don't care if I follow your point of view or not, Ms Jacobs. I need to be able to say what needs to be said without any constraints.'

'Well, of course you can, sir. You're the expert. We just want to make you comfortable.'

'When is this show?'

'Tonight, sir, right after the eleven o'clock news.'

'That's sudden.'

'We wanted to make sure we had everything in order and we were ready to proceed with the other guests, the background, the hotline volunteers and a strong promotional effort. We didn't want to waste your time if we could not pull it off tonight.'

Jake suspected that she didn't want to ask him before now because she didn't want him to have time to cause problems with any other aspect of the production. 'All right. When do you need me?'

'Come to the studio tonight at ten thirty or a little before. We can do a walk through, get you familiar with the set, fine-tune the blocking and make sure the lighting is appropriate to make you look your best.'

Jake wasn't certain what all of that entailed but he'd just go there and do as he was told. 'I'll see you at ten thirty then.'

He ran down the price he'd pay if it didn't go well tonight: grief from Goodman, punitive action from her or maybe even dismissal. He chuckled. Nah, she won't fire me. I've got a friend in the media right now. If I get canned for appearing on her show, Jeanne Jacobs will make sure everybody knows and Goodman despises bad press. Now, what will I say?

Twenty-Seven

Returning to the Justice Center, Lucinda went straight to the sixth floor, carrying the recorder as gently as if it were a fragile antiquity. She leaned against the door trim of DA Reed's office waiting for him to look up and notice her.

'What do you want, now, Pierce?' he snarled.

'I come bearing good news.'

'Forgive me for being dubious about your definition of good.'

'On this tape, I have an interview with Trevor Phillips, done in the presence of his psychologist and with the permission of his legal guardians.'

Reed's eyes squinted as he stared at her. 'More proof of prosecutorial misconduct, Pierce?'

'No, sir. Not at all. It's a confirmation that you did the right thing when you prosecuted his father. He distinctly remembers his first stepmother's so-called accident and his second stepmother's murder. He witnessed both.'

'Are you shitting me?' he said rising from his chair.

'No, sir. It's all here along with a good reason to have Phillips' bail revoked.'

'Really? Come in. Sit down,' he said, gesturing to the comfortable sitting area off to the side, away from his desk. He stuck his head out in the hallway and shouted, 'Cindy, could you get us some coffee?'

Lucinda remained a bit wary. She knew he'd be happy after listening to the tape but how long would it take to remember that he was still supremely pissed at her about the Sherman situation?

They listened to the tape together. Reed sat at the edge of the chair, the smile on his face broadening every minute. He pressed the pause button after Trevor finished his recollection of Gloria's plunge down the stairway. 'You know we can't charge him in that case – he's already been acquitted.'

'Yes sir, I know that.'

'OK,' he said with a nod. 'Just wanted to make sure that was clear.' He pressed the play button. When Dr Craig's voice came out of the speaker praising Trevor for the good job he'd done, Reed reached for the stop button.

'No sir, keep listening. There's more.'

Reed listened to Trevor talk about the text message and bounced to his feet. 'Is that it?'

'Yes, I think that's enough.'

Reed jammed his hands in his trouser pockets and rocked on his heels. 'Yes, indeed. Yes, indeed.'

'Sir, we need to rearrest him to protect Trevor.'

'It's past business hours on a Friday, Pierce. The judges have all gone home for the weekend.'

'Say that it's an emergency.'

'Can't do it, Pierce. He has not made a direct

threat. And he hasn't said that they're leaving this weekend. I'd just tick a judge off for bothering him with something that could wait till Monday.'

Lucinda jumped up from the chair. 'Reed, there is no knowing what Phillips will do. There's no way to know that he won't act this weekend.'

'If he did that, we'd lose a witness.'

The man's priorities exasperated Lucinda. 'For God's sake, Reed, the fact that an innocent boy's life is at risk is the important issue here.'

'Oh, chill, Pierce. I know that. I'll call the chief and tell him that we're about to take action and need eyes on Phillips round the clock. If he goes anywhere near the boy, they'll stop him in his tracks.'

'Fine. But if it even looks like he might be thinking about going near him, I want a call. Immediately.'

Reed nodded. 'I'll let the chief know.'

'Are you going to want me to testify at the revocation hearing on Monday?'

'No, Pierce. I've got the tape. I can handle it.' A coldness filled Reed's eyes and his facial features hardened. 'I don't want you anywhere near a courtroom on Monday.' He jabbed his finger in her direction. 'Is that clear?'

Lucinda's jaw clenched tight. She forced it apart and said, 'I understand what you want, sir. You've been very clear.' She turned and walked towards the door.

'You'd best not play any games with me, lieutenant.'

Lucinda turned around and faced him, enunciating each word distinctly. 'I do not play games, sir. Not with anyone.' She spun back around and walked away, knowing if she stayed a second longer, she might say something she'd regret.

Twenty-Eight

Jake went over to Mack Rogers' former home to check up on the progress of the evidence search and collection. All the human remains discovered had been removed but the stench of rotting flesh still filled the interior. It made him wonder if there might be more bodies yet to be found.

The upstairs of the home bore little resemblance to its appearance when he'd entered the first time. Some of the drywall had been torn down, exposing the bare framing, and the section of the original wood flooring above the crawl space, piled up in a stack on the side of the room, revealed the floor joists and the underground space beneath. Here and there he saw yellow flags sticking up from the dirt.

'Agent Lovett, how are you?' a woman's voice called out.

'Spellman?' he asked. 'Marguerite Spellman?'

'Sure is, sir.'

'Are you working for us now?'

'No sir, I haven't gone over to the dark side yet.'

'The dark side, Spellman? C'mon, give us a break.'

'I have worked with Lieutenant Pierce on many cases – certainly things are bound to rub off,' she said with a smile. 'You've got to admit, she's a strong personality.'

'No doubt about that,' he said. 'So, why are you here?'

'The lieutenant wanted me to keep an eye on everything you all do. I was afraid I'd just be standing around watching the dig, which moves so slowly, it's about as stimulating as watching a carrot grow. Fortunately, the forensic anthropologists and the lead forensic tech both decided they could use another pair of hands. So I've been pretty busy helping out wherever I was needed.'

'I'd guess that means you have a pretty good overall view of the progress here.'

'Pretty much,' Marguerite agreed.

'Get me caught up – like what's the deal with the walls and the floors?'

'We started tearing that up today after an evidence tech pulled on a loose piece of baseboard molding. Behind it, he found a box filled with newspaper clippings from Martha Sherman's trial.'

'That's a good find.'

'Yes,' Marguerite said with a smile. 'And I had one myself as well. I stepped on a spot in the floor and it didn't quite feel right – sort of loose and not quite as secure as it should be. I pulled it up and found another box. It was filled with candlelight vigil announcements and missing posters. There were more different missing women in that collection than we've found victims.'

'More bodies in the basement?'

'The anthropologist doesn't think so. The dirt's packed too hard below what they've already excavated. They're still finding little bits of jewelry, scraps of paper and things like that but she doesn't think we'll find anything of any size. So they decided to bring in the ground-penetrating radar equipment and check the back yard, see if he planted anyone out there, particularly in the garden patch that the landlady said he'd used for years.'

Marguerite crumpled up her face and said, 'And she told me he grew the biggest and best tomatoes and really spectacular watermelons. Thinking about what might have fertilized those crops made me swear off fruits and vegetables for a while.'

'Yuck. Not an appetizing thought. Well, thanks, Spellman. Appreciate the update. I'm going to muck about downstairs a bit.'

'Be careful, the anthropologist is a bear about the integrity of her dig – don't take a step without her approval or she'll bite your head off.'

'Thanks for the warning.' Jake descended the stairs and stood in the landing looking through the doorway to the crawl space. The small brushes and trowels used to remove every bit of dirt with slow deliberation made it all appear so tedious. He knew he didn't possess the patience for that kind of work.

He walked down the three remaining steps and over to the sifting area where three people stood over fine screens combing carefully through each small bucket that emerged from the hole. With a magnifying glass they studied each and every solid thing that remained on top – from teensy pieces of rock to even tinier bits of bone. He gave one last look at the hive of busy workers in the crawl space and went up the stairs.

Outside, he went out in the back, looking over the terrain, trying to guess where they might dig outside of the garden space. He wondered if the yard would yield resolution for any other families with missing loved ones. He wondered if any other people were sitting in prison for a crime they hadn't committed.

Lost in thought, he kicked at clods of dirt in the tilled garden area without any awareness of what he was doing until his cellphone rang. He looked down at his feet, and then pulled out his cell. 'Lovett,' he said.

'Jake, it's Lucinda.'

'Hey, how did it go with the DA?'

'He was quite excited and it wasn't until the end that he remembered that he was still pissed at me.'

'You never got around to telling me about that. What's the problem?'

She explained her run-in with him over the prosecutorial misconduct she'd uncovered in the Sherman case.

'But he didn't even prosecute that case. He wasn't even District Attorney then. What's his problem?'

'The former DA was his mentor. He feels he owes the man for where he is today. On top of that, Andrew Sherman is a major contributor to his campaign and old Andrew does not want Martha released from prison.'

'But he has to know she didn't kill his daughter.'

'Jake, I think he knew that all along. I think he pushed the investigation in her direction simply because he wanted to be rid of her at a minimum loss of assets that a typical divorce would have gotten him. But with her in prison for killing his daughter, she got next to nothing out of the marriage. And once she was gone, he was free to marry the wealthy Dora Canterbury, who, by the way, he was already involved with before the death of his daughter.'

'Oh, dear, a high society scandal.'

'Yeah, and he's willing to sacrifice Martha's life to keep the dirt away from his door.'

'Nice guy.'

'I wish I could think of some way to charge him with something. But he looks as if he went up to the line of obstructing justice but never crossed it.'

'Too bad.'

'Yeah. It's been a hell of a week – for both of us. Why don't we have a little down time without talking about any of the cases? I could pick up carry-out from that nice Italian place up the street – shoot, I'll even grab a couple of bottles of Chianti to set the mood. And after dinner, you could spend the night.'

'You mean, like, tonight?' Jake asked, the dread of the bad timing rising like gorge in his throat. He'd been waiting for an invitation; it had been a while. Why did she ask tonight?'

'Sure. What? Have you got other plans?'

'I just can't tonight. You see—'

'Oh, well, whoever she is, I don't want to hear about it. See you next week.'

'Wait, Lucinda. No, it's not like that. You see Jeanne Jacobs called—'

'Damn it, Jake. I told you I didn't want to know her name.'

'Wait, wait, no! She's a television producer, Lucy. I'm going to be live on her show tonight.'

'Oh, that's a good one, Jake.'

'You can watch me. It's tonight after the eleven o'clock news, *Virginia's Most Wanted*. And after the show, I'll be taking calls on the hotline they've set up. I'm hoping to get some leads to Mack Rogers' whereabouts.'

'OK, sarcasm jettisoned. That is a good one. I'll be watching. And good luck.'

'I'll need the luck – if something good doesn't come in the wicked witch will have my head.'

'You didn't clear it with her?'

'She'd only say no, so why bother?'

Lucinda laughed hard. 'Oh, my influence is sooo bad for you.'

'Can I blame you then?'

'Oh sure. Sic the wicked witch on me – she'll never know what hit her.'

Twenty-Nine

Lucinda went back to her apartment alone. At least Chester was there to greet her. He raced around, bounced off walls and meowed non-stop until she'd filled his bowl. She checked her phone for messages, speeding through the call from Dr Burns' office wanting to set up the next surgery in her facial reconstruction series and one from the veterinarian reminding her of Chester's appointment for his annual check-up next week. The third and final message broke her heart.

'Hi, Lucy,' Charley said. 'I know you can't talk to me. I think it's stupid but I don't want to get you in trouble. If you're there, do not pick up. I just wanted to tell you I love you and I miss you and I like that Mr Waller and he said you were a good cop and I told him I know that and he laughed. But, anyway, I'm not worried. Everything's going to be OK. And I love you and miss you and bye, Lucy.'

Lucinda wanted to call her despite her orders but she knew that would only drag Charley into her now rather messy professional life. She sighed. She had time to kill before Jake's television appearance but had no idea of what to do. She was too restless to sit down and read. She wasn't hungry; when Jake turned down her invitation she'd lost her appetite. She sure didn't want to open a bottle of wine; with the week she'd had, she'd fall asleep before Jake was on the air. She finally decided to take a walk on the river to see if that would settle her nerves.

Unfortunately, the walk was also a good time to think and Lucinda's thoughts were haunted. First by her sister Maggie and her latest interview; what had she done to turn her sister on her like that? Maybe it was all Maggie, maybe it's just the kind of person she is. That's a cop-out, Lucinda. There has been something I could have done differently or better or something. There has to be some way to set things right. But I have no idea of what that could be, she told herself.

Part of her said that Maggie would have to find that on her own and until Maggie accepted responsibility for the pain she'd inflicted on her sister and sincerely apologized for it, there would be no resolution. Still, Lucinda felt that as the oldest child, she should fix the problem but she had no idea how – everything that ever came to mind would make her more vulnerable to renewed attacks and magnified pain.

And what about Martha Sherman? The role she played in destroying that woman's life was unforgivable. Sure, she wasn't in charge but she also was not stupid. She chose to set aside her questions and concerns about the investigation and rely solely on Boz's judgment in everything. It was a rookie mistake but that did not relieve her of responsibility. Somehow, after Martha was out of prison, she knew she would have to do something to help set her life right again – or at least make it better.

And what about the deaths that lay at her feet? How many of the victims in the cellar were killed after Emily? How many lives could have been saved if she'd stood up to Boz and refused to accept some of his lame reasoning? What if she'd really probed and stopped the miscarriage of justice before he and the DA sent Martha away for all those years? How could she ever wash that sin of omission from her soul?

And Trevor? What harm had she done him? What if his father did get custody? Had she just set him up for more misery, for more abuse – or worse?

So what should she do? Just shuck her moral compass and reconsider all of her core beliefs? What if when she did, she ended up back in the same place? Then what? Somebody said an unexplored life is not worth living – or something like that. Maybe it was untested or unexamined or whatever. She tried to remember who was credited with the quotation; she thought of Thoreau and John Stuart Mill but knew neither was correct, but still the name eluded her.

She heard the bongs from a nearby church steeple ringing out eleven bells for the top of the hour. She hurried back home to catch Jake talking about Mack Rogers.

Thirty

Jake arrived at the television station a few minutes before ten thirty. Jeanne beamed at him when she retrieved him from the lobby and took him to the studio. There she walked him through his marks on the set – the position for the opening, the spot for the wrap-up plea. She had him read the teleprompter out loud from each spot.

He started to criticize the wording of some of the script, but Jeanne said, 'No, no, no, Agent Lovett, that is just there for practice and it will be up during the show in case you lose your train of thought. But feel free to say whatever you think will be appropriate in those segments. I just ask that you include the hotline number – nothing more.'

'Now, over here,' she said, leading him to a set within the set where a long open counter stood with six chairs behind it with a red telephone on the surface in front of each chair. 'This is the hotline set. When you are not talking, you will be over here, answering phone calls. The first seat is yours – go try it out.'

Jake sat down in his place; the chair was more comfortable than it looked. He leaned back and stretched out his legs.

Jeanne turned to the cameraman. 'There, see that. Make sure you get some long shots. I want you to capture those red chucks in the frame.'

Jake sat upright, pulling in his legs, checking his posture.

'No, no, no, Agent Lovett. When you're not actually taking a call, I want you to sit just as you were.'

'I'm sorry. But, it just wasn't very professional.'

'Oh, Agent Lovett, put that silly idea out of your head. We want you to look approachable – those cute red chucks do that for you. They make you look more human. Plus, when your phone rings, the movement from that relaxed pose to a more erect posture will be more dramatic – it will make the call appear very important – whether it is or not. And that's what we want.'

'But . . .'

'Come on now, Agent Lovett, slouch for me,' she said with a stern expression and pouty lips.

Jake slid down in his chair wishing it would swallow him whole.

'Now remember, Agent Lovett, you will have an earpiece on during the show. I will tell you when to move from one position to another. I will tell you when the camera is on you and when it leaves you. And if you're not slouching when I want you to slouch, I will nag you until you do. OK?'

'Got it,' he said, his face in a scowl.

'And remember,' she said wagging her finger from side to side, 'no scowling during the broadcast. Now, come with me. I'll take you to the green room. You can meet that professor I told you about as well as our other hotline volunteers. They've been briefed and they've all done this before but you can feel free to give them any specific instructions that apply to this case.'

Yeah, right, Jake thought, I don't know what the heck I'm doing, how am I supposed to tell anyone else what to do?

After the walk, a little of Lucinda's appetite returned. She fixed a bag of popcorn, poured a glass of wine and sat down in her recliner and clicked on the television. In minutes, the show began.

She thought the opening was a little cheesy but figured a local station was limited in what they could do. The host introduced Jake and he looked fantastic on the screen. And he delivered his lines about the case perfectly. He didn't look as if he were reading. Did he read that well? Or did he memorize it? Or was he just speaking off the cuff? She couldn't tell.

The host referred to the hotline, reminding everyone it would be open during the commercial break and the camera cut to a long shot of the phone bank. Her hand flew over her mouth as she saw his red chucks. It looked as if the lens was focused on his shoes. And look at his posture. He must not know the camera was on him, she thought.

As a criminal justice professor talked about Mack Rogers and his possible motivations, Lucinda could hear the pace of the incoming phone calls increase. When they cut to the hotline bank, everyone was on one of the lines. Jake was sitting up straight now – thank heavens.

When they returned from a commercial break,

Jake was on again, making a plea for calls to help him track down Mack Rogers. The host wrapped it all up and the camera returned its gaze to the hotline table where most of the lines were engaged again. Looks successful, she thought. I hope Jake gets something useful; I hope he finds Rogers before anyone else dies.

When the programming shifted to a *Friends* rerun, she scooped up Chester and went to bed. For a long while, sleep eluded her, as a cavalcade of worries raced through her head. Chester finally tired of her tossing and turning and abandoned her to find a more peaceful place to sleep.

Thirty-One

When the telephone beside the bed rang at four thirty that morning, Lucinda was anything but rested. She grabbed the receiver and mumbled, 'This better be good.'

'Better than good, it's hot.'

'Spare me. What is it?'

'I got a lot of leads that I need to follow up but one was particularly intriguing. It came in after the show. Some guy said, "597 Elm Street", and then hung up. I got a list of all the towns in the state with an Elm Street – do you have any idea how many there are?'

'No, I don't.'

'Well, I haven't counted them but there are a lot. I picked out the three closest ones since I think they are the most likely and I'm going there this morning as soon as the sun comes up. I thought you might want to come along.'

'Sure. Where are they?'

'One's right here in town. Then there's Hopewell and Waverly. I'll come by and pick you up at dawn.'

'You might have trouble finding an open guest spot in the garage on a Saturday morning. Give me a call when you get here and I'll pull out of mine and you can park there.'

'Oh no, Lieutenant Pierce. I'm driving today.'

'Jake, you know what I think of your driving.'

'This is not negotiable. It's supposed to be a beautiful day and I want to take our road trip with the top down in my car.'

'But it eats so much gas.'

'I won't ask you to pay for it. C'mon, you look so good in my baby blue Impala Super Sport.'

'The car's older than I am.'

'Ah, c'mon. She's not fifty years old yet, give the girl a break.'

'I suppose I could put up with your driving for one day.'

'Sure you can. I'll see you soon,' he said and hung up abruptly. Lucinda was certain he disconnected quickly to avoid the possibility that she'd change her mind.

She bolted down two cups of coffee and started a third while she dressed and left food for Chester. When the first streaks of light cut across the sky, she went downstairs to wait for Jake.

He pulled up, the convertible top already down, and a big grin on his face. 'Hey, good looking,' he said. 'Can I give you a lift?'

Lucinda didn't want to encourage his behavior but she couldn't help but smile. She climbed into the passenger's seat and said, 'Don't forget. We are working today.'

'It won't hurt to pretend we're out for a ride around the countryside.'

Lucinda shook her head.

Their first stop was at 597 Elm Street in town, the address of an apartment complex that appeared a bit too upscale for Mack Rogers.

They pulled up at the entrance where a manned gate blocked their way.

They waved their badges and the guard lifted the gate. Before pulling forward, Jake held out a photo of Rogers. 'Have you seen this guy?'

The guard took the picture and studied it, then shook his head. 'Don't think so.'

They started by driving around looking at cars, hoping to find Rogers' vehicle. No such luck. They stopped at the management office where they learned that Rogers wasn't a tenant and staff did not recognize him. The manager said he'd make sure all the guards saw his photo and promised to call if anyone had seen him.

They hit the road for their next stop in Hopewell. The drive was nice but the address was another bust: a piece of property with a burned-out house sitting on it. They poked around, looking for any place where Rogers might have taken shelter, but the roof was completely gone and pieces of the wall had fallen down.

They drove south and, in just over half an hour, reached the same address in Waverly. Going down the narrow road, they saw some newer, larger homes before encountering the older, much smaller ranch house at 597 Elm Street.

The surrounding tall oaks, maples and sycamores gave the white aluminum-sided home with gray shutters a comfy look. A faded red Toyota parked on the bare dirt driveway appeared as if it had left its best miles behind quite some time ago. No sign of Mack Rogers' pick-up truck but he could have ditched that for all they knew.

Stepping onto the porch, Lucinda saw the tips

of fingers pull back a curtain and quickly release. When Jake knocked on the door, however, no one answered. Lucinda retreated and circled around to watch the back of the house.

Jake pounded on the door and shouted, 'FBI, open the door now!'

Lucinda placed her hand on the knob of the rear door and turned; it responded, swinging open. She slipped inside, her weapon at the ready. Carefully, she moved through the kitchen into the living room and unlocked the door to admit Jake.

'FBI!' Jake shouted again. 'We know you are in here. Come out now with your hands up.'

In the living room, a folded blanket and sheet along with a bed pillow sat on one end of the sofa. They moved with deliberation toward the bedrooms. Rawhide chews littered the hallway testifying to the presence of a dog, but they heard no barks or whimpers of confirmation. The first bedroom was used as a storage area filled with stacked boxes with a bed frame, box spring and mattress leaning against one wall.

The bathroom appeared normal and they found no one hiding in the shower stall, the linen closet or under the vanity. Moving into the other bedroom, they saw a double bed, hastily made, with a pink terry cloth robe stretched out on the spread near the foot board.

Jake got down on his knees and lifted the bed skirt – nothing but dust bunnies and one battered shoe. The two moved silently to the sliding closet doors, one flanking each side.

Jake gave a sudden shove to the panel; as it

slid open a scream pierced their ears. A woman's voice shrieked, 'Please don't shoot me. He made me do it. He kidnapped Prissy.'

'Ma'am, we're not going to hurt you if you follow my directions. OK?'

The woman sobbed and said, 'Yes.'

'Put both of your hands on top of your head and walk out slowly.'

'I can't put my hands on my head and push the clothes out of the way, too,' she whined.

'Fine. Push the clothing aside. Put your hands on your head. And come out slowly.'

Lucinda trained her gun on the moving hangers as they shrieked against the metal rod. The woman made her nervous. If she were armed, she could easily come out shooting while they were distracted by the flutter of moving garments and the noise.

A thin, haggard woman with long, tangled hair and a tear-stained face emerged from the closet. 'Please don't hurt me.' Her eyes blinked rapidly and an ugly blue-black bruise marred her left cheekbone.

Jake exchanged a glance with Lucinda and said, 'OK, ma'am. You can put your hands down.' She wore a paper thin cotton dress that would have revealed a hidden gun or even a knife with ease. 'How about if Lieutenant Pierce here gives you a pat down to make sure you're not armed?'

'I'm not. I swear I'm not,' she said, her eyes darting like those of a frightened, cornered dog.

'Will you consent to a pat down, ma'am?'

'Yes, yes.'

Lucinda reluctantly lowered and holstered her

gun and stepped up to the woman. When she finished her check, she said, 'She's clear.'

'OK, ma'am, let's go sit down at the kitchen table. We have a few questions for you.'

'Will you find Prissy? Will you bring her home?'

'Let's go talk about that, ma'am.'

The three sat in the simple straightback chairs around a rectangular wooden table. The woman's hands were busy, she clutched at the right one with her left, then switched to wrenching on the left one with the right.

'First of all, ma'am, what is your name?'

'Helen – Helen Johns.'

'Do you know who kidnapped Prissy?'

'Yes. But, but . . . he said if I told you he'd kill me. He said if I even looked at a police officer he'd kill Prissy. He said, "Don't even think you can pull one over at me. I'll know anything you do, where you go and who visits you". He said after he killed Prissy, he'd come back and kill me. He said he's killed a lot of women in the last few years and he'd have no trouble killing me.'

Lucinda slid a photograph of Mack Rogers across the table. Helen looked at it and gasped. She threw her hands over her face and sobbed.

Jake put an arm on her shoulder. 'Is that the man who kidnapped Prissy?'

'Oh, why did you have to come here? You've killed Prissy,' she wailed.

'Does that mean you recognize the man in the photo?' Lucinda pressed.

'Oh, poor little Prissy. Oh, I hope she doesn't suffer.'

'Ma'am, you need to help us or we can't find Prissy and bring her home.'

She dropped her hands from her face. 'Yes. Yes, that's him. That's Mack. I don't know how he'll do it, but I know that he'll know what I said to you. And he'll kill Prissy.'

Lucinda reached across the table and placed a hand on top of Helen's. 'That's why you hid from us, because you think he knows everything that goes on in your house?'

Helen nodded her head.

'Well, then, Helen, he'll know you tried. That ought to count for something. Maybe it will save Prissy's life and we'll be able to bring her home to you. Do you have a recent photo of her?'

Helen nodded again, rose from the table and retrieved a small frame from an occasional table in the living room. She turned it toward Jake and Lucinda who looked at it and then at each other. It was a photograph of a small gray dog with fur pointing in every direction and a little pink bow on her head.

'So,' Jake said, 'Rogers kidnapped your dog?'

'She's not just a dog,' Helen protested. 'She's the most important person in my life. She's the only one who really cares about me.'

Jake opened his mouth to speak. Lucinda gave a sharp shake of her head and said, 'I know exactly what you mean, Helen. My little Chester – he's my cat, but he's one of the best people I've ever met.'

Helen looked at her and beamed. 'You understand.'

'I sure do, Ms Johns.'

'Oh, please, call me Helen.'

'Certainly, Helen. Now, I need your help to rescue Prissy, if you could please give me some background information, OK?'

Helen nodded, her demeanor noticeably calmer.

'How do you know Mack Rogers?'

'He's my cousin. Known him all my life.'

Jake said, 'Wait a minute. We checked for Rogers' relatives in the area, your name didn't come up.'

Helen nodded and pushed a strand of hair out of her face. 'We weren't really cousins, I suppose. I just always called his mom Aunt Irene and he called my mom Aunt Frances. We always thought of each other as cousins but I don't think we were really related by blood. Our moms worked together for a while and roomed together off and on.'

'Where did they work?' Lucinda asked.

'On the streets, if you know what I mean,' she said as the color rose in her cheeks.

'You lived under the same roof with Mack at times?'

'Yes, off and on. I think things were better for Mack when they lived with us. My mom might have been a whore but she always made sure that there was food on the table and she never brought work home. Mack's mother really didn't care at all. When the two of them were on their own, she'd leave Mack at home without even a pack of crackers in the house. And she often entertained men at her place – which usually was nothing more than a bedsit with everything crammed in one room – there was no place for Mack to go.

'I think that's one of the reasons my mom kept trying to get them to come back and stay with us. She said it was to share expenses but I think she worried a lot about little Mack. He and I were pretty close growing up but then he got a little weird. He talked too much about dead bodies. Gave me the creeps. Still, when he was in jail or prison, I'd write to him – sending a little spending money if I had it, visited him when I could. We only had each other – never knew who our fathers were – and both of our mothers died years ago, one right after the other.'

'When did Mack come here, Helen?'

'Oh, couple of weeks back. Now, don't get the wrong idea – he slept right over there on the sofa.'

'We noticed that.'

'Good. Well, he said that these guys were after him. They threatened his life and now they were trying to frame him for murder. So what could I do? I let him stay here. It felt like a family obligation, you know what I mean?'

Lucinda nodded. 'When did he leave – when did he take Prissy?'

'It was Friday night,' she said and pointing at Jake added, 'And it was all your fault.'

'He saw the show?'

'Oh yeah. And he cussed you out every time your face was on the screen. He said he was doomed now that the FBI was in on the conspiracy to destroy him and frame him for murder.

'I told him he oughta turn himself in to the local police – get them to protect him and straighten it all out. That's when he hauled off and punched me in the face.' She placed her fingers on the bruise and winced. 'Still pretty tender,' she said.

'You believe he's being framed?' Jake asked.

'Well, I did. Up until he punched me and took Prissy. And if he did what you said he did in that show, you ought not to arrest him – you oughta shoot him dead on the spot.'

'Where would he go now, Helen?' Lucinda asked.

Helen shook her head. 'If I knew, I'd tell you. He spent a lot of time with creeps he'd known in prison. Some of them came around here – tattooed head to toe a lot of them. He never introduced them and I never stuck around. I stayed to my bedroom until they left.'

'But he must have talked about some of them – anything you can tell us would help,' Lucinda said.

'There was this guy he called Tom Cat – he and Mack really got into it one day about money Tom Cat said Mack owed him. Mack called him a liar and I thought they were gonna start busting up furniture, but Tom Cat stomped out of the house saying that Mack would regret stiffin' him.'

Lucinda wondered if that argument was the instigation for the anonymous call about the fugitive's whereabouts.

'Let's see,' Helen continued, 'there was this other guy he called Mean Joe Green – but I'm sure he wasn't the football player – they seemed to get along just fine. And there were a few others – let me think a minute.'

Lucinda's cellphone rang. She pulled it out and saw the number for the Justice Center. 'I better take this,' she said, pressing the button. 'Hold on a minute,' she said to the phone and walked outside. 'Pierce.'

'Lieutenant, this is Brubaker. Cafferty has 'em all in here. The three girls, one boy and all three sets of parents. Each family group is in a separate room – except for the brother and sister. They divided them up and each one has a single parent at their side, though the boy looks old enough that it's probably not necessary but best that Cafferty is taking no chances.'

'I'll get back there as soon as I can. Call me back if anyone's arrested. And thanks, Brubaker.'

Jake was still probing Helen's recollections when Lucinda went back into the kitchen. For another half hour, he and Lucinda poked and prodded her memory but didn't come up with anything that seemed useful. They left the home with promises that they would do everything they could to find Prissy and bring her home.

'And, Helen, make sure you keep all your doors locked,' Lucinda said. 'You don't want Mack slipping in the back door like I did.'

Helen promised but Lucinda still felt uneasy leaving her there alone.

Thirty-Two

Jake pulled up to the front of the Justice Center to drop off Lucinda. She opened the door but before getting out, she turned back to Jake, leaned forward and planted a kiss on his lips.

She went up to the second floor, heading for Brubaker, but just before she reached his desk, Cafferty approached her and said, 'Too bad, lieutenant. Not one of them confessed. Guess it's all on your girl. You might as well kiss her goodbye.'

He turned and pressed the elevator button.

'Wait a minute, Cafferty.'

The elevator doors slid open. He stepped in and pressed the button to close the door.

'Cafferty,' Lucinda shouted.

He just waved and said, 'See ya,' as the doors closed.

She took a couple of steps toward the stairwell when she heard Brubaker call her name. She turned back to him. 'I've got to catch him.'

'He's just jerking your chain, lieutenant.'

Lucinda looked at the door for the stairs then back at Brubaker. 'What do you mean?'

'Come over here a minute,' he said. When she reached his desk, he said, 'The techs are in the interview rooms now, gathering up the soda cans and coffee cups. They're dusting them for prints to see if they match the ones that aren't

221

Charley's on the spray paint can. And getting DNA to match to the urine. Cafferty's doing what needs to be done. After meeting with them, he seems to agree with you about who's responsible. But he hates to admit he was wrong, so he's going to give you as much grief as he can before he has to acknowledge it. Steer clear of him until the forensics unit has results.'

Lucinda went to the forensics lab hoping to impress the urgency of the results on the department head Dr Audrey Ringo. When she got to the door, she encountered the doctor on her way out. 'Hey, Audrey.'

'Who?' the skinny redhead asked.

'You.'

'And my name is . . .?'

'Dr Ringo. Yeah, so I was checking on the evidence you gathered from the interview rooms a while ago.'

'It's Saturday, Lieutenant Pierce. I created my budget with built-in expectations that my field staff would have to go out and gather evidence without notice any time of day or night. My lab staff is a different situation. They work Monday through Friday.'

'No exceptions, Dr Ringo?'

'Certainly not for a petty crime like vandalism, lieutenant – even if the accused has an influential member of the police force on her side.' Audrey peered at Lucinda's face. 'Not quite done with the repair work, are you? I certainly hope you've scheduled another procedure soon.'

'Not yet, Audrey,' Lucinda said, trying and failing to keep the irritation out of her voice.

'Well, see that you do. We'll all be happy not to have to see the ugly consequences of the risks of police work every time you drop by,' she said, walking off toward the elevator. She stopped halfway there and spun around to face Lucinda. 'Oh, I saw your sister on the news talking about your recent screw-ups. Migod, lieutenant, what did you do to that woman to deserve that?' Audrey turned away without waiting for a response.

Audrey always made her want to scream but Lucinda bit down the urge. She knew Audrey pushed her buttons deliberately and she'd be damned if she'd let her see that she succeeded.

At her desk, Lucinda returned to her review of the files and her notes on the Sherman case in preparation for Monday's hearing. She'd been at it for a couple of hours when Jake called.

'His pick-up truck's been spotted at an apartment complex on the south side of town. I've got a patrolman watching it until I get there – you want to come along?'

'I'll be there in five minutes. Be out front. I'm driving.'

Jake chuckled. 'Yes, ma'am. See you in five.'

The maze of tired apartment buildings behind a brick enclosure looked as if they just wanted to fall down and rest for a while. Shingles were missing from roofs and the white paint on the window trim was cracked and flaking off onto the ground below.

Rogers' pick-up truck sat in a space in the back

223

of the building at the greatest possible distance from the entrance. It was locked with a security bar across the steering wheel. They went to the manager's apartment but he had no knowledge of the truck and didn't recognize Rogers' photo.

Lucinda and Jake went door to door, asking residents to look at his picture. They ran into a few hostile people but no one gave any indication of deception when they said they didn't recognize the man in the photo. One man even admitted that he looked vaguely familiar but could not recall why.

'We need to stake this place out,' Jake said. 'It doesn't make sense that he'd lock up the truck that tight unless he was planning to come back for it.'

'Could be what he wants you to think,' Lucinda suggested.

By the time they arranged for a stake-out that night, it was ten o'clock. They left two patrolmen in an unmarked car in the parking lot and headed home to grab some sleep before returning to relieve them at four the next morning.

On the way back, Lucinda said, 'Don't even think about using your car in the morning. It'll stand out in that shabby neighborhood more than a fur-covered, bejeweled matron. And besides, if we had to leave the car for any reason, it'd be stripped clean in five minutes fast.'

'No argument from me, Lucinda,' he said as they pulled up to his car. Before getting out, he leaned over and kissed her, and then he was gone.

When he got into his Super Sport and started the engine, Lucinda pulled out of the lot. This peck and run routine is lame, Lucinda thought. How old are we anyway? It's my fault, she had to admit. I always make him think if he presses too close, I'll cut him off at the knees. I've really got to make up my mind. I'm driving us both nuts.

Thirty-Three

No time of the week is lonelier than a Sunday morning at four. Lucinda and Jake were grateful for each other's company on the quiet streets. The only signs of life were feral cats that ran and hid at the slightest provocation.

They talked at length about the status of the cases foremost in their mind. Would Martha Sherman be released from prison on Monday? Would Mack Rogers ever be found and arrested? Would Chris Phillips walk away from his crimes and, God forbid, end up as their elected congressman once again? Would Charley ever be cleared and how would the experience change her? They shared their hopes and fears about outcomes in each one. Jake tried to help Lucinda cope with the guilt she felt over each situation.

When they ran out of thoughts to share, they sat in companionable silence until Jake broke it. 'Lucinda, I'm not telling you what to do and it won't make any difference to how I feel about you; but I really think it would do you a lot of good to get the final surgical procedure done.'

'I've been thinking about it, Jake. But one thing stops me every time.'

'What's that?'

'I am afraid that after it's done, Dr Burns will

say that I need just one more. I don't think it will ever be over.'

'You'll never know if you stall out now. And listen, I'll be at the hospital, waiting for you to come out of surgery. I'll be there by your bed when you wake up. I'll come to stay with you, if you'll have me. I'll run your errands, make your meals and if you get tired of my cooking, I'll pick up some take-out. I want to be there for you.'

'Shoot, you do that and next thing you know I'll get used to it and expect you to move in.'

'Would that be so bad, Lucy?'

She looked at him, trying to assess his seriousness. 'My place is too small for the two of us. Sometimes, it seems too small for me and Chester.'

'My place isn't any bigger. Maybe we should both find another place.'

A sharp intake of breath from Lucinda indicated her alarm at taking the relationship to the next step. 'I don't know, Jake. I don't know if I'm ready.'

'Sometimes, Lucy, you just need to take the risk and hope for the best.'

'Well, as my ex-mother-in-law put it, I'm easy to like on an occasional basis but once someone knows me well, I'm poison.'

'She's a fool and her son is a liar.'

Lucinda laughed. 'How about if I just think about the surgery first? If I go through with it, I'll take you up on the offer of temporary live-in servitude. Now, do you really think Rogers is ever going to show up?'

Before he could answer, Lucinda's cellphone rang. It was her brother Ricky. 'Hey, bro, what's up?'

'I just got back home from bailing Lily out of jail.'

'Lily? She was arrested? For what?' Lucinda turned to Jake and mouthed, 'My brother Ricky's wife.'

'Assault. Our dear sister Maggie filed charges.'

'Oh, dear. Start at the beginning, Ricky. How did this happen? Jake's here with me, do you mind if I put you on speakerphone?'

'No, not at all. Hey, Jake!' Ricky said. 'Well, we saw Maggie's little television performance and we were both pretty ticked off. Honestly, I just wanted to pretend as if she didn't exist, but Lily insisted we go over and tell her to cut it out. So we did.

'I started out being really diplomatic and trying to convince her that the attack on you didn't specifically matter to me, but you do know it does, right?'

'Yes, Ricky. I know.'

'Well, anyway. I wanted to make her think that I believed having a sister like you reflected on me – and on her – and she was making us all look bad. Maggie wasn't buying it. Lily was keeping quiet. Then Maggie said, "Our piece of shit sister", sorry, Lucinda but that's what she said.'

'I know, Ricky. Go on.'

'Anyway, she said, "our piece of shit sister shouldn't be allowed to use her badge to abuse people. She should be locked up for the rest

228

of her life. And I won't give up until that happens". I guess that was a bit too much for Lily. She got up in Maggie's face and said, "That woman saved my life. She saved your brother's life. And a long time ago, she saved both of you from the worst of it when your father shot your mother and then himself. Where is your gratitude?"

'And Maggie had to put in her two cents. She said, "We'd all have been a lot better off if Dad just shot Lucinda instead". Lily's response was to throw all of her weight into a shove that sent Maggie flying across the room. She hit her head on the edge of the fireplace mantel and boy, did the blood flow. Don't think it was that bad of a cut but you know how head wounds bleed.'

'Then what did you do?'

'The second Maggie got to her feet and started roaring at us, I grabbed Lily and got out of there. We went home and about two hours later, a couple of deputies were at the door. They cuffed Lily, put her in the back of the car and took her over to the county jail.'

'Is there anything I can do, Ricky?' Lucinda asked.

'For another one of your wife's breakfasts, I'll do anything you need,' Jake added.

Ricky laughed. 'You can come on out for breakfast any time, Jake. Lucinda, the lawyer said if we go to trial, we might need you to testify, but he's hoping it won't come to that. He said usually these family things can be worked out. I'm not sure I want it "worked out". You ask me, Lily's reaction is normal – it's been building for a long time, thanks to our sister's continued provocation. Maggie's out of control. Something needs to be done.'

'But what, Ricky? What could we possibly do?' Lucinda said as she watched an angry woman in a tight spandex skirt move across the parking lot as quickly as her garment would allow. When Lucinda realized she was heading for the car, she said, 'Listen, Ricky, something's happening here. I have to run. I'll catch you later.'

The woman's fist hammered on the passenger side window. Jake rolled it down and the woman said, 'You cops?'

So much for our undercover presence, Lucinda thought.

'Yeah,' Jake said. 'Is that a problem?'

'You vice?'

'No. I'm FBI. The lieutenant here is Homicide.'

'So you're not here to bother girls trying to earn a living?'

'No, ma'am,' Jake said.

'Well, then, somebody stole my damn car.'

'From this parking lot?'

'Well, I live here. Where else?'

'When did you notice it missing?'

'It was a couple of days ago. But I thought a friend borrowed it. I just found out she didn't.'

'Have you reported it as stolen?'

'What do you think I'm doing here? Are you sure you're cops?'

Lucinda tried to suppress her laughter and put her hand over her mouth to hide her spontaneous smile. The woman leaned into Jake's window and said, 'What you laughing at, girlie? You better not be laughing at me.'

'No,' she said, pointing a thumb at Jake. 'I'm laughing at him.'

'Yeah, well, he is a pretty sorry excuse for a cop. Maybe I should be talking to you.' She backed up and walked around to Lucinda's side.

Lucinda got out of the car and said, 'C'mon, let's sit over on that bench and call it in together.' Lucinda relayed the details about her car along with the woman's name and phone number and slid back behind the wheel.

'A 1998 green Hyundai Elantra – I can hardly believe it's still on the road. Nobody would steal that car unless they were simply desperate to get away. It has to be Mack Rogers. He's not coming back for his truck, Jake.'

'Damn, I guess we'll have to start looking for her ride and hope we find him with it. Did you emphasize the importance of finding it?'

'Yeah, they're sending it out to all the patrols as we speak. We'll find him.'

'I still don't feel right abandoning the truck.'

'You could just tow it in.'

'Yeah, I think I'll keep the watch up for another twenty-four hours first.'

'You love stake-outs that much?' Lucinda asked.

'With you, I do.'

'Don't start, Jake. I already agreed to a temporary living arrangement with you after my surgery – don't push your luck.'

Jake pressed his lips together and held his hands up, palms out.

'Jeez, Jake, you're even more juvenile than I am. If you do the little girly thing miming that you're locking your lips and throwing away the key, I'm getting out of this car and walking home.'

Thirty-Four

When their relief arrived, Jake and Lucinda
decided to go into their respective offices to
catch up on paperwork before a busy Monday
hit. Lucinda dropped Jake off at the FBI
offices and pulled into the Justice Center lot.
She was halfway to the back door when her
cell rang.

'Pierce,' she answered.

'I've got an arrest warrant for you.'

'For whom, sir?'

'Chris Phillips, who else?'

'But, sir, I didn't think you were going to take
action this weekend.'

'Do you want to arrest him, or not? I can get
someone else.'

'No sir, I would very much like to make that
arrest.'

'Then, get in here and pick up the warrant and
go get him.'

'Yes sir.' Lucinda was puzzled what changed
the DA's mind about not bothering a judge on
the weekend. In a couple of minutes, she was
on the sixth floor, walking into Reed's office.
'What changed since Friday?'

'Phillips' travel plans.'

'Where is he? At the airport?'

'Nah. Not yet, anyway. He went by his brother's house and dropped off the key to his front

door and asked him to stop his mail and home newspaper delivery. Apparently, his sister-in-law is not too fond of him. After Phillips left the house, a police officer knocked on the door. Phillips' brother got all belligerent about invasion of privacy but his wife blurted out that her brother-in-law had plans to leave the country for an indefinite period of time. That started a yelling match between the couple. The officer warned them not to get physical and left them to their squabble.'

'Where is Phillips now?' Lucinda asked.

'He's been circling around the neighborhood where Trevor's grandparents live. I suspect he's trying to figure out how to get Trevor out of the house. Keep in touch with dispatch, they're in constant contact with the cop on his tail. Get him – but do it easy. Don't cuff him unless it's absolutely necessary.'

'Excuse me?'

'We don't want to make a spectacle out of this. It could have far-reaching consequences.'

'To your re-election campaign?'

'Get out of here,' Reed said. 'And go do your job.'

Lucinda located Phillips parked at the curb, a block away from the home where Trevor lived with his grandparents. She pulled up behind him, got out and approached his silver BMW. She was beside the rear of the vehicle when the engine roared and Phillips peeled away.

She ran back to her car and set off in pursuit, with three other police vehicles just behind her.

She flipped on the multicolored lights and siren hidden in the grill of her car and slapped a portable round light on top of the roof. She was surprised when Phillips pulled to the side of the road.

She parked lengthwise in front of his car and called for a patrolman to do the same in the rear. Then, she got out of the car and approached Phillips.

He popped out of his Beamer and stood with his hands on his hips and his elbows jutting out at his sides. 'Looks like harassment to me, officer.'

She held up the warrant and said, 'Sir, you are under arrest.'

'I called my attorney as soon as I saw your lights. He's on his way. We have plans to sue your department unless you abandon your harassment immediately.'

'Sir, step away from your car and put your hands on top of your head.'

'And if I don't, what are you going to do? Shoot me?'

'I'm sorely tempted, Phillips, but I'll control myself. Step away from the vehicle.'

'I have witnesses – not just your cop buddies. Look around you. People are coming out of their houses. This is not the type of neighborhood where folks are used to seeing a gathering of cop cars.'

'Phillips, if you do not step away from the car, I will have to take steps to forcefully secure you. I have an arrest warrant and you need to comply with my orders.'

'I'm not going anywhere until my lawyer gets here.'

Lucinda sighed and caught the eye of the nearest patrolman who immediately moved towards her. Lucinda reached back to make sure her gun was secured in her holster and then took four quick steps over to Phillips. She grabbed one wrist off his hip, pulled it behind his body and bent it back.

Phillips squealed and tried to writhe out of her grasp. 'Police brutality,' he screamed. 'Somebody help me.'

The officer slapped a cuff on the wrist Lucinda held and grabbed Phillips' other hand and connected them together behind his back. Phillips yelled, 'Help! Help! Somebody help me!'

Lucinda made a quick visual assessment of the curious neighbors. Fortunately, none seemed willing to intervene. Some were on cellphones. I hope one of them is calling the media, Lucinda thought. It would be great if television cameras caught the former congressman making his perp walk from the car to the jail.

Thirty-Five

Monday morning, Lucinda woke up with a start, her heart pounding in her chest. She looked at her bedside clock, just past four a.m. She knew she'd never get back to sleep. Her anxiety about the coming day raced through her bloodstream and set off alarms throughout her nervous system. Her mouth was dry, her palms moist, her skin crawled and zings shot through her brain.

The last thing she needed was a jolt of caffeine but she convinced herself that a warm mug of coffee in her hands was just what she needed to calm down. In the short term, she was right. The first sip slid down with soothing warmth but by the time she'd finished her first cup and started on her second, her nerves jangled like a streetcar racing downhill.

She tried to cuddle with Chester but her anxiety oozed through her fingertips, causing him to wriggle away and take refuge on the window sill cleaning his hindquarters. Knowing she'd be in court that afternoon, she chose her outfit with care, deciding on her favorite suit in a muted gray, with a four-button jacket and pencil skirt. She selected her classic black pumps with four-inch heels to give her a one-inch height advantage over DA Reed – something she was certain would come in handy before the day was over.

She drove out of the parking garage as dawn shot pink slivers through the skyline. Arriving at the Justice Center, she checked her email and voice messages and grew restless once again. Looking at her watch, she knew it was too early to find anyone in the lab or to locate someone in the court clerk's office willing to update her on Phillips' bail revocation hearing scheduled that morning in the criminal court.

Not knowing what else to do, she dug into the Sherman files again, making sure she'd memorized every little detail she'd need when she testified for the defense that afternoon. When her cell rang, she was grateful for the interruption.

Pulling it out, she looked at the screen. Charley. She knew she shouldn't answer it but she just couldn't bring herself to ignore it.

'Lucy, Lucy, I don't know what to do,' Charley wailed.

'What's wrong, Charley?'

'At first, I thought I should rip it off my locker and tear it limb from limb and stomp on it. Then, I thought it would be better if I just ignored it. Pretend it wasn't there and that it didn't bother me at all. But then I thought, maybe it's evidence. And so I called you. I know I'm not supposed to but I–I–I . . .'

'It's OK, Charley, I'm glad you called. Now, you need to talk slower and start at the beginning.'

'I was so scared when I saw it,' Charley sobbed.

'Breathe, Charley, breathe. Take a deep breath

in and let it out slowly.' Lucinda listened as Charley did as instructed. 'Now, one more time, atta girl. OK. Tell me what scared you.'

'The doll,' she said in a quavering voice.

'What doll, Charley?'

'The one hanging from my locker with a noose around its neck.'

Lucinda jolted to her feet. 'You stay right there, Charley.'

'But I'm already late for class.'

Lucinda hurried to the stairwell, going down the steps as quickly as her heels and tight skirt would allow. 'Don't worry about class. You stay by your locker. If anyone gives you any difficulty with that, you have them call me or police head-quarters. Understood?'

'Yes, Lucy. I'll be here.'

Lucinda popped the light on top of her car again, amazed that she'd had to use it two days in a row, when she'd gone for weeks without even thinking about it. She sped down the road with siren blaring. She pulled up in front of the school, screeching to a halt in a no-parking zone.

Grateful for the PTA Open House where Charley had given her a tour of the school that included a visit to her locker, Lucinda headed straight there without stopping in the office – a clear violation of school policy. Rules, however, were never her priority in a crisis situation.

She found a frightened-looking Charley standing by a locker. Next to her a rag doll with blonde yarn hair hung from a noose tied to the handle of the door. Someone had colored a red tongue lolling from its mouth and drawn block Xs over its eyes.

Lucinda wrapped her arms around Charley and gave her a hug. 'Now, another lesson in evidence collection,' she said with a smile.

'Cool!'

Lucinda pulled out her cell and snapped photos from a couple of angles and distances before she touched anything. She slipped on latex gloves, gathering fingerprints first, even though she suspected that there might be too many overlapping prints for it to be worth the effort. She was surprised when she lifted a few very sharp whorl patterns.

Down the hall, a voice rang out, 'Hey, hey! What's going on here?'

Lucinda turned and saw a woman in a red suit barreling in her direction, the large key ring on her waist jingling. She whipped out her badge and held it up. The woman slowed her pace. 'You're supposed to report to the office before going out into the school.'

'Sorry,' Lucinda said, gesturing toward the locker.

'Oh, my,' the woman said and reached a hand to Lucinda. 'Camilla Stovall, principal.'

'Pleasure to meet you,' Lucinda said, holding up her glove-clad hands. 'Afraid I can't shake hands right now.'

'Of course not, I'm sorry.' She turned back to the locker. 'Who in heaven's name would do a thing like this?'

'I think you probably know, Ms Stovall. You

spoke to Agent Lovett about three girls last week.'

'Yes, those girls. You think they did this? Well, I'll get them all called out of class right now.'

'I wish you wouldn't, ma'am. I'd really like to get this evidence back to headquarters for analysis without giving them any warning. But I did need to see you about Charley. I don't think she should be attending school until this matter is settled.'

'I agree. If you'd charge those girls, I could have them transfer to the alternative school.'

'Hopefully, that will happen soon. Right now, I need to get back to this,' Lucinda said, pointing to the locker.

'Of course. Charley, step over here, we'll talk about what we need to do to keep you from falling behind in your courses.' The principal and Charley moved over to the other side of the hall.

Lucinda cut the rope in between the doll and the handle; then bagged and labeled the doll with the noose attached. She took a few close-up shots of the knot still tied to the locker, before removing and securing it, too.

When she'd packed up the supplies and evidence, she stood quietly, waiting for the other two to finish up their conversation. Lucinda thanked Camilla and finally shook her hand. 'Ready, Charley?'

'Yep,' she said, bouncing down the hall, her fear gone as if it had never existed, as if the doll and its accompanying threat were nothing more than a momentary distraction.

Lucinda parked at the condominium tower and went inside with Charley. Charley begged her not to leave. 'I've got to get that evidence down to the lab, girlfriend. Duty calls. I'll check in with you later today.'

'Won't you get in trouble for calling me?'

Lucinda almost said, 'Screw it,' but stopped just in time. 'Don't worry. I'll take care of that.'

'Thank you, Lucy.'

'Love you, sweetie,' she said as she planted a farewell kiss on the young girl's forehead.

Back at the Justice Center, Lucinda went straight to the forensics lab. She peered through the windows in the door, hoping to avoid Audrey Ringo. When she saw no sign of the woman anywhere within her range of sight, she slipped through the entrance and went to Beth Ann Coynes' work station.

'Lieutenant,' Beth Ann said with a smile. 'What brings you here?'

She handed the evidence to the technician, explaining the morning's events as they signed the transfer of custody papers.

'That's right,' Beth Ann said. 'That's the little girl that Cafferty busted for vandalism, right? You've known her for a while.'

'Yeah. Has any of that evidence from the interview rooms been processed yet?'

'I'm running DNA profiles right now. But fingerprint analysis is already completed. Lesley matched the prints on two of the soda cans to the ones on the can of red spray paint.'

'Excellent,' Lucinda said. 'Has anyone spoken to Sergeant Cafferty about that?'

'No, he said he'd be down at lunchtime. But if you want to let him know now, that's fine.'

'Actually, Beth Ann, if I call him, he'll probably stall for a while. But if someone else lets him know about this morning's incident at the school, he might take it more seriously.'

'I can take a hint, lieutenant,' Beth Ann said with a smirk. 'I'll give him a call; tell him about the prints and the school. I'll tell him we recovered evidence from that scene this morning. When I say "we", I am including you; but he doesn't need to know that.'

'Thanks. Let me know how it goes. My debt to you increases every month.'

'Just doing my job, lieutenant.'

'Don't short sell yourself. I'd say something to Audrey but I doubt that'll do much good. I'll try to talk my captain into putting in a good word for you.'

Lucinda went down to the first floor where both sides of the hall were lined with courtrooms. She peered around corners and columns to make sure she didn't accidentally bump into DA Reed. She approached a pair of deputies outside of Judge Thurston's chambers. 'Has the bail revocation hearing started in the Phillips case?'

'Just underway,' one of the deputies said, pushing open one of the double doors.

Lucinda ducked back. 'I can't go in.'

'Why not? It's your case, isn't it?'

'Yeah, but Reed warned me to stay away.'

'Why do you listen to him? It's your case; you have the right to be there.'

'Sometimes, deputy, you have to choose your battles.'

'I hear you on that. C'mon,' he said with a jerk of his head. 'I've got the perfect solution for your problem.' He led her into the sheriff's closed circuit control center.

Multiple screens lined the wall, showing camera shots of every courtroom and pivotal locations in the main lobby and at the entrance. 'Hey, Bucky. Bring up camera five in the viewing screen. Here, lieutenant, have a seat. Headphones are hanging under the table. And this knob here adjusts the sound.'

The screen flickered on. 'Thank you, deputy,' Lucinda said as she settled into place and tweaked the volume.

The defense attorney waved his arms in the air. 'Your honor, I am outraged at these allegations and disturbed by the attitude of the state. They have taken a simple wish of a father to spend some enjoyable time with his son and perverted its meaning. All my client was saying in his message to his son was that he wanted to spend some time together, relaxing, enjoying each other's company. My client has been a victim of a great injustice. Locked away, kept from his son by the actions of the state.

'Soon, the state will either drop the charges or we will be back in this courtroom to defend the innocence of my client. Either way, with the previous court decision overturned, my client should have the benefit of the doubt. He deserves, like any defendant, to be considered innocent until proven guilty, anything less is a deliberate and provocative perversion of justice and an insult to the judicial system of this great nation.'

Judge Thurston turned to the district attorney. 'Mr Reed, do you have anything further to add before I rule on this matter?'

'Yes, your honor, we'd like to submit the following documents that we obtained this morning from the airlines. Two reservations on a flight to the Cayman Islands scheduled for 6:10 this morning. The reservations were in the name of Chris Phillips and Trevor Phillips.'

'I object, your honor,' the defense attorney said, rising to his feet. 'I object. This is the first I've ever heard of these documents. I question their validity and I question the timing of the state's introduction of this evidence.'

'Your honor,' Reed interjected. 'I was already in this courtroom when I received this document. In less than a minute after it arrived, you'd taken your position behind the bench. I had no time to do anything else.'

'Your honor, I strongly object—' Phillips' lawyer began.

'Save it,' the judge said. 'The defense team does have the right to review this evidence and reach their own conclusions. The court defers its decision until Friday when you can present your arguments once again.' The judge banged down the gavel.

Lucinda smiled. Good, she thought. She stayed in place, watching deputies cuff Phillips and escort him out of the courtroom. Then, she snuck out the side entrance of the Justice Center and went over to the deli for lunch, with high hopes that the afternoon in court would turn out as well as the morning had.

Thirty-Six

Lucinda placed an indulgent order for lunch – a big, fat Reuben on dark rye with melted Swiss cheese, with a baton-sized kosher dill on the side. When it arrived, though, her appetite was already gone.

She nibbled on a corner of the sandwich before giving up. She got the waiter to box it up and went back across the street to the Justice Center where she went to the break room. She wrapped the box in yellow police tape before putting it into the refrigerator. Even with that precaution, she knew her sandwich wouldn't be safe for long. Hopefully, she'd feel like eating once the hearing was over.

She dawdled in her office not wanting to get downstairs in time for Reed to intercept her but knowing she had to be there before the proceedings started or risk alienating the judge. Outside the courtroom, reporters spotted her.

Cries of 'Lieutenant! Lieutenant!' filled the air around her. She looked straight ahead and did not pause to acknowledge their presence. 'Why are you here, lieutenant? What do you know? And when did you know it? Do you feel any responsibility for ruining this woman's life?'

Martha's attorney Nelson Culver spotted her first and nodded in her direction. The district

247

attorney saw the gesture and turned to see who had drawn Culver's eye. His brow furrowed and his nostrils flared as he saw Lucinda. He leaned down to the assistant DA, whispered and then strode down the aisle. 'I told you not to show up in this courtroom, Pierce.'

'I was subpoenaed. I had no choice.'

'Leave this courtroom right now before the judge arrives and I'll forget this ever happened.'

Coming up behind Lucinda and placing a hand on her shoulder, Captain Holland said, 'No one under my command will ever ignore a subpoena.'

'Captain,' Lucinda said, surprised by his presence.

'Lieutenant,' Holland acknowledged.

'Holland, her presence in this courtroom will not only damage the office of the district attorney but it will also blacken the reputation of your department.'

'What happened, happened,' Holland said. 'I wish the lieutenant was not subpoenaed but she was. We all need to adapt to that reality and right now, we all need to take a seat.'

Lucinda moved toward the side aisle on the defense side of the chamber but the captain put a hand on her arm and guided her over to the prosecution side. 'It's not a wedding; you don't have to sit with who invited you.'

As they settled into a row, the clanking of chains drew their attention to the left side of the courtroom where Martha Sherman entered, escorted by two deputies. She spotted Lucinda and gave her a nervous smile.

The judge was announced and took his position behind the bench. He slipped on a pair of reading glasses and shuffled through the papers before him. 'I've read your motion for the immediate release of your client, Martha Sherman, counsel. Do you have any additional argument or witnesses to call in support of your motion?'

'Yes, sir, your honor,' Culver said. 'The defense calls Lieutenant Lucinda Pierce.'

'Objection, your honor,' Reed shouted.

'The state knew full well that we planned to call this witness, your honor,' Culver said. 'They were aware that we had served her with a subpoena.'

'Mr Reed?' the judge said.

'May we approach the bench, your honor?' Reed asked.

'You are aware that this is a hearing, not a trial, aren't you, Mr Reed? You do know there is no jury in this courtroom, don't you?'

'Yes, your honor, but there is a sensitive matter with the lieutenant's testimony that I do not think would be appropriate to address in the presence of the media.'

'Very well, both attorneys please approach the bench.'

Lucinda couldn't hear anything but mumbles from where she sat. She tried to read lips, but Reed and the judge both kept a hand up blocking their mouths. She settled for watching their body language. Reed was clearly angry. The judge, with a scowl on his face, appeared more than a little annoyed. Only Culver seemed relaxed and unperturbed. That, she thought, was a good indication that all might go well for Martha.

When the lawyers walked back to their respective tables, Culver smirked and Reed looked as if he might spontaneously combust at any moment.

'Mr Culver,' the judge intoned, 'you may call your first witness.'

'The defense calls Lieutenant Lucinda Pierce.'

Lucinda timed the pace of her walk to the witness stand. She did not want to appear too eager or too reluctant to testify. She raised her hand to be sworn in as a witness and then took her seat.

After the preliminary questions about her identity and experience, Culver asked, 'Did you review the records of Ms Sherman's criminal investigation and trial?'

'Yes, sir, I did.'

'Did you uncover anything that raised your concerns as a law enforcement officer?'

'Yes, sir, I did.'

'Did you find any evidence of prosecutorial misconduct?'

'Objection, your honor,' Reed interrupted. 'The lieutenant is not an attorney, not an expert on that point of law, and she is not qualified to present what amounts to a judicial decision.'

'Sustained. Just ask her what she found, Mr Culver.'

'Yes, your honor. Lieutenant Pierce, when you were searching the files on this case, were you concerned about the integrity of any of the documents?'

'Yes, sir. I found a problem with one interview transcript. Only clean originals should be in the file but I found a document marked with redactions.'

'What were your initial thoughts when you discovered this anomaly?'

'I thought a mistake had been made. I thought that somehow a version of the transcript prepared for public release inadvertently went into the file.'

'What did you do then?'

'I went through the audiotape archives to find the actual recording of the interview to listen to it in its complete form. But when I played the three tapes, they were blank.'

'Another mistake, lieutenant?'

'It did not appear to be an error. It seemed to be deliberate. The hiss on the tape sounded like erasure noise.'

'Did you take any additional steps, lieutenant?'

'Yes, I went to interview the original subject on the tape.'

'And what did you learn?'

'She told me that—'

'Objection,' Reed shouted. 'Hearsay.'

'Sustained. Lieutenant, you can answer to the nature of the information she provided but not the specific content of what she said. Do you understand?'

'Yes, your honor.'

'Proceed. You may answer, lieutenant.'

'She shared with me the exculpatory information that she had given to law enforcement during that interview.'

'Are you saying that the interview contained information that would have helped the defense in her case?'

'Yes, I am.'

Culver shuffled through papers. Lucinda hoped he didn't ask her about visiting Martha in prison. Reed knew she had been there but he didn't know about the conversation and she would not lie about that under oath. If she was asked, she'd answer truthfully. But she hoped she was not asked. To her great relief, Culver said, 'That's all, your honor. I have no more questions for the witness.'

The judge said, 'Your witness, Mr Reed.'

He stood up and leveled a hard look at Lucinda. 'Were you the lead investigator in the Emily Sherman murder investigation?'

'No, sir, I was not.'

'Were you a homicide detective at the time?'

'No sir, I was not.'

'You were simply an officer assisting Homicide in an investigation, is that correct?'

'Yes, sir.'

'In fact, you didn't know what you were doing, did you?'

'Objection, your honor. Badgering the witness.'

'Sustained.'

Reed looked down at the papers piled on the table and continued, 'You didn't have much experience with murder investigations at that time, did you?'

'No, sir.'

'Is it true that the only reason you ever got a position in the homicide department was because of the untimely death of Lieutenant Boswell?'

Lucinda refused to give him what he wanted. She looked over at the captain and recalled his words and said, 'It was one of the reasons, yes, sir.'

Holland nodded at her.

'But you wouldn't have gotten the job if he hadn't keeled over—'

'Objection. Asked and answered,' Culver interjected.

'Sustained,' the judge said. 'Move on, counselor.'

Lucinda never liked a defense attorney more than she did Nathan Culver at that moment.

'Despite the fact that Lieutenant Boswell died to give you a job, you—'

'Objection, your honor,' Culver said. 'The state's attorney is testifying, not asking a question.'

'Your honor, there is a question in this sentence.'

'Sustained. Reword the question, counselor. The lieutenant is not on trial here.'

'In the course of that investigation, did you do something you regret?'

'Yes, sir, I did. I regret I accepted too much at face value and—' Lucinda started.

'Please stick to yes or no answers, lieutenant,' Reed interrupted.

'Objection,' Culver said.

'Overruled,' the judge answered.

Reed beamed like a cat ready to pounce on its prey. 'When you realized that your actions during the original investigation may have played a role in the conviction of an innocent woman, did you attempt to pin the blame for this wrongdoing on a dead detective?'

'I did not.'

'Then, why did you set out to destroy his reputation?'

'Objection,' Culver yelled. 'Badgering the witness.'

'Gentlemen, please step up to the bar. Lieutenant, you can step down but remember you are still under oath.'

Lucinda was disappointed. She thought she'd get to hear every word from the witness box. Again, she tried to translate the meaning of their interaction without the benefit of sound. Once again, Reed looked very unhappy.

When they returned, Reed glared over at her before turning to face the judge. 'Your honor, I have no further questions for Lieutenant Pierce at this time.'

'You are dismissed, lieutenant,' the judge said. 'Any further witnesses, Mr Culver?'

'Yes sir, the defense calls Lisa Pedigo.'

Lucinda smiled. It was all over now.

Lisa reiterated her original interview with law enforcement, including the victim's treatment of Martha Sherman, theft of Martha's car, and the complication of Andrew Sherman's affair with heiress Dora Canterbury.

Culver asked, 'Who was present for that interview?'

'Lieutenant Boswell.'

'Was Lieutenant Pierce present – or Sergeant Pierce as she was at the time?'

'No, sir. I never spoke to her. I never saw her until she came to my home last week.'

'Was the district attorney present at your interview?'

'No, sir.'

'To your knowledge was he aware of your interview?'

'Yes, sir, I know he was. We talked on the telephone about it. We went through the whole thing. I must have been on the phone for more than an hour.'

'Did you hear from anyone else at the time of the investigation or trial?'

'No, I thought that was odd.'

'Odd, in what way, Ms Pedigo?'

'I had expected someone on the defense to contact me. I was surprised that they didn't want to question me, too.'

'Why did that surprise you?'

'Mostly, because I knew that Martha did not have access to her automobile at the time of Emily's disappearance. I knew that Martha had not left her house between the theft of her car by her stepdaughter and the discovery of her car stained with Emily's blood. I knew that Martha couldn't have done anything to Emily.'

'Why didn't you assert yourself to make sure that information was known to the defense at the time?'

'I called the detective and the district attorney but got no response to my messages. I know I should have made the same effort with the defense lawyer but . . . but . . .' Lisa paled, threw her hand over her mouth and seemed to shrivel in front of Lucinda's eyes. On the surface, the detective didn't think it was a fair question to ask Lisa, because it seemed to cast blame on her. She hoped there was more to it.

'Your honor,' Mr Culver said, 'perhaps we should take a quick break to allow Ms Pedigo to compose herself?'

Lisa shook her head. 'No, please. I'm sorry. I am ready to continue.'

'Are you certain, Ms Pedigo?' the judge asked.

'Yes, your honor.'

'Do you recall the question, Ms Pedigo, or do you need me to repeat it?' Culver asked.

'I can answer. A few months before the trial, my daughter grew ill, very ill, gravely ill. She had a brain tumor, malignant as it turned out. All my focus was on her. All my concern was about her. We lost her . . .' Lisa said and choked on her words. 'We lost her but I have no idea if it was during the trial or after the trial. I just don't know. I was an emotional disaster zone. I wasn't even aware of the verdict until years later.'

'Thank you, Ms Pedigo,' Culver said quietly and sat back down behind the defense table.

'Your witness, Mr Reed.'

'We have no questions for the witness, your honor.'

Lucinda sighed out her relief. She had thought Reed would try to tear Lisa apart, too.

'Do you have any additional witnesses, Mr Culver?' the judge asked.

'No sir, your honor.'

'Mr Reed, do you wish to call any witnesses in opposition to this motion?'

'Your honor, I would like to approach the bench.'

The judge stared at him, shook his head and said, 'Granted.'

Culver and Reed whispered with the judge. Culver walked away with a smile on his face and squeezed his client's hand as he returned to his seat. Reed's head hung down and he looked as if he was slouching to a fate worse than death.

'Mr Reed? Did you have something to tell the court?' the judge asked.

'Yes, your honor. The state is in accord with the defense motion. We have no objection to Ms Sherman's immediate release.'

'The court orders the immediate release of Ms Sherman from the state department of corrections. And also orders that her criminal records be forthwith expunged. And, Mr Reed, if the state does anything to delay the execution of the court's orders, you will be found in contempt. I want this woman released this afternoon.'

Martha swiveled around in her chair and mouthed, 'Thank you. Thank you,' at Lucinda. As she turned her head back, she froze halfway, a look of horror on her face.

Lucinda looked in the direction of her stare and, for the first time, noticed Andrew Sherman's presence in the courtroom. He pushed his way over and around people in his rush to get out of the courtroom. Reed's behavior toward her before the judge now made more sense – a very ugly, political sense.

Thirty-Seven

Outside of the courtroom, Lucinda turned on her cell. She had three voice messages. The first was another call from Dr Burns' office wanting to know when to schedule her next surgery. The second was from Dr Craig: 'Lieutenant, I want to thank you for what you did this weekend. Chris Phillips has withdrawn his custody petition and tomorrow's scheduled CPS interview with Trevor has been cancelled. I am grateful. Trevor is grateful and so are his grandparents. Again, thank you.'

Smiling, Lucinda went to the third message. It was from Beth Ann Coynes in the forensic lab. 'Just wanted you to know we recovered all three girls' fingerprints from the locker and the doll. And the DNA profiles are complete. The DNA in the urine matches that of Tyler Pruitt and two other unknown males. And, before you ask, yes, Sergeant Cafferty is aware of these results. Later, lieutenant.'

Turning out to be an excellent day, Lucinda thought, and headed down to roll call for the evening patrol where she was scheduled to address the officers before they hit the streets. She walked through the men and women in blue, exchanging greetings with those who called out to her as she moved to the front of the room.

'I'm here to draw your attention to one

particular stolen vehicle report. A '98 green Hyundai,' Lucinda began.

'A '98 Hyundai? Shouldn't the owner be counting his blessings?' shouted one officer whose remark was rewarded with chuckles all around the room.

'I know, I know.' Lucinda raised her hands to settle the mounting hilarity. 'There's more to this car than meets the eye.'

'I thought there was always less with a Hyundai,' someone joked, spawning another round of laughter and boisterous exchanges.

'Hey! Hey!' the patrol supervisor shouted. 'Straighten up. Listen to the lieutenant. This is not fun and games here. Show a little respect.'

The laughs and talk in the crowd died as quickly as if someone flipped a switch. 'That's better,' he said. 'Lieutenant, please continue.'

'We believe this vehicle was stolen by a suspected serial killer, Mack Rogers. As I am sure you've heard, we found five bodies in various stages of decomposition in the basement of the house he'd been renting for years. We tracked him down to the home of a childhood friend – he stole that woman's car and kidnapped her dog.

'If you locate this vehicle, do not approach. Consider the suspect armed and dangerous. Call in the location and keep your eye on the car. If he moves, follow him. Do not lose him – blow your cover if you have to. I'd rather have him know we're on to him than to lose track of him again. Any questions?'

'You got a description of this perp?'

'Look at your briefing report. He's on the top of the most wanted list. All the details are there. Anything else?'

She was greeted with silence until the patrol supervisor said, 'Thank you, lieutenant.'

She nodded and left the room, heading straight for Sergeant Cafferty's office. It was empty. She roamed through the halls asking others in the property division where he was. She only got shrugs in return so she went to see if Brubaker was on duty.

'Cafferty's out making arrests, lieutenant,' he said.

'Anybody I know?'

'Yes indeed: Jessica and Tyler Pruitt, Madison Sinclair and Ashley Dodson. Looks like Charley will be off the hook soon.'

'Excellent,' Lucinda said. 'Thanks, Brubaker.'

In the elevator on the way up to her floor, Lucinda's cell rang. 'Pierce.'

'Lucy, oh, Lucy,' Charley said, her voice breathless. 'You have to come over here. You have to come over right now.'

'What's wrong, Charley?'

'Hurry, Lucy, hurry!' she said and the call was gone.

Lucinda pressed the button for the first floor. She tried to call back but got no answer. 'If you get this message, Charley, I'm on my way.'

In the parking lot, she popped on the lights and turned on her sirens. It was the tail end of rush hour and traffic was still dense. She pushed her way through, adding the cacophony of her horn when necessary. She ran into the condo building and paced while she waited for the elevator to take her to the tenth floor. She ran down the hall, unfastening her holster as she went.

The door was slightly ajar but not even a whisper of noise came from inside the Spencer home. She put one hand on her gun, without drawing it. With the other she edged open the door. All the lights were out, and the faint glow of the dusk did little more than create ominous shadows in the room.

A shout made her grip her weapon but then she realized the word shouted was 'surprise', and the room lit up and everyone was smiling. She blinked and looked around. Hundreds of balloons decorated the space. A banner stretched over a long table filled with food. It read: 'Congratulations to the Best Detective in the World.'

Charley ran up and threw her arms around Lucinda's waist. 'Thank you, Lucy! Thank you! Did you see your sign?' she asked pointing at the banner.

Bill Waller approached her and clapped her on the shoulder. 'Good job, lieutenant.'

'I really didn't do much of anything.'

Evan said, 'You believed in Charley even when I had doubts about her. You held Cafferty's feet to the fire. Without your intervention, my daughter could have been dragged through this mess for months. Thank you, lieutenant.'

Ruby tugged on her jacket. 'Lucy, Lucy, we got all the stuff you like. Look. We got shrimp. And we got the dingy crabs.'

'Ruby, Dungeness crabs,' Charley said.

'And well, Lucy knows what I mean. And Lucy, we've got mudbugs – but Daddy said I won't like them 'cause they're so hot. Do you like bugs, Lucy?'

'They're not really bugs, Ruby,' Charley said in an exasperated tone of voice. 'They're crawfish – they're like little bitty lobsters. Lucy loves them and she wouldn't eat bugs.'

'And I brought a few six packs of Blackened Voodoo beer to wash them all down.'

Lucinda spun around. 'Jake!'

Jake smiled and handed her a cold beer. 'Who do you think told them about the Cajun crawdads?'

Lucinda gave him a hug. 'I'm so glad you're here. That sign, this celebration should be for you. You did more to help Charley than I did.'

'Maybe, but I only did it at your request – not on my own initiative. So you get the credit for that, too.'

Ruby tugged again at Lucinda's jacket. 'Lucy, Lucy . . .'

'Yes, Ruby.'

'And we got corn on the cob and potato salad and cold slaw.'

Charley sighed and rolled her eyes. 'Cole slaw, Ruby.'

'It's cold – it is.'

'Yes, Ruby,' Lucinda said, with a smile. 'It is cold.'

'Lucy, if you agree with her when she makes mistakes, she'll never learn,' Charley rebuked her.

'I'd say tonight's not for learning, Charley. It's for having fun.'

'But at her age, you cannot pass up any learning opportunity,' Charley opined.

Lucinda hugged her tight to keep her from seeing the amusement in her face. 'Yes, Charley, you're right. You're a good big sister.'

'I have to be, Lucy. Ruby doesn't have a mom.'

That simple statement of fact stirred up ripples of pain. Lucinda squeezed her tight, let her go and said, 'OK, girlfriend, come on, let's eat!'

Thirty-Eight

Lucinda tucked Ruby into bed that night, reading her a story while Charley sat on the floor feigning indifference, but the light in Charley's eyes gave away the pleasure she received participating in the nightly ritual that she insisted was for little kids. After Ruby fell asleep, Lucinda went with Charley to her room.

Tucking the covers around the girl, Lucinda sat on the edge of Charley's bed. 'Do you want a story, too?'

'Yes,' Charley said.

'I thought you said you were too old for bedtime stories?'

'Not for the one I want to hear.'

'What's that, Charley?'

'I want to know when you're going in for that last surgery.'

'Charley, I . . .'

'I called Dr Burns today, Lucy. He told me he's been trying to get you to set an appointment.'

'I'm a little busy right now, Charley.'

'You're always busy. You need to make time. You know you'll feel a whole lot better once he fixes that cheek.'

'Well, maybe, but . . .'

'No, Lucy. You know I'm right. I've seen you running your fingers over it as if you're trying to hide it when you talk to people. I've

264

seen you make faces when you walk past a mirror.'

'I don't have time right now, Charley.'

'Then, I guess I'll have to stop seeing you so that you'll have more time.'

'OK, Charley, I promise. As soon as I get this one last bad guy locked up, I will call and make an appointment.'

'I want it in writing,' Charley insisted.

'What, you don't trust me?'

'Not when it comes to taking care of yourself, no I don't.' She pulled a spiral notebook and pen out of the top drawer of her nightstand and handed it to Lucinda. 'Here: write it down, sign it and date it. I will sign as your witness. Then if you don't do it, I'll sue you for breach of promise.'

'Breach of promise? Where did you pick that up?'

'Mr Bill.'

'Your attorney, Bill Waller, gave you this idea?'

'Sort of. I heard him talking to one of those other lawyers from his office tonight. And decided it made a lot of sense.'

Lucinda hid her amusement at Charley's odd application of the law as she wrote out her promise. 'Here you go, Charley.'

Charley countersigned the handwritten document and ripped the page from the notebook. 'I'll make a copy on Daddy's printer and give Mr Bill the original for safe keeping. You can't wiggle out of this one, Lucy.'

Lucinda kissed her on the forehead and said,

'You've got me locked in, Charley. I've got to run now.'

'No. Stay and talk. Daddy's already told me to sleep as late as I want in the morning. He'll write me an excuse and drive me to school.'

'Sorry, girlfriend. Duty calls. I have to talk to the night shift of patrol officers before they hit the streets.'

'Why?'

'I need their help to catch that bad guy I mentioned.'

'Oh, then go, go, and tell them it's real important.'

After addressing the night watch, Lucinda headed home for a few hours' sleep before she had to show up for a repeat performance with the morning shift. After that, she headed to her office to work on the self-perpetuating stream of paperwork that never seemed to end. She kept her eye on the time, waiting for the hour when DA Reed would be in his office. She was angry with him still but she wanted to mend bridges enough to help him in any way she could with the prosecution of Chris Phillips.

At nine that morning, she set aside her reports and went upstairs. Usually, the door to Reed's office was wide open but now it was shut tight. She walked towards it to knock but was stopped by Cindy. 'Lieutenant, I am under strict instructions, barring you from the DA's office.'

Lucinda looked at her, then turned and took two more steps toward the room.

'Lieutenant, he locked the door. He told me

he was doing it in case you barreled past me over my objections.'

'Oh, for crying out loud. I know he's as pissed at me as I am at him, but really? We do have to work together.'

'Well, not this morning, lieutenant.'

Lucinda paused, wondering whether to sit and wait him out or hope to catch him when he was loose in the building or out in the parking lot.

'He also left a message for you.'

'Is it fit for repetition?'

'Yes, lieutenant,' she said with a smile. 'Actually, he said I probably wouldn't be able to get rid of you unless I tossed you a bone.'

'Oh, nice,' Lucinda said and sighed. 'OK, what is it?'

'He received a call this morning from Chris Phillips' attorney. He wants to make a deal. Mr Reed is meeting with him and his client at the jail this morning at eleven.'

'A deal? He's not going to fight through a trial?'

'Apparently not. Mr Reed has not lost a single opportunity to spread the word that he might be seeking the death penalty.'

'The death penalty?'

'Yes, he's been going out of his way to casually "bump into" a number of lawyers and parale-gals to mention that since he got a life sentence for Phillips without a witness, he should be able to get the death penalty with one. And you know how fast gossip spreads through the legal community.'

'Oh yeah. I think they have the cops beat on

267

this one. You have any idea what the defense wants in exchange for a plea?'

'His initial offer was ten years minus time served and he wanted half the time to be probation instead of incarceration.'

'That means he'd be out in what? Two years? Is Reed going for that?'

'Nah. Right now, his counter-offer was the same sentence he got at trial, life without parole. I imagine they'll settle on something in between. But Mr Reed is very serious about this case. He's hoping to find enough evidence to tack on another murder charge for the death of his first wife, too. He's not going to come down much.'

'I hope not,' Lucinda said. Her faith in prosecutors sticking to principle was eroded a long time ago by experiences she'd prefer not to remember.

Thirty-Nine

Mack Rogers stared out of the front of the convenience store after handing over twenty-five dollars to put gas in the miserable excuse for transportation he was using since he'd stolen it out of the apartment parking lot where he'd abandoned his truck. He was annoyed that he'd been so careless. He should have left the pick-up at least a mile away and walked back for the other car. But he'd been panicking when he made the switch and hadn't taken the time to think.

Seeing nothing that looked the least bit suspicious, he pushed open the door and walked over to the gas pump. He pumped the fuel, his eyes roaming without pause around the parking lot and up and down the street. He saw no reason for concern as he finished up and pulled out of the lot.

A block later, at a stop light, he realized a cop car was right behind him. Panic beat a tattoo in his chest. When the light changed, he pulled away carefully, not wanting to give the cop any reason to pull him over. He made sure he drove at the speed limit, not a mile over or under. He worried the speedometer was not accurate in the old piece of junk. But the cop showed no interest in him, in fact, the distance between them seemed to have increased a bit. He hoped there wasn't a busted tail light or any other stupid reason for the cop to pull over the crappy little car.

He turned into a side street and his anxiety rose when seconds later, he saw the cop car enter the neighborhood, too. He fought off the urge to flee, maintaining a speed of twenty-five miles per hour. He came to a complete halt at a four-way stop sign. He then moved forward slowly and deliberately.

He relaxed a bit when the cop made a complete stop there, too. Then sighed in relief as the car took a left turn. He pulled into the driveway and entered the open garage door. He jumped out of the car, rushed to the button and stared underneath the lowering door to make sure the cop hadn't doubled back and followed him. He didn't notice anyone or anything moving outside. He did have a flash of concern about the obstruction to his view caused by the tall row of shrubbery across the back of the property; but dismissed that worry as quickly as it arose.

He entered a home he'd been in many times before. He'd worked here: building bookshelves, replacing broken window panes, hanging pictures on the walls, unclogging toilets and any other thing the prosperous but mechanically challenged couple needed. It seemed like they had one little job after another every couple of weeks. He put away his purchases, grabbed a beer and sat down to make plans for his immediate future.

He knew his time here was limited. The owners, his occasional customers, were away on a long cruise encircling the entire South American continent. They'd been kind enough to let him know they wouldn't need him while they were away. He laughed out loud at their misplaced trust.

He wondered if he could find enough in the house to sell for a few quick bucks – enough to get him far, far away from Virginia. He wondered if it would be possible to get out of the country. He expected the only way possible would be if he sneaked across the border into Mexico or Canada on foot.

He grew angry as he thought of the reason he'd abandoned the home he'd rented for all those years. The smell wasn't really that bad. If only he hadn't been spooked when Mrs Plum asked him about repairs he made to the home. She'd talked about coming by to admire his work. He should have stalled her, brazened her out. It would have worked. She was so grateful to have a long-term tenant who kept the premises in good condition. But no, he'd panicked and fled.

He'd been such an idiot. If he hadn't done that, no one would have found the bodies. No one would be looking for him. That thought brought Martha Sherman to mind and a smile to his face. He'd loved watching that trial on Court TV. On days he'd had jobs, he'd taped the coverage so he could watch it at night. It was thrilling to watch someone else take the blame for his actions. It was a real high to watch her parents sobbing after the verdict.

But now, he had problems – serious problems. He needed to find someplace he could hide permanently. Someplace where no one would see the news. No one would ever recognize him. He'd started growing out a beard and mustache; that would help but only so much. He needed an isolated place where he could live cheaply. It would have to be Mexico.

The other problem, though, felt more pressing. It demanded his attention no matter how hard he tried to suppress it. The hunger was building. It gnawed at him when he tried to sleep. It burned inside when he caught a glimpse of a young woman walking past the end of the driveway. It ate away at his concentration when he tried to focus on his escape from pursuit.

A cavalcade of dead women rode relentlessly through his mind. One pretty little face after another. Their desperate pleading for their lives. Their screams as they died. He closed his eyes and savored those moments, pausing on the most delicious few seconds of all, the time he spent staring into their eyes as the light faded and their lives slipped away.

He would have to do something about it before he made his run for the border. He had to find someone new. He'd be too careless if he didn't take care of the need first.

Forty

Jake raced over to Mack Rogers' former home as quickly as traffic would allow. The anthropologist had called. Another body had been found in the garden. He wanted to see it for himself.

When he arrived, he walked to the back of the house, tiptoeing around the marked, strung areas scattered across the yard. In the spot where vegetables once grew was a barren section of earth. The sun shone down on the unmistakable curved shape of the top of a human skull.

The anthropologist, holding a trowel in one hand and a small brush in the other, said, 'The only one, so far, but I wouldn't be surprised if it isn't the only one in this garden patch. We also had indications of disturbed earth and suspicious shapes, over there, there and there,' she said pointing to three yellow flags further out in the yard.

'What about those?' Jake asked pointing to the flags toward the markers closer to the house.

'That's where they started rolling through with the equipment. At that point, even the slightest indicators merited a flag. The best hits were at this spot and beyond. We'll go back and check the others but want to check out the most promising locations first.'

'Makes sense. Do you have any idea of how

this body fits into the chronology of the ones found in the basement?'

'Can't give you a definitive answer at the moment but if you want an educated guess, I'd say he planted this one before any of the ones inside.'

'How long before you think you'll finish up back here?'

'You do know that we don't just shovel up dirt like we're digging a ditch, right?'

'Yes, ma'am. I—'

'It'll take as long as it takes, agent. I'll alert you of any important developments as they happen.' She crouched back down to the earth and brushed at the skull.

Jake, realizing he'd just been dismissed, backed away and went into the house to check on the progress made by the forensic techs. All the walls had been stripped of drywall and nothing remained but the bare wood framing. Planks stretched across floor beams now that every piece of oak flooring had been removed. Jake felt a little giddy staring through the gaps into the basement below.

'Agent Lovett,' the lead tech greeted him. 'We've just about torn everything out of this place. Haven't found anything of significance in days. Of course, they're still finding little bits of bone and other artifacts down in the crawl space. That process moves at its own speed – sort of like traffic at rush hour when accidents are blocking the road.'

'Don't call it quits on the rest of the house until you're certain. The landlady said she's bringing in a crew to level this place when we're done.'

'Can't say that I blame her. Who'd want to live here after what we found? Is she going to rebuild?'

'Last time I talked to her, she hadn't decided,' Jake said. 'I think she's inclined to hold on to the property and sell the lot after the news dies down. I told her that might take some time. We gotta find the guy first.'

'And who knows how long till trial?'

'Exactly. What do you have left to do?'

'The bathroom has a shower that doesn't look more than ten years old. We'll rip that out and then I'll be satisfied that we've taken care of everything – unless someone decides they want us to jackhammer out the concrete floor in the finished section of the basement.'

'Do you think that's necessary?'

'I don't but I'm not calling all the shots. C'mon down the hall and look through to the old crawl space on the far end of the house.'

In a back bedroom, Jake stared down a deep hole, where workers in blue Tyvek suits labored away in the dirt. The floor was now much further away than it had been the last time he was at the house.

'As you can see, they're still at it. They think they've gone deep enough in the main area where the bodies were found, but now they're working at the far corners. They want it flat and a bit deeper than the finished basement floor, all the way across the whole area. Glad I'm not working down in that hole.'

'You and me both,' Jake said. 'Give me a holler if you find anything.'

'Will do, Agent Lovett – but don't hold your breath. I suspect we played this thing out a couple of days back.'

On the drive back to the office, Jake called Lucinda and told her about the discovery of yet another body.

'Whoever it is, I'm glad for the family; but I sure hope I haven't been involved in another wrongful conviction.'

'That would be too much of a coincidence.'

'I don't know, Jake. I feel very disillusioned about my department and the DA's office. I'm questioning everything.'

'Well, in this case, you're probably in the clear. The anthropologist said that she thought the skeleton she found pre-dated the bodies in the cellar.'

'I can take some personal comfort in that, Jake. But what if Boz tampered with more than just the Sherman case? What if his high closure rate was based on the unlawful concealment of evidence?'

'At one time, you said he was a good cop. Do you really think your judgment is that impaired? Isn't it more likely that the situation with Martha Sherman was an anomaly?'

'I hope that's true, Jake. But if it's not, the department is going to have to clean up the mess. I only hope the captain is proactive about investigating old claims of innocence. It would be better if we found it instead of some muckraking reporter.'

'Now just hope we can find Mack Rogers

before he kills again. That would give the press even more ammunition to shoot at your department and my agency, too. They're already calling any time a young woman goes missing to ask if I think he could be involved in the disappearance. So far, every one of them has been a runaway, or someone who just left town for a short while without explaining her absence to anyone. I'm afraid, though, our luck won't hold out forever.'

Forty-One

Tuesday morning, Lucinda drove to the Justice Center worried about the outcome of the plea bargain negotiations in the Chris Phillips case. She didn't trust the DA or any prosecutor to reach an agreement that would leave any of a perpetrator's victims or their loved ones with a shred of peace of mind.

She went straight up to the sixth floor, hoping to find out what transpired the previous day. On the way up, she grew progressively peeved that Reed did not bother to inform her on his own. She brightened up when she saw the door to his office hanging wide open.

Cindy shot down her rising optimism. 'He's in a staff meeting with the ADAs. I don't expect them to wrap up for at least an hour.'

'Do you know what's happening with the Phillips plea bargain?'

'Mr Reed said they were considering his offer overnight. He wasn't sure if they'd accept it or make a counter-offer.'

'What did Reed offer?'

'That's something you'll have to ask him – but I'm not sure if he's talking to you yet.'

'You're kidding me,' Lucinda said. 'Just how old is he and when will he stop pouting?'

'Lieutenant,' Cindy said as she tried to stifle a grin, 'you know I can't answer that question.'

'Yeah, yeah, yeah . . .' Lucinda said as she walked away. Back in her office, she got busy on reports. She despised the time spent on paper-work and was relieved when Brubaker called offering a distraction.

'Lieutenant, I thought you'd want to know that Cafferty just hauled in those two other high school punks involved in the vandalism.'

'Really? How did he manage to identify them?'

'Got me. But he's letting them stew in separate rooms for a while. Might be a good time for you to ask him.'

Lucinda disconnected and took a flight of stairs down to the second floor. As she entered the property crimes division, she spotted her prey sipping from a mug of coffee as he spoke to a colleague. 'Hey, Cafferty!'

Cafferty spun around. 'You,' he said, pointing a finger in her direction. 'If you say "I told you so", you're really gonna piss me off.'

'Jeez, sergeant, settle down. I came to congratu-late you for identifying the other two little hoodlums in the case.'

Cafferty gave her a sidelong glance through eyes narrowed to slits.

'Aw, c'mon, Cafferty, ease up. How did you manage it?'

'You really want to know?'

'Yeah. Honest,' she said, raising her hand in a two-finger scout pledge. 'I come in peace, Cafferty.'

'OK. Well, it was kinda lucky, I guess. I told each set of parents about the evidence against their kid, or kids in the case of the Pruitts. At the time, they were all sticking to the stories their children gave in the interviews – the maybe-the-other-kids-were-involved-but-not-my-little-darlings line.

'Apparently, Mr and Mrs Pruitt were putting on a false front till they got their "little darlings" back home. Then, they came down on them hard – even told them not to expect any visits or spare change after they were locked up in juvie hall.

'Finally, they wore 'em down. Not sure which one cracked first. But after they pulled the whole story out, they marched the pair of them back into my office and made them tell me the complete sequence of events. Jessica admitted that she made the 9-1-1 call reporting that there was vandalism in progress even though she knew that wasn't true. She said that she wanted to see what her friends had done and just happened to arrive at the apartment complex when Charley was climbing through the window – not sure if we've gotten the whole story there, but I let that slide.

'Tyler gave up the names of the other two guys but begged me not to make him testify against them. His father clapped him on the back of the head and told him that he'd do what needed to be done and feel good about it. One of the kids he named is seventeen, the other eighteen, so we can question them without their parents present. Might call the younger one's father in to play it safe – it sounded as if he was a little worried that his dad might find out and that could work to our advantage.'

'Not really luck, Cafferty. You planted the right

seeds and the parents simply harvested them for you. Good job,' Lucinda said.

'But, I really was about to pin it on the little Spencer girl.'

'Yeah, but you would have seen the holes in that theory eventually. I just helped move along the process a bit, that's all. See you around, Cafferty,' Lucinda said and walked out of his division toward the stairwell.

She had one hand on the door when her cell-phone rang. Jake started talking before she could even say her name. 'Lucinda, the car's been spotted. My office is in between you and the location.'

'I'm on my way,' she said. 'My car. I'm driving.'

'You got it.'

Lucinda screeched into the parking lot, braking hard beside Jake. When he got inside the car, she asked, 'Where to?'

'Turn left,' Jake answered.

She squealed out into the traffic, causing horns to blare.

'And you think my driving is bad?' Jake said.

'Don't start, Jake. Just tell me where to turn.'

In ten minutes, they were one block from the location where a patrol car sat, hidden from a possible sighting by anyone in the home housing the Hyundai inside its garage. The officer got out of his patrol car as they pulled up.

'You the one who spotted the vehicle?' Lucinda asked.

'Yes, ma'am, lieutenant.'

'Tell me about it.'

'I saw the car pull out of a convenience store parking lot on Wright's Crossing Road. It seemed like he spotted me, so I turned onto another street at that four-way stop down that-away. I parked my vehicle and followed on foot. I went from cover to cover to minimize the possibility of being seen but still managed to catch him turning into the driveway there. I ran up to those bushes in time to see the garage door lowering with the vehicle inside. The car hasn't come out of there since. I called for backup and now another patrol car is on the street running past the front of the house, in case he goes out that way on foot.'

'Sharp eyes and quicker thinking, officer. We're going to go up and see what we can see from behind that line of bushes. There's an extraction team on the way. Tell them where we are and make sure they know that there is a possibility that he has abducted another woman since we lost track of him – we have nothing to confirm that one way or the other; but we don't want to take a chance that he's been behaving himself since the last kill and could have a potential hostage in his control.'

Lucinda and Jake crouched as they ran down the line of shrubbery toward the driveway entrance. They found positions where, between them, they could have eyes on all the windows and doors of the home. Lucinda was settling in place when she heard yipping and whining coming from the side yard. She sidled down and looked. A small ball of gray fur was tangled up in a chain wrapped around a tree. It looked as

282

if it might choke itself to death if it didn't stop fighting with the restraint.

Lucinda scurried back to Jake's location. 'I think I found Prissy.'

'Who?'

'The dog – Helen's dog.'

'Oh, right,' Jake said. 'I'd forgotten.'

A hacking, choking sound came from the side of the house. 'Damn. She is going to kill herself,' Lucinda said and took off up the driveway and cut into the yard with Jake begging her to come back. Lucinda didn't pay the least bit of attention to his pleas or warnings. She moved as fast as she could while staying as low as possible to the ground.

Jake moved down the bush line to keep her in sight. As she tried to untangle the leash from the chain, the little dog fought her in desperation to get free. Out of the corner of her eye, Lucinda saw a flash of light in a window. At the same time, she heard Jack shout, 'Get down.'

She threw herself flat as a shotgun blast erupted from inside the home embedding pellets in the tree trunk above her head. She stopped trying to untangle the mess and just jerked the collar over the little dog's head. She grabbed the dog and held her tight.

Jake yelled, 'Game's up, Mack. Come out or we're coming in.'

Lucinda heard movement inside, followed by the sound of breaking glass and another blast from the shotgun that she assumed was aimed in Jake's direction. She took off, running straight for the line of shrubbery instead of returning the way she had come across the yard and down the drive. She heard the crack of a revolver and felt even more urgency to get back to Jake to stop him from firing on the house when they didn't know if Rogers was alone or if he was using a victim for a shield.

She looked for a gap to slip through and saw no way out except for crawling through at the bottom. She got down on her knees just as another blast fired; this time right over her head, sending little bits of shredded leaves and branches tumbling down on her back.

The falling debris sent Prissy into a state of panic, whimpering and struggling to get free. Lucinda tightened her grip and forced her way through the lower branches, scraping her arms and face in the process. On the other side, she moved away from her escape route before another shot could barrel through the bushes.

'Have you lost your mind?' Jake shrieked.

'What about you, Jake!' Lucinda yelled back. 'Firing into a house when we don't know who is in there?'

'Damn it, Lucy, give me a little credit. I fired a shot into the chimney hoping the distraction would give him pause and give you a little time to get out of the open. But you took a horrible risk for that mangy little beast. I like dogs as much as the next guy, but really . . . .'

'How could I possibly explain to Helen that we sat here, minding our own damn business while Prissy choked herself to death on that damn chain? Or even one of us hit her during a gun battle. I don't know which would be worse.'

'Jeez, Lucinda. What do you think I would do if you were hit?'

Lucinda shrugged.

'And what are you going to do with the dog now?'

At that point, three members of the black-clad extraction squad raced up. One of them said, 'Shots fired. Who's down?'

'I don't think anyone was hit.'

'The perp fired?'

'Yes, three, four times.'

'Either of you fire?'

'Yes, I fired once, shooting the chimney as a distraction.'

'Stand down. We'll take over from here.'

'I don't think so,' Jake said. 'It is possible that he has a hostage – another potential victim.'

Lucinda's mind flashed back to another shooter in another house – the time she aimed at a shadow and hit the little boy a man had held up to the darkened window. She struggled to keep the emotion out of her voice when she insisted, 'We have to make sure – absolutely sure – that no one else is in that house.'

As they talked, another seven black-clad men joined the group. The man with sergeant's bars, who acted is if he was the leader of the pack, said, 'Don't tell me you want to negotiate with the bastard?'

'We'll do whatever the hell we need to do to make sure no innocent life is lost in the apprehension. Is that clear?'

'Oh, yeah, lieutenant. I guess you've gotten cautious after all your screw-ups.'

'Jake!' Lucinda said and thrust the dog into his arms. She stepped up, face-to-face with the sergeant, her nose nearly touching his forehead. 'I would love an excuse to screw you over. Make one wrong move, violate just one of my orders and your ass is mine.'

He waited until she backed off and said, 'No need to pull rank, lieutenant. We're all on the same side here.'

'Just don't forget it,' she snapped. Turning to Jake, she recovered the dog and walked down to the manned patrol car and handed Prissy to the officer for safe keeping.

She started her return trip, realizing that all eleven pairs of eyes – the ten-man team and Jake – were staring in her direction. 'What?' she shouted. 'You can't make a move without me?'

They moved around in place in a definite state of unease. When she got closer, Jake said, 'These are all police officers, Lucinda. You call the shots this time – not me.'

The sergeant quickly added, 'Just waiting for orders, lieutenant.'

'Holy crap, sergeant. You know how to deploy your men in preparation for a takedown. Just do it. Maintain your positions and hold your fire till I say otherwise.'

Forty-Two

Everyone moved into place, including snipers perched high atop nearby houses. Patrol officers evacuated the homes within two rooftops of the location of the fugitive. Others circled the home on a reconnaissance mission, checking any possible means of entry and egress, looking for weaknesses to exploit in an aggressive maneuver and those that needed coverage in a defensive action. Thirty minutes had passed without a single shot fired.

A negotiator called the telephone in the house but it rang until it flipped over to voicemail. A message was left for Mack but they had no way of knowing if he listened to it.

The reconnaissance team reported back that they'd seen no signs of life within the home, prompting the negotiator to ask if it were possible that Jake missed the chimney and hit Rogers instead.

Jake stared at him dumbfounded. 'He wasn't on the roof. Do you really think I'm that inept, that I'd aim way up there and hit someone inside the house?'

'Sorry, Agent Lovett, but I've seen stranger things.'

'Could he have committed suicide with the last shot he fired?'

Jake insisted that it wasn't possible since they

saw the results every time he pulled the trigger. Nonetheless, the speculation didn't end. Jake and Lucinda were guessed and second-guessed in one discussion after another, making them both frustrated and a bit testy.

The negotiator pulled out the megaphone and delivered the standard, scripted speech about the force surrounding the building, the desire for a peaceful ending without any deaths and the plea to surrender. When no response came from inside the house, the sergeant from the extraction team argued, 'It's time to go in and pull him out whether he's dead or alive. If he had a hostage, he would have responded, using the captive as a bargaining chip. We need to go in now, without warning.'

'No,' Lucinda said. 'A forced entry is premature at this time. We've been assembled and in our places for what? An hour now? Patience is a vital part of a successful effort – haste is a recipe for disaster.'

'You have learned that the hard way, haven't you, lieutenant?'

Lucinda reminded herself not to say what was in her mind; strip the personal out of his attack and lob back a gentler ball. 'Sergeant, you don't want – no one here wants – to go home wondering if something was done differently, would an innocent person still be alive? You do not want to carry the burden of knowing that the capture could have been done without the taking of life, if you'd only taken your time to do it right. Patience, sergeant, we'll move when we feel we know all we can possibly know. We will not make a foolhardy rush into the house simply because we are growing antsy.'

The sergeant walked away grumbling. Lucinda believed she heard him threaten to call his captain to set her straight. It was his right to contact his superior officer under any circumstance but she hoped office politics wouldn't inflame an already volatile situation.

For an hour, positions shifted as the team worked to find out what they could about the situation inside. Repeated attempts to communicate by telephone or megaphone produced no results. Movement was spotted from time to time and directional mikes picked up the sound of someone inside. But no voices were heard.

Lucinda was contemplating the firing of a flash-bang grenade followed by a forced entry, when a voice in her ear said, 'Lieutenant, this is Briggs. I have a clear view of the subject. I see no one in the immediate vicinity.'

'Take the shot. But shoot to wound. Everyone else, hold fire.'

Glass shattered. Followed by a loud crash. And then nothing.

'Briggs, did you get him?' Lucinda yelled in her headpiece.

'Don't think so, lieutenant. Sorry.'

'Look for another opportunity.'

Snipers crawled across roofs and other team members checked windows. For five long minutes, no sound came from the house. Then, the back door opened ever so slightly and a white T-shirt moved up and down in the crack.

'Hold fire,' Lucinda said as she scrambled over

to the negotiator with the megaphone. She held the device to her face and said, 'Rogers. Mack Rogers. Throw out your weapons and come out with your hands up.'

The door opened further and a shotgun thumped on the grass four feet from the house. Crouching, a black-clad man raced up, grabbed the weapon and backed away.

The door slammed into the wall and Mack Rogers, hands held high, walked through the doorway. He stumbled, his hands dropped down as if to steady his balance but when they came back up, he had a revolver in his hand. He fired and hit an extraction team member's bulletproof vest, sending him falling backwards, stunned but unharmed. Without Lucinda's order, an immediate volley of fire opened up, making Rogers' body dance before falling face first into the yard. Lucinda screamed, 'Hold your fire! Hold your fire!'

Quiet roared in the aftermath. Then, sirens shrieked in the distance, coming closer with every second. Lucinda held her gun on Rogers as she carefully approached and kicked the man's revolver out of the way.

Jake bent down and checked the body. He shook his head.

Lucinda blew out a sharp exhale. 'Damn.'

The team swarmed around and past them, entering the home to search for any others inside, dead or alive.

'Too many questions left, Jake.'

'Yeah, I know. We've backtracked up till his last prison stay. Checked out every place he lived. Never was in one place for long before he rented from Plum. No signs of foul play at any of the others.'

'So, if there were other victims, he must have killed them and dumped bodies away from his residence. How many families are missing someone because of Mack Rogers? How many will never get resolution because the only person with answers is now dead? I wonder if I should have sent the team in sooner.'

'It probably wouldn't have mattered, Lucinda. He was hell-bent on avoiding capture. Up-close contact with him could have resulted in an officer's death. You never know. You used your best judgment and now, you'll deal with the consequences. Looking back, no takedown is flawless. No sense in second-guessing your actions when it's over.'

Lucinda only sighed in response.

From the house, a man in black hollered, 'Lieutenant, the house is clear but there's something you should see.'

Lucinda and Jake followed the officer into the kitchen. A spiral notebook lay open on a small breakfast table. Handwritten on the exposed page were notes about a girl: 'Short, long blonde hair, blue eyes, very pretty. Leaves the school, walks down Campbell, turns right on Greene and then a left on Sycamore. House third on right. Arrives 3:45. X=thick shrub and overhanging trees at corner of Greene and Sycamore.'

Lucinda pulled a pen out of her pocket and flipped the page. 'Average height, baby-fat pudgy, short brown hair, brown eyes, cute. Gets

291

off school bus at Trinity and Glass. Walks down Glass to eighth house on left. Uses key to open door. X=inside the shrubbery encircling property.'

Lucinda kept flipping pages. One after another filled with notes of young women he stalked as he searched for his next victim. Each one with X= at the end, indicating, it seemed to Lucinda, the place he'd make the snatch. A couple of the entries had a question mark rather than a specific location.

Jake, looking over her shoulder, whispered, 'Holy shit,' several times as each page turn revealed yet another girl. 'Wonder if any of these notes apply to bodies we've already found? Or are they all safe because he's dead?'

'There's also the question of whether or not all of his victims were planned. Emily, for example, appeared to be spontaneous.'

'Unless she agreed to meet him,' Jake said.

'Another question without an answer,' Lucinda said. 'At least no one else will die at his hand.'

'And you rescued the only hostage.'

Lucinda furrowed her brow. 'Hostage? Oh no, Prissy. I forgot all about her.' She rushed up the street to the patrol car where she'd left the little dog. The driver's door was open. A few feet away, an officer held a clothesline tied loosely around the dog's neck as she squatted in the grass attending to an urgent need.

'Thank you, officer. I'll take her off your hands now and get her back to her owner.'

'She wasn't much trouble. But when one of the guys brought me a burger, I thought she was going to steal it out of my mouth so I shared it with her. Didn't seem like she'd been fed for a while.'

'Probably hadn't,' Lucinda said. 'Thanks again.' Lucinda took the rope and led the little dog back to the side yard, where she untangled the leash and collar from the chain and replaced the rope around her neck. She walked her over to the evacuated house next door and secured her in the fenced back yard while she took care of processing the scene.

Dr Sam arrived to take possession of the body. When he looked down at the bloody corpse, he said, 'Pierce, did you do this?'

'No sir, I didn't fire a shot. Multiple weapons were engaged. If you find any bullets in the body, I'm sure they'll match the weapons of the extraction team.'

'I'm seeing a lot of exit wounds, Pierce. Might not find any inside.'

A team of FBI forensic techs arrived and started to process the scene, collecting evidence to add to what they'd recovered earlier from the rental house where Rogers once lived. They found bullets in the side of the house, embedded in the dirt, and then went inside where they recovered several more. Before they were done with the house, they removed everything that seemed to belong to or had been used by Mack Rogers.

With the departure of the black-clad team, the police presence dropped down to a few officers, giving Lucinda a moment to call Helen Johns. 'Ms Johns, this is Lieutenant Lucinda Pierce. We found Prissy.'

'Oh, my, is she OK?'

'She certainly is. I'm not sure when I'll be able to get away from here and bring her to your place.'

'Can I come and get her?'

'Yes,' Lucinda said, giving her the address. 'The area is taped off but if you tell an officer, they'll find me and I'll bring Prissy to you.' Lucinda got busy at the house again, supervising the removal of the Hyundai on a flat bed tow truck. She signed the paperwork, sending it to the forensic garage to be processed under the oversight of an FBI tech. That made her remember how grateful she was that the person in charge of the local federal law enforcement office was Jake Lovett. A lot of the others would have shut her out of the case, leaving her on the sidelines wondering what was happening.

She'd have to remember to let him know how much he meant to her professionally. And what about personally? she thought. Isn't it about time I let him know how I feel? She pushed that subject firmly out of her mind; she had work to do.

A half hour later, her cell rang. 'Lieutenant, there's a woman at the barricade who said you told her to come get her dog.'

'Keep her there. I'll be right out,' Lucinda said. As she walked over to the porch next door, the little dog made excited yips and turned in circles as she bounced up and down. 'It's all over now, Prissy,' she said, scooping her up in her arms.

As she neared the barrier, Helen lurched forward, stopped only by the arm of an officer.

'Prissy, Prissy, Prissy,' she cried. 'Come to Mama, Prissy.'

Lucinda handed over the wriggling gray ball of fur. Helen squeezed her and kissed her face. Prissy licked Helen's lips, nose, chin and eyes.

'Eww!' Helen said. 'She smells like onions.'

Lucinda laughed. 'An officer shared his burger with her.'

'A hamburger? You fed little Prissy a greasy hamburger?'

'She was hungry, Helen.'

'Poor little babe-ums,' Helen said, snuggling her face in Prissy's fur. 'Poor little thing. You gonna have an upset tum-tum for days, aren't you, baby? Nasty old policeman.'

Oh, Jeez, Lucinda thought and turned away from the barrier, shaking her head at Helen's non-stop string of baby talk. If I treated Chester like that, he'd run away from home.

It was after ten that night before Jake and Lucinda could leave the scene. On the drive home, Lucinda said, 'I'm not good for anything but sleep tonight but I can offer you a warm, comfy spot beside me and fresh coffee in the morning.'

'You got a deal,' Jake said. 'Just so long as your only expectation is sleep. I'm beat.'

As Lucinda lay in bed, drifting away, she thought about how nice it was to have him lying there beside her.

Forty-Three

Lucinda woke first to find Chester wedged between them with his head on her pillow. She hoisted him up and carried him into the kitchen. She started the coffee brewing and filled Chester's bowl with dry food and placed a spoonful of tuna feast on his plate.

She fixed two cups of coffee and carried them into the bedroom where Jake still slept deeply. She poked his rump with a toe and then her whole foot while balancing the two mugs in her hand. 'Sleeping Beauty, arise. Coffee's served.'

Jake grunted, rubbed his eyes, rolled over and smiled. 'I could get used to this,' he said, reaching for the coffee.

'Don't think this service in bed establishes a precedent, Mr Special Agent man,' she said as she smiled and climbed back into bed.

Jake and Lucinda went off to their respective offices to drown in an ocean of paperwork and face scrutiny about the death of Mack Rogers. Jake got dressed down by the wicked witch who made a special trip just to give him a hard time. Lucinda faced Internal Affairs who questioned every decision reached and every move made. Near lunchtime, Lucinda picked up a phone call from Jake.

'Word is that Martha Sherman is going to be rearrested.' Jake said.

'What? On what grounds?'

'They found one of her credit cards in the excavation of Rogers' basement graveyard.'

'So?'

'Apparently there are those who believe that indicates that she was involved.'

'You mean Andrew Sherman thinks she was involved.'

'Well, I also heard that your DA is taking him seriously.'

'Damn it,' she said. 'I've got to run.'

'Lucinda, I don't know this all for a fact. It's just what I've heard.'

'Later, Jake,' she said, disconnecting the call.

She flew up the three flights of stairs to DA Reed's office. Once again, his door was shut tight. 'Cindy, am I still barred from his office?'

'No. Not unless you've done something new to get him annoyed.'

'My breathing annoys him.'

Cindy chuckled. 'He's got someone in his office right now and he said he should not be disturbed.'

Lucinda took two steps toward the door.

'C'mon, lieutenant, you're putting me in a difficult position.'

Lucinda sighed and dropped her shoulders. 'OK. Who's in there with him?'

'You're not going to like this . . .'

'Who is it, Cindy?'

'Andrew Sherman.'

'You're kidding me. Damn it,' she turned toward the door, stopped, looked at Cindy and stormed out of the office. She went to her desk, grabbed her car keys and tore out of the parking lot. She pulled into the long circular drive leading up to the Shermans' home. Three stories of brick topped with gables rose up above her. White columns marched across the edge of the porch.

She walked about the steps, smoothed her skirt and rang the doorbell. A woman in a simple green shirt dress answered. 'Dora Sherman, please.'

'May I say who's calling?'

Lucinda whipped out her badge. 'Lieutenant Lucinda Pierce.'

'One moment,' the woman said and shut the door in Lucinda's face.

She was about to press the doorbell again when the door opened and Dora stood framed behind it. She was a striking woman with carefully coifed jet black hair and unusually brilliant green eyes. Lucinda wondered if they were naturally that color or enhanced by tinted contact lenses.

'Good day, lieutenant,' Dora said. 'I really can't speak with you without my attorney present. I've called and he's on the way.'

'Ma'am, if you're not willing to answer my questions here, then maybe we should go down to the Justice Center and you can wait for your lawyer there.'

'Don't be silly, lieutenant. That is so unnecessary. Besides, he's already on his way to the house. We'll all be more comfortable here. Marcie, please take this person to the kitchen to wait.'

'Excuse me?' Lucinda said with images of film clips running through her mind, where beggars and other undesirables were sent to the back door and into the kitchen to await the pleasure of their betters.

Marcie appeared out of nowhere and snapped, 'You can't expect to be treated like an invited guest, miss. This way, please.'

Lucinda looked skyward. 'Mrs Sherman, I am a public servant but that does not entitle you to banish me to the kitchen as if I am your personal hired help.'

'Oh, dear, I wasn't thinking how that might sound. I didn't mean to be dismissive. Come with me. You can sit in the garden. It's lovely this time of year.' Dora led her down a hallway, into a sitting room and out of a pair of French doors. Outside, she gestured to a sitting area on a stone patio. 'I'll send cook out with some refreshments.'

'That won't be necessary.'

'Oh, nonsense,' she said as she went back inside.

A woman in a floral print dress with a white apron tied around her middle stepped out onto the patio. Her graying hair was pulled back in a bun and wrinkles creased beside her merry eyes. 'What would you like? Coffee, tea, soft drink, beer or something else? I'm sure we'll have whatever you'd like.'

Feeling perverse, Lucinda decided to ask for

something that few people had on hand. 'How about a diet ginger ale?'

'No problem,' she said. 'Back in a minute.'

After she left, Lucinda thought, I should have asked for a Blackened Voodoo beer – surely she wouldn't have that in the house. Or maybe some fruity sweet screw-top wine; they'd probably die before allowing a bottle of that to cross the threshold.

The woman returned faster than Lucinda thought she could have reached the kitchen. She set a glass with its fizzing beverage poured over ice on the table and added a bowl of pretzels and another of cashews down beside it. 'If you need anything else, just press that buzzer and I'll be here as quickly as I can.'

Lucinda sipped on her drink and nibbled on the nuts as her patience rapidly dwindled away. Finally, she heard the doorbell ring and the sound of a male and female voice in conversation. She reached over and opened the door a bit, hoping to hear what they were saying. 'Fine, whatever you want, Miss Canterbury. But let me do the talking.'

Miss Canterbury? Lucinda thought. Why is he referring to her by her maiden name? She slouched back in the chair, leaning away from the door.

A tall man in an expensive suit stepped outside with Dora by his side. 'Miss Canterbury believes that you are here inquiring about Mr Sherman, is that correct?'

'Yes, it is.'

'And that your inquiries involve his former wife Martha Sherman?'

'Correct.'

'Miss Canterbury wants me to inform you that she is in the process of having divorce papers served on Andrew Sherman. She has a locksmith on his way here to change all the locks on the house.'

'Is she aware of where her husband is and what he is doing at this moment?'

The attorney turned to Dora. She shook her head. 'I thought he was at his office.'

'Actually, he's at the DA's office. Plotting the rearrest of Martha Sherman.'

'I will say that does reinforce Miss Canterbury's decision to terminate her marriage. She has kept up with developments and Andrew Sherman's continued persecution of that innocent woman is part of her reason for wanting to dissolve the relationship.'

'That's noble. It's all on principle, then?'

The attorney looked at Dora. 'Go on,' Dora said. 'Don't be an ass. Tell her the real reasons and ask for her cooperation.'

The lawyer's face flushed. He nodded his head at his client and turned back to Lucinda. 'The two issues of most concern to my client is that Andrew Sherman's actions will put her on the front page of the news, reminding everyone of her poor judgment when she became involved with him while he was still married to Martha. The other thing is that there is a strong possibility that Martha will sue Andrew and Miss Canterbury does not desire to be financially tied to her husband when and if that happens.'

'So just throw penniless Martha to Andrew and his lions?'

'On the contrary,' the lawyer continued. 'Miss Canterbury accepts her unsavory role in the break-up of Andrew and Martha's marriage and the fact that she did, unwittingly, enable Andrew's persecution of an innocent woman. For that reason, she has made a generous settlement offer to Martha in exchange for her agreement not to involve her in any legal clashes Martha has with Andrew in the future.'

He turned from Lucinda and toward his client. 'Did I leave anything out, Miss Canterbury?'

'Nothing but a thank you. We would have never known Andrew's location if not for your information, lieutenant. I appreciate that. We can send the man serving the papers over there. I want this over and done with as soon as possible.' She extended her hand toward Lucinda, who accepted her firm grasp and returned one of her own.

'Thank you, ma'am. Thank you for not keeping me in the dark.'

'One more thing, lieutenant,' the lawyer said. 'We would appreciate it if you would keep Miss Canterbury's name out of the media.'

'Sir, I have no control over that. I, for one, will not say anything publicly about her, but I cannot control what anyone else does.'

'As long as you agree not to feed the fire, that will be quite satisfactory. And, just so you know, I plan to deliver a message loud and clear to Andrew Sherman: I am prepared to stretch out any financial settlement connected to the divorce indefinitely as long as he persists in harassing Martha Sherman. We have every reason to believe he will comply since he lost most of his personal wealth because of a few unwise investments – and frittered away a considerable sum of Miss Canterbury's funds in the same foolish ventures.'

Lucinda smiled as she walked back to her car.

Forty-Four

Lucinda returned to the Justice Center and to DA Reed's office. Loud voices were bouncing off the walls behind the closed doors. 'You think that's something, you should have heard it when the process server arrived,' Cindy said.

The door flew open, slamming into the wall. A red-faced Andrew Sherman stomped out of the office. He spotted Lucinda and said, 'And you helped him, too, didn't you? I'll get you for this, too.'

What did that mean? Who does he think I helped? Rogers? Lucinda wondered.

'Ah, Pierce, just who I wanted to see,' DA Reed said.

Lucinda swung around and glared at him. 'Oh right, you wanted me to catch you pandering to one of your campaign supporters.'

Reed smiled. 'And that bothers you?'

'Have you listened to anything I've said?'

'Actually, I have,' Reed said.

'It doesn't exactly look like it, Reed.'

'Where have you been in the last few hours?'

'That's irrelevant.'

'Not really,' he said and then turned to his secretary. 'Cindy, was the lieutenant aware that Andrew Sherman was in my office this morning?'

Cindy blanched. 'Well, sir, uh . . .'

'Yes, I was, Reed,' Lucinda interrupted.

'Did you tell anyone else?'

Lucinda ran her tongue across the inside of her lower lip, as she tried to think of a way to evade the question and failed. 'Yes.'

'Dora Sherman?' he asked.

'She prefers to be called Dora Canterbury now.'

'Ah ha! I thought it had to be you. He accused me of informing his wife that he was in my office so that she could corner him here and serve the divorce papers. He has, of course, withdrawn his financial support from my re-election campaign. But the funny thing is that the only money Andrew Sherman will probably have after the divorce will likely be tied up in attorney's fees and the judgment in the civil suit brought by Martha Sherman.'

'Dora Canterbury's lawyer said much the same thing.'

'The divorce removes Andrew Sherman from my base of contributors with big pockets,' Reed said with a grin. 'Thus making everything he says and thinks irrelevant to my political future.'

'So you're not rearresting Martha Sherman?'

'Of course not.' Reed said.

'Because the person who wanted you to arrest her has now been rendered financially impotent?' Lucinda asked, hoping somehow she was reaching the wrong conclusion.

'I hate that word.'

'What?'

'Impotent. It makes my skin crawl.'

Lucinda dropped her head and shook it. He's such an ass, she thought.

'Hey,' Reed said, 'give me credit. I'm doing the right thing.'

Lucinda blew a sharp gust of air through her lips. 'But for all the wrong reasons, Reed. You're hopeless,' she said, turning to leave.

'Oh, wait. One more thing.'

Lucinda hesitated before turning back around. Did she really need or want to hear his political excuses any longer? 'What, Reed?'

'Phillips. Chris Phillips. We got a plea bargain worked out.'

Lucinda felt nauseous. What had he done now? She steeled herself for the worst bargain with a killer she could imagine and then realized she probably couldn't conceive of how bad it could get. 'OK, tell me, how soon is he going to get out?'

'Oh, ye of little faith . . .'

'Oh, please, you're quoting from scripture now? How bad is it?'

'You gotta let me start from the beginning,' Reed said, bouncing on his toes.

Lucinda shrugged and sighed. 'Go ahead.'

'At first, I said I was going for the death penalty and the lawyer thought I was bluffing. But then I led him to believe I had enough evidence to charge him with first degree murder in the death of wife number one. And two murders and an attempted murder – with financial motives one and all – add up to the death penalty.'

'You just led him to believe? So you lied, what else?'

'As I suspected, Phillips panicked over that possibility. The lawyer came back with a counter-offer. Twenty years minus time served.'

Lucinda ran the math in her head. With good behavior, he'd be out in seven years. 'Oh, no . . .'

'No, no, no, no, no! I didn't agree to that. I came back with life without parole if he pled guilty to the death of wife number three. And, then I added – you'll like this – I said he had to admit in open court that he was responsible for the death of wife number one and the assault on wife number two.'

'You know these women have names?' Lucinda snapped.

'Of course, of course. Numbers are easier to keep straight. Anyway, the lawyer objected strongly to that. He said that they'd take their chances at trial if I didn't include the possibility that he'd get out of prison one day.'

'So of course you went along with that?' Lucinda said.

'Yeah, but wait, it gets better. I threw in something else. I said, OK, a life sentence with the possibility of parole and his willing agreement not to fight the permanent termination of his parental rights.'

That's something, Lucinda thought. 'And then?'

'I said I'd leave them alone to talk it over. And reminded them that if they didn't agree to that offer, then I could put the death penalty back on the table. I said if a jury found him guilty of two murders, even if he didn't get death, he would surely get two consecutive life sentences. The lawyer accused me of bluffing again but I just shrugged and walked away.'

'So it's still up in the air?'

'No, they called me back in an hour. There

307

must be something out there that can prove Phillips murdered wife number one and whatever that is, Phillips thinks I found it. His attorney said that he decided to accept the offer because – and you'll just love the piety of this one – he said that Phillips accepted because he didn't want to put his son through the ordeal of testifying against him on the stand. Can you believe it?'

'Sure, Reed, a lot of people do the right things for all the wrong reasons.'

'Oh, you're back to that now. What's wrong with you? Everything turned out like you wanted and you're still giving me a hard time? I just don't get it.'

'No, I don't doubt that, Reed,' she said, walking away.

'Wait. I still don't understand your problem,' he objected.

'And you probably never will.'

Epilogue

With Chris Phillips back in prison, Mack Rogers dead, Charley cleared of wrongdoing and Martha Sherman rebuilding her life, the only case hanging over Lucinda's head was the assault charge filed against her sister-in-law by her sister. There was not a thing she could do to influence the progress of that situation and no telling when it would be resolved. She knew there'd never be a better time for her to take an extended absence from work. Not being able to hang on to the 'middle-of-the-case' excuse, she succumbed to the pressure from Charley, Jake and Rambo Burns and scheduled another surgery despite her misgivings.

When the doorbell rang two days later, Chester ducked behind the sofa and peered around the corner, his eyes on the apartment door. Lucinda opened it to Jake and three suitcases.

'Good grief, Jake, you need all that for one week?'

'No. You're on leave for a month. I'm here for a month. I only have ten days of leave and after that I'll have to go back to work but I'll still be here evenings and weekends to run errands and keep an eye on your recovery.'

'Jake, that isn't necessary.'

'Maybe not for you. But it is for me. I need to be here, Lucy.'

'Jake, I don't want you to feel obligated . . .'

'I don't feel obligated, Lucy. I feel committed. How about you?'

Lucinda turned away. 'One step at a time, Jake.'

As they lugged his suitcases into the apartment, Jake asked, 'If you moved out of this place what would you miss the most?'

Lucinda set the suitcase she was carrying on the floor at the entrance to the hallway and went into the kitchen and got out a bottle of wine while she considered the question. 'I'd have to say the view of the river – it soothes me and gives me a sense of grounding to the earth.'

'I guess finding another place with a river view would have to be a priority for you then.'

Lucinda had a suspicion that this conversation was leading someplace she was not ready to go, but it was best not to acknowledge her awareness and force him to be more direct or drop the subject entirely. Pouring two glasses of wine, she said, 'That or the pounding surf.'

'You're not going to get that here. So if you stayed here in town, what would be your ideal place?'

'The Spencer condo – or something like it with a balcony jutting out over the river and that is way out of my reach.'

'If we pooled our resources, we could get something a bit smaller but with the balcony over the river that you like.'

Lucinda swallowed hard and reached for one of his bags. 'Well, let's get your stuff put away in the bedroom. I hope we can find a place to put everything. I only cleared out one dresser drawer and the closet isn't the biggest. As you know, I stretched my budget a bit to afford this place and . . .' she rambled on.

Jake placed a hand on Lucinda's forearm. 'Hey, it's OK. Relax. One day at a time works fine for now. No pressure. I promise.'

Under Chester's watchful eyes, they managed to find a place to stow Jake's clothing and toiletries. To Lucinda's relief, the empty suitcases slid easily underneath the bed.

'OK,' Jake said, 'how about we go get some dinner, maybe catch a movie. We can't stay out too late. You need to get a good night's sleep before your surgery tomorrow.'

Lucinda looked into his eyes, a smile on her face.

'What?' Jake asked.

'First things, first, Mr Special Agent man,' she said, grabbing his hand and leading him towards the bed.